THE SPIDER HOUSE

LINDA ANTHONY HILL

Hill House Publishing

ISBN: 13: 978-1-7330814-1-2
 PUBLISHED BY HILL HOUSE PUBLISHING
www.HillHousePublishing.com

Printed in the United States of America
Suggested retail price (SRP) 14.95

The Spider House is printed in Palatino Linotype

DEDICATION

I'd like to dedicate this book to my father, Robert (Bob) William Anthony Sr. He encouraged me to write from as far back as I can remember. He was in my corner when I decided to publish a neighborhood newsletter. My father was responsible for his Elks Clubs Newsletter, so I guess he saw me following in his footsteps. He made me feel special every time I wrote a new poem. My dad died before I took up writing seriously. I like to think that he would be proud to see me publishing my second novel. This one's for you, Dad

ACKNOWLEDGMENTS

There are so many people to acknowledge. Always first is my husband, Del. He helped me stay focused without pushing too hard. He talked me through the slump I fell into when I realized I had written three chapters that didn't belong in this book. He keeps me on track, and reminds me to take my meds.

I'd also like to acknowledge Teal Gray, a fellow author and paranormal enthusiast. She's a practicing psychic and occasionally I run ideas past her. She's also a spiritual teacher and coach. Look for her on Amazon.

C. Derick Miller, a fellow author, can also be found on Amazon. He has been an inspiration to me for many years. His advice has helped me in the writing process, but also in the publishing process.

Prologue

Welcome to the world of Madam Celeste. She is a spirited woman who also speaks with spirits as the Gloryville psychic. She and her apprentice, Emma, get involved in mysteries on a regular basis. After all, if you need a mystery solved, who better to go to than the psychic that has worked with the FBI?

Emma is a college student at Gloryville's Community college and works for Madame Celeste when she isn't in class. She is still undecided, but is leaning toward following in Madam Celeste's footsteps to get a degree in psychology or social work.

Madam Celeste has told Emma that she is more powerful than Celeste. She needs practice and training, but the raw talent is there and Madam Celeste has agreed to mentor Emma to achieve her full potential. While both women can see spirits, Emma can also hear them. Madam Celeste has to work much harder to communicate with them.

Though Madam Celeste has many Christian clients, she is a practicing solitary—she doesn't belong to any formal group. Her beliefs and practices are uniquely her own. While she is teaching Emma, she is also encouraging Emma to think for herself and formulate her own conclusions.

Madam Celeste lives within walking distance of the courthouse, in a very old house where she also sees clients. She prefers to schedule between nine and five with an hour for lunch. Most of her friends—including her beloved cat, Chaos—are alive, but at least one is a spirit named Paul, who she met while working on a case with the FBI.

She has been napping this afternoon and apparently, she's having a vision . . ..

CHAPTER 1

Where did all these spider webs come from? she thought.

She'd seen pictures of old abandoned houses with sheets draped over the furniture. They never seemed covered to the floor with spider webs. This was ridiculous.

Finding a broom off the back porch, she tried to go in from the back through the kitchen. It was just as bad. She swept the broom through the air like a mutant lunging for food. It was comical to see, but Cheryl found no humor in the situation, wishing she'd never agreed to come here.

Her mother had asked her to go over to the old house to look for some paperwork about the deed. Cheryl thought her mother didn't want to confront all the old memories of the place. Now she knew the spiders were what her mom didn't want to confront.

Her mother had said to look in the study. There was a beautiful oak cabinet that was actually a filing cabinet. All the paperwork about the house would probably be in there. If she hurried, there would be time to find the papers before sundown.

The house had been well lit so far. It was late afternoon, and there was plenty of sunlight, but the study had no windows. It was pitch dark and a little spooky. Cheryl was glad she brought a flashlight.

She had never spent much time in the study. It was her father's private room, and no children were allowed. If he caught you in the study, you were in deep trouble. If he *took* you into the study, you better start to pray.

It gave her chills to remember, and she found there was still a little of that childhood fear while looking around for the filing cabinet in disguise. *This must be it,* she thought after opening the top drawer and thumbing through the well-organized files, then moving to the third drawer and finding the paperwork there. *Good,* she thought, *I'm ready to get out of this spider village.*

A strange noise came from the corner of the room. It was loud enough to hear, but not loud enough to startle. It sounded like something shuffling. *Gawd, does this place have mice, too?*

She swept through the dark room with the broom in hopes of clearing all the spider webs from her path. Not curious enough about the noise to investigate, she was getting a little creeped out by the webs, the dark, and the noise. She worked her way back to the door, which was now open. She didn't remember leaving it open . . .. Had she let a small animal in? *Dang! Now I'll **have** to investigate!*

Cheryl wasn't a scaredy cat, but spiders and who-knows-what she might have let in made her more than a little nervous. Broom and flashlight in hand, she swept her way into the dining room. No signs of life in there. She looked at the room and tried to remember what the furniture looked like under all the sheets.

There were a lot of ghosts from her childhood here, especially in this room. The family had always come together for dinner in this room. No TV trays at Dad's house. "We will dine in the dining room like civilized people," he would say when the children begged to eat in front of the TV.

2

Dad's word had been law in this house. Of course, so had Mom's, but they could sometimes wear her down or at least, negotiate a little. Dad never wavered once he had rendered a decision. If he and Mom disagreed, the children never heard about it. Dad was like a landmark, always there, never wobbling, never giving in—he was their foundation.

She was happy to remember him and somehow sad at the same time. She pushed on to the living room, constantly sweeping the air in front of her in case there were webs hidden in the shadows. It was all too creepy to run into one with your arms. It felt like someone was running a finger over your skin, and not in a good way.

Mom hadn't left much of the living room furniture here. The room looked vacant and that much spookier because of it. The sun had gone behind the trees, and the light was fading. Turning on the flashlight caused her to jump when her reflection appeared in the mirror by the hallway. She had forgotten it was there. *Wonder why they didn't cover that.*

Cheryl's heart was racing from the brief fright. Heading back to the study where the sound had been, she looked for signs that something had been disturbed. The room still filled her with that childhood dread. She walked over to the corner the noise seemed to have come from and saw a trash bin on its side and some wadded-up paper on the floor. The dust looked like it might have been disturbed here. She thought it could be a small animal like a cat or raccoon. Then she saw the sheet on the adjacent chair had been disturbed. Still, it could be a cat. Yes, the cat could have jumped up on the back of the chair. That would explain it . . ..

"Here, kitty, kitty," she called softly.

The sheet moved. Cheryl let out an involuntary gasp and raised the sheet hoping to find a kitten. But there was nothing there. She had shined her flashlight around the floor and could see her footprints in the dust. There were no other prints. No paw prints.No mouse prints. Nothing.

3

Was the sheet moving just her imagination? A chill ran up her arm. Startled, she dropped the flashlight, and it turned itself off. Alone in the dark, in the room of dread—the room reserved for her father only—she swallowed hard and started to feel for the flashlight, finding more spider webs instead. *Ugh!*

Finally, her fingers found the flashlight, and she immediately turned it back on. *Whew!* What to do. It would be right to stay, methodically checking out the whole house, but . . .. Maybe she could come back tomorrow with some friends. Yes, that was the thing to do. For now, with papers in hand, she would leave and come back tomorrow with more light and some friends. She turned and looked directly into Celeste's eyes and said, "Do you know what's going on here?" which startled Madam Celeste awake from her nap, realizing the dream had been a vision. The difference being that a vision had either already happened, was happening now, or would happen in the future. She sensed this was happening now and life was going to get interesting in the weeks ahead. She made a sticky note for Emma to leave some time open next week, preferably in the afternoon. There would be an emergency popping up this weekend or early next week. A girl named Cheryl would be calling or someone on her behalf. Celeste eased back into her nap to dream some real dreams this time.

"How often do I get a Thursday afternoon off to nap anyway, and I have to spend it having a vision?"

4

CHAPTER 2

On the ride back to her mom's, Cheryl thought about who to bring back with her. Which of her friends would be helpful? It couldn't be anyone who scared easily and needed to be someone who could help with an animal in case there was actually one in there. Who did she know? Mia liked to watch creepy stuff on television with her. They watched all the ghost hunting shows together. They had even gone to a cemetery one night to take pictures and record sounds looking for EVPs—what people called Electronic Voice Phenomenon, or in other words, spirits talking on a voice recorder. Cheryl wondered how Mia would do in a real-life situation. There was one way to find out.

Cheryl called Mia and explained the problem.

"I think we should ask Brooke to come with us," Mia said. "She's a professional photographer, you know, with pro equipment and skills."

"I don't know her very well," Cheryl said. "How would she do on a real investigation? Is she going to get scared and want to leave?"

"Maybe, but I don't think so. We should also ask Robert. He actually goes ghost hunting all the time."

"I don't think it's ghosts," Cheryl answered. "I think it's a stray cat or an opossum or something like that."

"It wouldn't hurt to have him along," Mia countered.

"Okay, if we're going to turn it into a full investigation, we might as well invite Tony, too. He's into the paranormal."

"Sounds good to me," Mia said. "I'll call Brooke and Tony. You can call Robert. We'll meet on Saturday afternoon. Details to follow."

"Great," Cheryl said before she ended the call.

Cheryl took the papers to her mother and told her about all the spider webs. Her mother nodded and waved her off. She was knee-deep in paperwork about another property and didn't want to discuss her daughter's activities.

"Mother, that's plain rude. I may be your daughter, but I'm also a person, and I did just wade through a jungle of horrid spiders for you."

"Mmmm, hmmm," her mother replied and nodded slowly, pretty much ignoring Cheryl.

"Mom? Really? I need to find out what you know about this. There were strange noises and some paper moved by itself. This was not a fun trip to the old house for me."

"Sweetie, go make some tea and relax. You saw some spider webs, and a breeze made some paper move. It's hardly an episode of Monster Hunters, now, is it?"

"I understand this doesn't seem serious to you, but I have a couple of friends that are going over there with me on Saturday afternoon. We're going to do an investigation just like they do on Monster Hunters. Something is going on over there, and I intend to find out what it is!"

With a little help, she organized Mia, Brooke, Robert, and Tony to come with her on Saturday afternoon. They all brought multiple flashlights and a camera, and Robert brought his digital voice recorder. He was the only one who had ever done a real paranormal investigation before, while Cheryl, Mia, and Brooke had only seen them on TV and gone to that cemetery. Cheryl wasn't sure how much investigating Tony had done, but felt it was probably a lot less than Robert.

Robert became the self-designated leader of the group, even though it was Cheryl's mother's house. They entered through the back door since Cheryl had already swept a path through the spider webs.

"I thought you said you had swept the cobwebs out," Mia whispered. "This is terrible."

Who knew spiders could repair webs so quickly? "Imagine how it felt being here by myself," said Cheryl. "How did they rebuild them so fast? I was just here Thursday afternoon."

"Nature doesn't wait long to reclaim things, I guess," Tony said.

"It's not like there are vines growing everywhere or trees in the house. It's just all the spider webs," Robert said. "I've been investigating for years, and this is the worst I've ever seen in a house with furniture."

"Well, it gets more interesting. There was definitely something in here, but the only marks in the dust were made by me," Cheryl said.

As they made their way into the dining room, Robert stopped them. "Everyone, stop! We're going to ruin any evidence by walking and touching things."

"So, what do you suggest?" Mia asked.

"I'd like before and after pictures of the floors in every room. I want evidence if a room is undisturbed before we go in. In fact, if it's undisturbed, then we should stay out of the room," Robert answered. "We can investigate every room from the hall or just the doorway. The kitchen, the dining room, the study, and the living room already have footprints from Cheryl being here the other day, right, Cheryl?"

"Yes, those are the only places I went, and I didn't leave much in the study. I was looking for signs of the intruder if that's what it was, but I never saw any track of anything but me,"

Robert gave everyone a station in an area that had already had some traffic. He put his digital recorder in the study.

"The first rule of investigating is, don't whisper. If you whisper, it's hard to tell if you are a person or a spirit leaving an EVP. So, *if* you need to say something, just say it in a normal voice. Now let's do a voice check. Each of you will say your name in your normal voice."

They took turns doing that.

"This gives me a baseline if we get an EVP. I will be able to separate our voices from anything paranormal," Robert explained.

"What if they can mimic us?" Tony asked as he looked around. "They could, couldn't they?"

"Good point, Tony," Mia said. "How do you tell that, Robert?"

"It is a good point, but I'm not sure of an answer. I can separate out spirits sometimes because of the frequency they are on. It's not an exact science."

"What about pictures? When should we take pictures?" Brooke asked, who had brought her professional Nikon.

"Take pictures whenever and wherever you feel like something is there. Take pictures of the room you've been assigned to and after a half an hour or so, we'll all change places," Robert said. A loud crash punctuated his sentence, almost like a lamp had fallen over or something.

"Where was that?" Robert asked, his eyes growing wide.

"It seemed to come from down the hall where no one has been yet," Brooke said.

"Who is closest?" Robert asked.

"I am," Cheryl said. "Do you want me to walk down the hall and see what I can see?"

"No, Brooke needs to be the first one to walk down there and take pictures, especially of the floors and her professional-graded camera. Remember, I want those before pictures for comparison with the ones we take when we leave. If there is an undisturbed room, I especially want pictures of those floors. Got it, Brooke?"

"I'm on it," Brooke said to Robert. "I'm passing Cheryl now. I'm going to switch to movie mode and record the whole thing. Then I'll come back and get some stills."

"Be careful," Mia called after her.

"Thanks for trying to scare me, Mia," Brooke called over her shoulder. "I had almost forgotten we're in an old house with spider webs everywhere and strange noises." The sarcasm in her voice made Tony chuckle.

"You don't have to be mean," Mia said with a pout.

"I'm sorry. You're right."

She swept her way down the hall while filming the whole thing, stopping at each room and shooting videos of every aspect available from the door. Then she stopped the video and took stills.

"There's going to be a lot of evidence to review," she said as she worked her way back.

Tony grinned. "That's the fun part."

Robert smiled. He enjoyed evidence review, too, but it was usually difficult to get anyone else to help. He was going to like working with Tony and Brooke. He hadn't decided yet about Mia. Of course, Cheryl was an old friend and gave them access to the house, so at least for this investigation, she was a key member of the team.

"I like going through the pictures and videos, but listening for EVPs puts me to sleep," Mia said. "Well, listening to any audio that isn't music puts me to sleep.

"Really?" Robert said. "That's my favorite part."

"I just really want to find out what is in this house and I'd be perfectly happy to find out it's a raccoon or a cat or an opossum," Cheryl said.

"Brooke? How's it going?" Robert called out.

There was no answer.

"Brooke?" he said louder.

"OMG! Where is she?" Mia squealed.

Robert turned to Cheryl. "Cheryl, were you watching her?"

"I saw her stop at a doorway to take pictures. Next time I looked up, she was gone," Cheryl answered.

"I'm out of here," Mia yelled as she ran for the door. "Tony, are you coming?"

Robert turned toward Tony. "I'll give you a ride if you want to stay."

"Mia, go ahead without me. I'm staying."

'Thanks, man," Robert said. "Cheryl, are you okay? Have you seen or heard anything?"

"I'm okay, but where is Brooke? Will you come with me to look?"

"Tony and I will both be right there."

They moved toward Cheryl's location at the beginning of the long hallway. They followed Brooke's footprints in the dust until they came to the last room. All they found was undisturbed dust and her camera on the ground.

"This doesn't look good . . ." Tony said.

Robert let out a low whistle. "This house is way bigger than it looks. Cheryl, you know the house better than we do. Where does this hallway go to?"

"Oh, it goes—"

"Hey, guys, you should come down here," Brooke yelled. Her voice sounded like it came from the bottom of a staircase that went to a landing then doubled back to the bottom.

"I believe you were about to say the basement, weren't you?" Robert snickered to Cheryl. "You left your camera up here, Brooke. You were supposed to get the before pictures, remember?" he yelled down to her.

"You try using a flashlight while sweeping the stairs and walking down them, all while carrying an expensive camera," Brooke called.

"You were brave to come down here alone at all," Cheryl said. "And thank you for clearing away the webs."

"I got some before video, and there was some kind of marks in the dust coming down the staircase. I got pictures. Oh, Tony, thanks for picking up my camera," Brooke said as she pointed to the camera at Tony's feet.

Tony shrugged. "I didn't bring your camera down. This must be someone else's."

"No, I recognize my camera, and that is it. It has my initials on it," Brooke said and paused. "So, if you didn't bring it down, who did?"

Everyone looked at each other. No one stepped forward. They all said some version of "not me" together. Apparently, Brooke's camera had made it to the first landing on its own.

Just then the door to the upstairs slammed shut. Cheryl was closest, so she ran to the top of the stairs. She heaved a sigh when she realized it was not locked. "It must have been the wind . . ." she said, not believing it. "Ghosts don't leave footprints, do they?"

"It's never been established," Robert answered. "Well, while we're down here, we might as well look around. Brooke, did you see anything in the rooms upstairs that looked like it had fallen over or caused the crash?"

"No, it all looked fairly undisturbed. But I want to look around down here before going back up."

"You go ahead and look. I'll stand guard at the door," Cheryl said.

"That works," Robert said. "We wouldn't want anything to lock it. Brooke, can you video this room before we trample all over it?"

"First thing I did after someone brought my camera down," Brooke said. "Just let me get some stills, and we can have a closer look. What happened to Mia?"

"The crash scared her and she left," Cheryl said.

"So, we're down to four?" Brooke said. "Sounds like the makings of a scary movie."

"Please, don't say that. I'm scared enough already, and this is my house."

11

"I thought it was your mother's?" Tony asked.

"Same thing," Brooke and Cheryl said in unison before they both laughed.

"Standing at the bottom of the stairs, I don't see anything out of the ordinary and nothing is knocked over. What about the rest of you? Do you see anything?" Robert asked, trying to get the team back on track.

"From up here, it looks like there is a container by the washing machine that's been kicked over," Cheryl said.

They all pointed their flashlights in that direction. No one had been over there yet, but the dust, however, showed the tracks of some kind of animal. It didn't look like a cat or dog; it was bigger and had sharp claws by the look of the tracks.

"Is there any way a cat or dog or something could be living here?" Tony asked. "Maybe there's another entrance or window in the basement?"

"Not that I remember," Cheryl murmured. "Wouldn't there be light coming in if that was the case?"

"Good point." Robert nodded. "Turn off all the flashlights and look for any source of light. Cheryl, would you close the door up there as well?"

"Dang, it's dark in here," Brooke whined. "I am going to get claustrophobic."

"It's so dark my eyes aren't even adjusting," Tony added.

"I know, right?" Cheryl said. Standing by the only light source, she felt marginally better with the sliver of light coming from the crack under the door.

"Let's give it a few minutes," Robert pleaded. "Stay where you are and be very quiet. Wait until you hear something to turn your light on and point it directly at the sound source."

They sat quietly waiting for any kind of noise. There was only the darkness and silence. The group was sufficiently scared within five minutes, at which time Robert called for everyone to turn their lights back on. Cheryl was the only one who did not comply.

12

"Cheryl?" they called.

The whole group directed their lights to the top of the stairs. Cheryl was gone.

"Cheryl!" they all screamed.

The door at the top of the steps opened slowly. "What?" Cheryl asked sheepishly as she stepped into the basement.

"When did you open the door?"

"After we all turned off our flashlights . . ." she said. "It was too scary for me."

Robert glared at her. "You can't do that during an investigation. You have to tell someone you're moving locations. Otherwise, we'll think we have evidence when we don't."

"I did tell you. I said I couldn't take it and I was going out to the hall," Cheryl said, meeting his glare.

"I didn't hear you," Robert said dismissively. "Did anyone else hear her?"

"Nope," Tony and Brooke agreed with each other.

"Did anyone notice the door open?" Robert asked.

"Nope."

"Well, this is a new one for me," Robert said. "Usually we see and hear things we shouldn't. This is the first time I've *not* seen something when I should have."

"Well . . . how do you explain it?" Brooke asked.

"I don't." Robert shook his head. "I don't."

"So, what now?" Brooke asked.

"I think we need to look at your video and pictures, and then Tony and I will listen to the recording to see if we found anything interesting and if we can hear Cheryl on the recorder. If we can hear her on the recorder, then we have a reverse anomaly. I've never heard of it before so we could be the first."

"We're not going to do all that here, are we?" Cheryl asked.

"Nah, I'm thinking we go get a pizza or two and do it back at my place. Plan?"

"Plan," they all agreed.

13

CHAPTER 3

Since Mia had left, they were all in the same car. It was Robert's, and even with only four, it was a tight fit with all his ghost hunting equipment.

Cheryl looked out the back window at her old house. Her mother had moved out of it after her father had died. Was it ten years ago? Mrs. Brently wouldn't sell it or let any of the furniture be sold. Cheryl's uncle had taken her over there one day to help him put sheets over the furniture. She was only twelve, but she remembered it vividly.

The house didn't look any different from the outside. It was a red brick ranch style with a formal living room, a formal dining room, a family room, three large bedrooms, a study, and a half basement. The garage was in the back, so the driveway was all the way to one side of the house.

The trees had gotten bigger in those ten years, but the house looked just like it did when they lived there. Her mother would not set foot in it, saying it held too many memories, but she wouldn't let it go for the same reason. Cheryl would have it when she was ready to settle down. Or at least, that's what her mom had said.

Cheryl was torn back to the present when she saw someone standing in the front bedroom window next to the study.

"Look," she yelled. "Look at the bedroom window! Do you see someone? Who is in there?"

Robert stopped the car. They could all see a figure in the window. Brooke had the presence of mind to take a picture.

"Do we need to go back in?" Tony asked. He didn't sound too keen on the idea. He had his fingers crossed that the answer would be a resounding no.

Everyone looked at Robert. He was their leader, right?

Robert looked at their faces and knew they didn't want to go back inside. "Let's look at Brooke's picture first," he said.

Brooke pulled up the picture on the back of the camera. It was too small to see much, but it was big enough to know that once she got it onto her computer, she would have a detailed picture of whoever it was.

"Let's go get the pizza as planned and review what we got today. Whatever or whoever was in the window will still be there another day if it's a ghost. And if it's human, we could get lucky and it will be gone," Robert said.

The car filled with sighs of relief. They had all had enough frights for one day. They were ready to relax, eat, and review the evidence together.

Cheryl called and ordered the pizza for pick up, and it was ready by the time they arrived. Everyone chipped in, and Cheryl went in to get the pizzas. From there, they went directly to Robert's apartment where everyone else had left their cars. Brooke went to her car and retrieved her iPad.

Robert's apartment was a large one-bedroom with a good-sized living room and a small dining room off the kitchen. He used the dining room as a study/office and used the kitchen as little as possible. His idea of eating at home was to drive through a fast-food place and bring it home.

Robert did one better and set Brooke's memory card into his TV. They all had a seat in the living room to eat and look at the videos and pictures. They went straight to the last picture. They wanted to see who or what had been standing in the window.

"Even on a big screen, I don't know what that is. Is it a person or a shadow?" Cheryl murmured. "It looked like a person when I saw it, but this is more of a shadow . . .."

"Shadow man," Tony and Robert yelled together.

"Yes, that's what it looks like on this TV, but I'm telling you, I could see some facial details and a shirt. Brooke, is there any way to lighten it or something?" Cheryl asked.

"I can on my iPad," Brooke said. "Let me have the card, and we'll see what it looks like with some light added."

Robert popped out the memory card and handed it to Brooke.

"I'll create some new files with the edits, and we'll be able to look at them on the TV," she said. "It'll only take a few minutes. Go ahead and eat. Just be sure to save me another piece."

"Ready," Brooke said after a few minutes. "I have set up a file of only the pics and moved them to my computer, so if you need something lightened, I can do it while you study the original."

She gave Robert the card, and they were looking at the picture again in seconds.

"It does look like a man," Tony said. "But there's something odd about him . . .."

Cheryl's phone rang. It was Mia. "Can I help with evidence review? I know I chickened out at the house, but I never said I would be any help at the location. I'm a chicken."

"Come on over," Cheryl said after Robert nodded his head. "We're doing it at Robert's place, and you're not going to believe what we got."

"Thanks, Cheryl."

Cheryl ended the call and slid her phone into her pocket. "Mia's on her way over to help with the review. But she won't be going back to the house, especially after seeing this picture."

Tony thought about it and said, "I don't know if I want to go back to this house either. What is this guy? We know he's not real. We were in there. There was no one in that house except us.

17

We didn't even find any sign of animals except for the strange prints in the basement. I'll gladly do EVP review, but I don't think I want to go back inside the house."

"That leaves just Cheryl, Brooke, and me. That should be enough. Are you ladies in?" Robert asked.

"I'm obviously in," Cheryl said. "I have to find out what's going on in my house. What if this is a real man and he's staying in the basement or something? I have to find out."

"I'm in, too," Brooke said. "You can't rely on camera phones to get proper pictures."

"Well, let's review what we have so far and then we'll know what to bring next time. Speaking of time . . .. Does anyone know exactly what time we left?" Robert asked.

"I have time stamps on my photos," said Brooke. "Let me look. Here it is . . .. It was seven-thirty. Right about dusk."

"If we don't find anything next time we go back, we will have to look at the time factor in case it is something residual," Robert said.

"What's residual?" Mia asked as she walked in without so much as a knock on the door.

"Residual is something that happens when the area displays a past incident over and over at the same time of day, week, or year. It happens all the time," Robert explained.

"I know what it means," Mia said. "I was asking what was caught that might be residual."

Robert laughed. "I should have known you would know what it was. You watch all the ghost shows and read all the books, right?"

"Are you making fun of me?" Mia said.

"I'm sorry," he said mocking her, "I couldn't resist. You make it so easy."

"Mia, look at this picture," Cheryl piped in.

"Wow. Where did you get this?" Mia gasped. "This is the clearest picture of a ghost I've ever seen. He almost looks alive except for the aura around him and the wispiness of his face."

"So, you have no doubt it's a ghost? You don't think it could be a living man?" Brooke asked.

"No, it couldn't be. Look at his face. You can practically see through it and look down here at his hand. It's like the end bits are missing." Mia was standing in front of the flat screen pointing to what she was seeing. "And finally, notice the aura around him. It's even and slightly tinted with blue. Brooke, have you ever caught anyone's aura with your camera?"

Brooke shook her head. "Mia is right. I would never have these anomalies on real people."

"We can have someone stand in the window, and you get a shot of it next time we go. We'll recreate the scene and circumstances to verify. Sound good to everyone?"

They all nodded.

"Let's watch some video," Mia suggested. "You were doing video almost from the beginning, weren't you?"

Brooke nodded.

Robert selected the first video, and they all watched. The house was so dusty and filled with spider webs, and there were thousands of orbs. When there were that many in a dusty environment, Robert ruled them out as any kind of evidence.

Cheryl appreciated the opinion because eventually, she was going to own this house and didn't want everyone thinking there were thousands of ghosts in there.

They documented the footprints Cheryl had left the last time she was there. Other than those, they saw no footprints in that room or the rest of the bedrooms until they saw the basement floor.

"Can anyone here identify those tracks?" Robert asked.

Everyone looked around. None of them were trackers in the first place, so it came as no surprise that no one could identify the tracks. All they could do was validate they were not human or cat or dog or anything they'd ever seen before.

"We'll have to get a bona-fide tracker to look at a picture," Robert said. "Brooke, can you get me a picture?"

"Already on it . . .. It should be in your mailbox . . . now."

"I have found an internet group that might be able to identify it," Mia said.

"On it," Brooke said. "I'm emailing everyone a copy of the footprint if you need it to show an expert or something. And whatever else you want prints of, just say so and I'll email a copy to each of you."

"Then let's continue with the video," Robert said.

The sheer volume of spider webs in the video was enough to make a lot of people stay away from the house. Where there's smoke there's fire, and where there's spider webs there's bound to be spiders.

"Do you think I should put some insect bombs in the house to get rid of the spiders before we go in again?" Cheryl asked. "I could put a bomb in every room, and then we could clear out the webs once and for all."

"No," Tony said.

"Yes," Mia said quickly.

"You don't get to vote, Mia," Cheryl said. "You left."

"Nobody gets a vote," Robert said. "It's your house, Cheryl. You do what you think you should, but it *would* be much safer without so many spiders in there."

"I'll do it tomorrow if someone will come with me," Cheryl said looking around at the group.

"I'll go with you," Robert offered. "We always follow the buddy system."

"Can I come, too?" Brooke asked.

"Don't see why not," Robert said with a nod. "Anybody else?"

"Not me," Mia said. "I'm just as happy to do evidence review."

"I'll go," Tony offered.

"Let's meet here," Robert said. "We can do a little more investigating before we set off the insect bombs."

"I'll need some time to go buy them. Can we meet at eleven?" Cheryl asked.

"Eleven it is." Robert nodded. "We'll meet here and take my car. We'll set up some cameras and a couple of DVRs. It'll be interesting to see what a house looks like while it's bug bombed. And who knows? We could get some spirit activity."

They went back to viewing the evidence from earlier in the day. There were, of course, thousands of orbs. There were a few actual light anomalies, and they marked those for extraction from the footage. Brooke was going to have a lot of work to do, but she looked forward to it.

After reviewing all the pics together on the big screen, they found only five shots that *might* be evidence of something paranormal, and three of those five were of the man in the window. The other two were just light anomalies.

CHAPTER 4

"I just heard back from the tracker club," Mia yelled.

"Cool. Did anyone in the club know what kind of track it was?" Robert asked.

"This is weird . . .. He said they don't get involved in hoaxes. This is the track of an animal which went extinct a hundred years ago on a different continent."

"Ask him if he wants to come to see it for himself," Robert snapped, feeling marginally offended by the insinuation.

Mia frowned. "He lives over two hundred miles away."

"See if anyone in their group lives closer. They could come have a look and take some pics," Cheryl suggested. "We could hold off bug bombing the basement until they see the tracks for themselves."

"He has one man in this area. He's contacting him now to try to get him in on the conversation," Mia said.

"I don't like that he automatically assumed we were trying to pass off a hoax," Robert grumbled.

"Well, imagine how it looks to him. If this animal has been extinct for a hundred years or more, what would you think if someone brought you pictures of his tracks?" Brooke asked.

"None the less, we started off on the wrong foot with this group. Maybe we should call the University in Denton. Someone there might be interested."

"Aren't any of you curious about the creature that might have left this? Do you realize what this means? This could be a species coming back from extinction. This is newsworthy," Cheryl said excitedly.

"Of course, you're right. What branch of science would be interested in it?"

"I don't know. Let me ask the tracking group," Mia said, her fingers flying over her phone screen.

"So, are we still going tomorrow?" Tony asked.

"I hope so," Robert said. "Cheryl? It's up to you."

"I think we should get rid of the spiders, but maybe leave the webs for now. And definitely stay out of the basement until we find out more about this three-clawed creature. I don't even want to set off a bug bomb down there. What if the creature is still there? If the stuff can kill people, it would definitely kill a little critter like this."

"Let's split up for tonight and meet back here in the morning at eleven," Robert said. "We have a possible shadow man to recreate and a lot more to do before we set off those cans tomorrow."

They all gathered their things and started to leave. Tony grabbed the last piece of pizza and was the last one out the door.

Cheryl was up early Sunday morning. She wanted to get a can of bug bomb for each room and knew that would probably mean going to more than one store. The house had at least nine rooms if you counted the bathrooms, so she needed a lot of cans.

It turned out they came in packages of six so she would be able to reserve a few for the basement.

Mia called her around ten to tell her the tracker club had a member who lived in the area and was interested in the case. He wanted to know if he could come look at the house today at one p.m.

"If he doesn't mind meeting us there," Cheryl said. "Robert's car won't hold another person."

"I thought since I am his contact, I should come out, too. I'm just not going inside the house. I'll do whatever I can from outside, but I'm not going inside."

"I don't care if you go in or not," Cheryl said. "But I sure appreciate you finding this guy. What is his name?"

"Jeremy," Mia said. "I don't have his last name yet."

"Did you give him the address?"

"Yes, I didn't want to give a lift to a total stranger. He seemed just as happy to go straight there in his own car."

"Did you tell him about all the spiders?" Cheryl asked.

"I did. Jeremy didn't think it was a big deal. He said he's been in some pretty bad situations when tracking. He should be fine."

"Okay, well, we'll see you around twelve-forty-five. Did you tell Robert?"

Mia chuckled. "Nah, I thought I'd surprise him."

Cheryl wasn't sure if Mia was joking or not. They had been friends for years, but she couldn't always tell when the girl was just kidding around.

Cheryl arrived at Robert's place at exactly eleven. Brooke was already there, and Tony pulled in minutes behind Cheryl.

"Okay, rookies, today we bring out the big guns. I'm going to show you how we set up the video cameras, infrared lights, and DVRs. We're going to be running wires for the cameras to every room in the house."

"Not counting the basement, there are nine rooms," Cheryl said. "Oh, by the way, Mia found a tracking expert who will be here at one p.m. She's going to show up just before Jeremy does to introduce him to us." Cheryl looked at the group as they nodded. "So, we'll want to keep the basement closed up until then. Don't want to compromise or contaminate the data."

"Good attitude, Cheryl." Robert grinned. "We need to treat this like professionals, even though we're not yet."

"Yet," they all said in unison.

"Can we pull through and pick up some sandwiches on the way?" Tony asked. "I'm going to be hungry before we finish."

"Anybody else?" Robert looked at everyone.

"Sounds like a good idea," Cheryl said.

"I'll eat one or two," Brooke added.

Robert pulled into the Burger Barn.

"Give us twelve burgers, four fries, and lots of napkins," he said into the menu mic. "Salt, pepper, ketchup, mustard, and mayo packets for four."

"Any drinks?"

Everyone wanted something different, but they sorted it out.

"Are we ready now?" Robert asked a bit impatiently.

"That's all I need," Tony said from the backseat. "What are you guys going to have?"

The drive to the house was quick. When they arrived, Robert started to bark orders for what needed to be done. There was a table to be set up. He had an adapter for the car that allowed him to use it as a generator when there was no electricity and a super long extension cord for situations like the current one.

He set up a monitor capable of tracking twelve cameras. Today they would be using ten, one for each room and one at the top of the stairs in the basement.

They worked well together, and by one o'clock the house was ready for them to set off the bombs.

Mia drove up at one-ten. and Jeremy followed in his car. Apparently, he had gotten lost and asked Mia to meet him and lead the way. Introductions were made all around, and Jeremy turned out to be a pretty nice guy.

"Cheryl, let's show Jeremy to the basement. That's where these tracks are, Jeremy. There is no light except flashlights. We have the house ready to set off bug bombs, and we will record from outside all afternoon."

"You are welcome to join us. When we entered yesterday, there were tracks on the floor. The other tracks are ours from before we noticed the anomalous tracks."

"I can see most of that," Jeremy said. "Where are the tracks?"

"Right here." Robert shined his light on the tracks they had found."

"These tracks are pretty old," Jeremy murmured. "Look how pronounced your tracks are compared to the others. And these older tracks are partially filled in with newer dust."

"What does that mean as far as identifying it?" Robert asked.

"It means there was a chicken that walked across part of this foundation when it was poured," Jeremy answered.

"What?"

"These tracks are in the cement." Jeremy pointed. "They have been filled in over the years with dirt and dust, until they resemble what my friend online thought was an extinct bird from Indonesia."

"Are you kidding?" Robert asked.

"No, man. I can see this wasn't meant as a hoax. I'll let everyone know. What are you guys up to here anyway?"

"My friend thought there might be some paranormal activity in the house, so we decided we'd better check it out. I've been an investigator for years, though my friends have only ever seen it on TV."

"So, what have you decided? Have you found anything more than chicken tracks?" Jeremy laughed.

"We haven't really started the investigation yet," Robert said defensively. "Once you finish, we are going to bug bomb the house and then clear the cobwebs. We have documented our footprints in the dust and set up surveillance cameras throughout the house. We will be monitoring what happens from the backyard."

"Sounds like you are taking it pretty seriously," Jeremy said.

"Well, we saw someone standing in the window when we left yesterday. We caught it on a professional camera, too. There shouldn't have been anyone in there. Also, the girl who owns the house heard noises when she went in to get some papers. She saw movement, but there were no tracks in the dust. I think it's worth investigating."

"The biggest problem right now, though, are the spiders. My people are freaking out over all the spiders. We swept out some pathways yesterday, and today they were all filled in with new webs. I haven't actually seen a spider yet, but the webs are everywhere."

"Sounds like an interesting case." Jeremy nodded. "I might just stick around to see what the inside of a house looks like when it's bug bombed."

"Feel free," Robert said. "It should start in the next ten minutes or so."

Cheryl walked up and told Robert she had a plan for setting the bombs off in a certain order so no one would be overly exposed to the poison.

"Listen up, people," Robert yelled to get everyone's attention, "Cheryl has the strategy set for who will release what, where, and when."

Cheryl walked them through the plan and checked on the cameras to make sure everything was working as it should.

"Let's do it," Robert called.

Everyone put surgical masks on and started in the farthest bedrooms from the back door, setting off one canister per room. Cheryl took care of the basement and then joined the line of people opening canisters on the main floor.

As they each finished, they ran to the monitors to see what the bombs looked like being dispersed. They watched as the house slowly filled with the foggy fumes. The spider webs became iridescent as the poison settled on them. It was a bizarre scene.

"We should have cleared all the webs before we released the poison," Tony said. "That way the spiders would have been out making new ones, and we'd have a better chance of killing them."

"We'll be sure to do that next time we have a house to investigate that is full of spiders," Robert said shaking his head.

"It was just a thought," Tony mumbled.

What happened next could not have been predicted. Slowly and very deliberately, a ball of light formed in the back bedroom. It grew larger as it moved through the rooms. It seemed to float through the webs as if they weren't there. Slowly it took on a shape.

"Does anyone else see what I'm seeing?" Robert whispered.

"It's beginning to look like what we saw in the window last night," Tony said.

"Let me pull up the photos I took," Brooke offered.

She pulled them up on her computer. It was amazing to see the figure form in front of their eyes.

"Does this kind of thing happen often? Or is this as out of the ordinary as it seems?" Jeremy asked.

"Oh, this is extremely unusual," Robert said. "I've never seen this before in my life."

"I wonder if it has anything to do with the spiders," Cheryl murmured.

"Good question." Robert nodded. "It does seem to draw on the spider webs for its essence."

"How long do we have to wait before we can go in?" Cheryl asked.

"According to the package, at least three hours," Tony said, holding the empty bomb box. "Whatever that is we're looking at, it can't be human. It wouldn't have made it through the first round of fog."

"What room is that in, Cheryl?" Robert asked.

"That's the room where we saw the man standing in the window. That was Pete's bedroom when he moved back home."

"Who's Pete?" everyone asked at once.

"My older brother. He was in college briefly, and Mom turned it into a craft room, then he moved back home. Then he moved to Los Angeles, and Dad turned it into a media room but then Pete moved back home. They finally quit converting it into anything else since he always came back home."

"Where is he now?" Brooke asked.

"He died when my father died. They were in a boating accident. They were both knocked unconscious, and neither of them had a safety vest on. Dad apparently died from the impact, and Pete drowned," Cheryl said.

"Where were they boating?" Mia asked who had joined the team monitoring the house cameras.

"Lake Texoma. They had gone out early while it was still dark to get some fishing in."

"What happened?" Jeremy asked.

"A guy was drunk, traveling full speed. He must not have seen their lights. He ran smack into them. He died on impact with a huge boulder," Cheryl said.

She was tearing up now at the thoughts of her father and brother and thinking of her mother who would no longer come to this house. The tears welled up and began to flow.

The strange figure inside turned to look directly at the camera. It seemed to know it was being watched. It didn't seem very happy about it, either. It peered into the camera, turned bright blue before it vanished. Without warning, a spider crawled across the lens. Cheryl jumped and Mia squealed, putting her hand out to swat it away. The spider stood in the center of the lens long enough to make Robert back up a bit.

It was as if the little guy was looking at them instead of vice versa. And on top of the general creep factor of having a spider trying to stare you down was the fact that he was neither dead nor giving any indication of dying. How many of these guys were there, and how many were immune to the poison?

CHAPTER 5

The spider seemed firmly planted in the middle of the camera lens, blocking their vision of the center of the room. Soon, another spider joined him, then another and another. Within minutes, the spiders were blocking their view of the entire room.

"It's like they're working together on a plan," Robert said. "I've never seen spiders do this. Of course, I've never seen so many spiders gather together like this for any reason before."

"I have," Tony said. "Daddy Long Legs will gather like this. There will be so many you can't even tell they're spiders. They look like a fur ball or fuzz, but if you touch them, they'll scatter in every direction. If you don't know to expect it, it'll startle or scare the wits out of you."

"These aren't Daddy Long Legs, though," Robert said.

"No, they would be black if they were," Tony said. "These are iridescent white. And it's not dark enough for the video to be using infrared yet. Besides, Daddy Long Legs have really long legs."

"Then what the hell are we watching?" Robert asked.

"I don't know," Tony said. "Spiders aren't my specialty. I just know about Daddy Long Legs."

"They only seem to be focused on that room where we saw the ghost," Brooke said. "None of the other cameras are being covered up with spiders."

"That doesn't even make sense," Robert said. "The spider webs are no worse in that room than they are in the rest of the house. And there is no more or less poison in that room. The only possible explanation would have to be the shadow man we saw in there."

"I wouldn't go that far," Jeremy said. "There has to be a reasonable explanation that doesn't involve the paranormal. You just need to find it."

"Like what?" Robert asked with more than a hint of agitation.

"I don't know. I don't investigate the paranormal, but surely someone has run across something similar before," Jeremy said.

"Not that I've heard of," Robert said. "And I go to a lot of conferences. It's all moot until we hear the recording."

"True," Jeremy replied.

"How long before we can go back in?" Brooke asked.

"Two and a half hours."

"Plenty of time to check out the rest of the cameras and see if we can see any spider movement in them," Jeremy said.

It seemed that Robert was beginning to develop a strong dislike for Jeremy. Who did he think he was? He was acting like the team leader when all he was, was a guest. But it *would* be their best use of time, so Robert agreed.

There was a picnic table behind the house where Robert had set up his monitors and other equipment. They all took a seat on the built-in benches. Robert zoomed in on the first bedroom. "Does anyone see anything that looks like a spider in this room?"

They all agreed they did not. Robert zoomed on each room, and the only one with evidence of a live spider was the room the stranger had been seen in. They still couldn't see in that room because the lens was covered with spiders.

"Let's go look in the window," Cheryl said. "We should be able to see most of the room from there."

"Great idea," Robert said, standing up to take the lead. But Cheryl was excited and sprinted off ahead of everyone.

Before they rounded the front corner of the house, they heard a blood-curdling scream. Everyone started to run to see if Cheryl was in any danger. There she stood at least two feet from the window. As they approached, each one stopped before they were even with Cheryl.

The window was covered with spiders, completely blocking out the room. What seemed to have stopped Cheryl was the fact that some of them were on the outside of the window. Cheryl backed slowly away from the house. This was going to call for a professional exterminator.

"I don't know if I can go back inside this house," Cheryl whispered.

"Welcome to my world," Mia muttered. "Even one spider is too many for me."

"These are just so unusual," Cheryl said. "And that blue light and the shadow man . . .. What was that all about?"

"No exterminator is going to fix that!" Robert said. "This house has already yielded more evidence of paranormal activity than any place I've ever been. And I've been to some famously active places."

"I found an exterminator on my phone. I'm going to call them," Cheryl offered.

"On a Sunday?" Brooke asked. "Who's going to be open on a Sunday to kill bugs?"

"Let's find out!" Cheryl said, still shaking from the experience of facing live spiders outside the house, who seemed to have a plan that didn't include her in any good way.

Cheryl started making some phone calls, wanting to find someone who would come out now while the spiders were covering the lens and the windows. She wanted them to see what they were up against.

"Hello?" someone at Rocky's Pest Control answered.

Cheryl explained the situation and Rocky agreed to come out and give them an estimate. Cheryl breathed a sigh of relief.

"We have a lot to look into here," Robert said. "We have eliminated the footprints in the basement, but there is still the fact that Cheryl left the basement when all the lights were off and no one noticed. We still have a shadow man that has shown up twice. We have a floating blue light. We will leave the spiders to the bug guy for now, but I suspect they are related to the blue light or to the shadow man or both."

"Where do we start?" Jeremy asked.

"You're here as a guest. You are not on the team," Robert said in his most authoritative tone.

"I know, but I'd like to be. This is really interesting," Jeremy said, looking at Cheryl, knowing it was her house.

"We have enough help," Robert said.

Cheryl did not disagree.

"Well then, I guess I'll be going . . .. You have my number if you change your mind. Call me anytime," Jeremy said looking directly at Cheryl.

"Cheryl! Jeremy was flirting with you!" Brooke whispered after Jeremy had driven off.

"I thought he was a little creepy," Cheryl said.

"I thought he was kind of cute," Brooke countered.

"I think we should get back to reviewing evidence," Robert muttered. "I think we might want to call in a medium."

"What? Like a psychic?" Brooke asked, chuckling at the thought.

"Exactly." Robert nodded. "Things are going on here that defy logical explanation. I know a woman one town over from here who might be interested in helping. They call her Madam Celeste. The problem is she doesn't drive. I would have to go get her."

"Let's see what the bug guy says first," Cheryl offered, "before we go all Ghost Whisperer on it."

As if on cue, Rocky drove up in his well-marked truck. Cheryl and Robert escorted him around to the front of the house to look at the spiders on the window. He walked up to the window and with a gloved-hand, picked up a spider, pulled a small plastic jar out of his pocket, and placed the spider inside. The lid was a magnifier, and Rocky seemed to be able to see the details better through it.

"This is just a common house spider," he said. "They're pretty harmless."

"Even in numbers like these?" Robert pointed to the window.

Rocky looked up at the window and jumped back a foot without thinking. "I thought those were curtains! Where in the hell did this many spiders come from?"

"We just set off bug bombs in the whole house," Robert said. "But this is the only room we can see spiders in. But there are spider webs everywhere inside the house."

"That's unusual . . . .. I wonder if there is a crack in the window or something that drew them here when the bombs went off. That's usually what happens. The bugs head for a space the bomb doesn't get to. That must be what happened here."

"Follow me," Cheryl said as she led everyone back to the monitors. "Do you see this blank screen?"

Rocky nodded.

"Those are spiders. It's like they don't want us to see inside that room. Can you explain it?"

"No, but I can probably fix it. When did you set off the bombs?"

"It's been about three hours," Mia piped up.

"Let me go get my mask out of the truck and something to spray them with. I'll be right back."

He looked like an astronaut or something when he walked back up. He had put on a white bodysuit and a helmet that covered his whole face and head. He walked alone into the house as the team watched on the monitors until he entered the room. In a minute, Rocky had wiped off the lens with his gloved-hand and they could see the room clearly. He waved at them and showed them the spiders on the lens were dead.

He walked over to the window and began to scrape with his hand, but not all the spiders were dead. They began to scurry around, and many climbed on his suit. He turned on his sprayer and aimed first for his arms. He then turned his attention to the window. Again, they were stopped in their tracks. They were dying so fast there was a pile of dead ones rising from the floor.

After spraying the window, he looked around the room for any stragglers. He found a few near the lens and sprayed that area down, trying to avoid the camera itself. When he was satisfied he had killed them all, he turned to leave. He couldn't see the foot-long spider hitching a ride on his back. Everyone started to scream, trying to warn him.

They ran to the door to tell him before he took off his helmet, but they were too late. He had taken it off in the kitchen as he approached the door. The spider bit him and leaped to the ceiling, scurrying out of sight.

CHAPTER 6

Rocky was pretty calm for someone who had just been bitten by a spider the size of a small dog.

"It hurts a little," he said, "but they're not poisonous. I'll be fine."

"No, this is my fault. I'll take you to the ER. I know where the closest one is. They have to check and make sure it didn't give you some disease or something. Have you had your rabies shots?" Cheryl asked.

"Spiders don't carry rabies," Rocky said. "I'm fine, really."

"No arguments. I'm taking you, and I don't want to hear another word about it."

"I'll go with you," Mia offered. "I have nothing left to do here today."

"I am feeling a bit dizzy," Rocky added. "Maybe it wouldn't hurt to see a doctor."

The three of them left in Mia's car.

"I guess that's a wrap for today," Robert said with a shrug. "I don't think we need to go back in there until we find that spider and get rid of it and make sure it's the only one in there."

Brooke and Tony agreed. They started to pack up all the equipment outside. They left the cameras and cords inside. Better safe than sorry.

Meanwhile, Cheryl and Mia took Rocky to the closest Emergency Clinic. They only had to wait a few minutes because Rocky was bleeding from the bite on the back of his neck.

The doctor looked at the bite and whistled. "You say this was a spider bite? This is too big to be a tarantula."

"It was a very large spider. I've never seen a spider so big, but we have pictures."

The doctor waited for Cheryl to produce them.

"We didn't bring them with us. Those pictures are on someone else's camera."

"There must be some form of blood thinner in the venom. I don't know of a spider that delivers a dose of blood thinner, though. But this is bleeding too much for a spider bite, even from a "very large" spider. I'm going to give you something to counteract that and then we'll clean up the wound. We'll give you some antibiotics, but first, we're going to do some blood tests. Someone will be in shortly to do all that," the doctor said.

Robert, Tony, and Brooke went back to Robert's to do some evidence review together. Robert still wanted to find out if the recorder had picked up the sound of Cheryl leaving the basement. He also wanted to look for Madam Celeste's phone number. He had a feeling she might enjoy this case.

They turned on the video from one of the cameras and sat down to watch while Robert put in his earbuds to listen to the basement audio. When he reached the part where Cheryl had left the room silently, it was anything but silent. Robert heard the door open, he heard Cheryl say she was leaving because of her claustrophobia, and he heard the door close.

He paused the video and set the recorder on speakers. "Hey guys. You gotta' listen to this!"

They sat in silence, not believing what they were hearing. How could this be? They had all been there, and not one of them had heard her leave. What's more, none of them had seen the light that should have leaked in when she opened the door.

"Play it again," Brooke prodded.

Robert obliged. It was the same. He played it three more times.

"How did we not hear that?" Brooke asked in disbelief. "That's clear as a crystal bell. We should have heard it."

Robert nodded. "I agree. That is some paranormal crap, right there. I'm calling Madam Celeste in the morning."

"Isn't there a charge for her services?" Brooke asked.

"She's friends with my aunt. I'm hoping she'll be interested enough to do it for free. Speaking of services, I wonder how Rocky is doing. Can you text Cheryl and see?"

"On it," Brooke said as she pulled out her phone.

"Can I use your earbuds to listen to the rest of this recording for any normal EVPs?" Tony asked Robert.

Robert still couldn't believe he had found someone who enjoyed reviewing evidence as much as he did. "Sure. I'll watch the videos."

Brooke had moved to another room to talk with Cheryl. Apparently, there was too much to text.

Brooke returned to the living room saying, "They think he's having a mild reaction to the spider bite, but not a poisonous one. They're going to be sending him home soon. Cheryl's going to call when they leave the clinic so one of us can meet her at the house to pick up his truck. He's not to drive tonight, though."

"Just bring him here and let him sleep it off on the couch. Then I'll take him to get his truck in the morning. Guess he won't be going back in the house after this," Robert said.

"On the contrary, he wants to get that "monster" as he calls it before it decides to relocate."

"Good on him, then," Robert said. "I'll be happy to come out and film it. Haha."

"I'll tell her to bring him here. She says he's a little loopy. The meds they gave him are going to keep him knocked out for at least a few hours, maybe all night, so he shouldn't be any trouble."

"Great. You look like you're ready to go, Brooke. Don't you want to stick around and see our new friend all doped up?"

"I have to work in the morning. I'd better get home. Let me know anything you find out. And if you need me to look for anything on the camera, just let me know."

"Will do," Robert and Tony said in unison.

Brooke left as Robert and Tony were ordering pizza. Shortly after, Cheryl arrived with Rocky. Mia didn't even come in; instead, she went straight to her car and headed home.

Robert and Tony got Rocky settled in on the couch. He was sound asleep. "Guess that's more pizza for us," Tony said with a laugh.

Robert shook his head. "We'll leave him a couple pieces. He'll probably be hungry by the time he wakes up. Grab some, Cheryl. You have to hear this reverse EVP and see a couple of these pics."

"Thanks," she said, picking up the smallest piece. "I want to hear it and catch up on the evidence."

"I'm going to call Madam Celeste in the morning," Robert said. "I want to get her out here as soon as the giant spider is out of there. She might pick up on who the shadow man is or what's up with the blue light. She might even have an idea about what's going on with all the spiders."

"That would be great. I don't want to tell my mom about this until we have some answers for her. She won't even go into the house as it is. This would all really take it over the top for her."

"We'll solve this, Cheryl. I promise," Robert said. "Celeste is really good, you'll see."

CHAPTER 7

Rocky didn't wake up until morning. He was thoroughly confused. Fortunately, Robert was already up and dressed. He offered Rocky some eggs while he explained what had happened yesterday. Rocky's memory jarred pretty quickly, and he was ready to go back in search of that monster spider.

"Let's eat and see where Cheryl is. Then I have to call someone," Robert said.

Robert called Celeste, but her assistant answered. "I really needed to talk to Madam Celeste herself. My aunt is an old friend and client of hers."

"What's her name? I may know her, too," Emma, the assistant, said.

"Her name is Margie."

"Margie Pettijohn?" Emma asked.

"Yes."

"Oh! I know Margie. What do you need help with?"

"I really wanted to ask Madam Celeste for a favor on a paranormal case we're working on right now. At least, we think it's paranormal. So far, we have some particularly strange evidence. There is a shadow man we all saw with the naked eye, and we also have it on video."

"Wow! That does sound interesting. I can tell you right now that Celeste is booked all week, but I could come if you don't mind a trainee," Emma said, who was genuinely curious as she was picking up some bizarre images just talking over the phone.

"Would you have to charge us for it?" Robert asked timidly.

"No, not for the first consult. If I like the case, then we will talk money. I can't promise it will be free, but it won't be nearly as expensive as it would be if Madam Celeste were to do it."

"Can you come today? I'll be happy to pick you up just like I would for Celeste."

Emma paused, checking through her schedule. "It would need to be this morning."

"I can be there in forty-five minutes. Would that be early enough?"

"That works for me. I take it you know where Madam Celeste's is?"

"Yes. I've driven my aunt there a couple of times," Robert said.

"Then I'll see you soon," Emma said before ending the call.

Madam Celeste had been listening to the call and fully approved Emma taking her place today. If it became complicated, she trusted Emma to call her. This would be free of charge because this would be a practice run for Emma to see how much she had learned so far, while also gaining some experience in the field. Celeste had a feeling she would be getting involved in this one before it was over. Her favorite spirit appeared and nodded in agreement.

Robert dropped Rocky off at his truck. "Are you going in to look for the spider," Robert asked.

"How long are you going to be?"

"I should be back here in an hour," Robert said.

Rocky nodded and checked the time on his phone. "I'll wait for you, then."

"I'm going to spend a little of that hour setting up the monitors since the cameras are already in place. You can watch them for any signs of the spider, and besides, Cheryl should be around soon," Robert added.

"I'll still wait for you," Rocky said.

Robert took off for Gloryville to pick up Emma. Gloryville was only about ten minutes away from Bella View where they all lived, but he had allowed time for dropping Rocky off at Cheryl's childhood home. He would be a little early picking up Emma, but "better early than late," he always said.

Emma was ready when Robert arrived, and she grabbed her bag full of her tools of the trade. They would be back a lot sooner than he had told Rocky.

"So, what exactly is going on in this house?" Emma asked as they drove toward Bella View.

"Well, like I had said, we have all seen a shadow man with our own eyes and then again on a camera monitor. Then, the next day, we saw a light that changed from a small light to a large blue light to the shadow man." Robert glanced at Emma. "Then, we saw some spiders acting as if they were being controlled by one brain. Then, Rocky was bitten by a spider that was at least a foot long."

"Spiders?" Emma squeaked. "I really don't like spiders."

"The guy that was bitten is an exterminator. He has killed most of what was in there, and it's had a whole day to air out. I think it will be okay," he lied. He knew the biggest spider was probably still in the house, but why worry the psychic?

"What are you lying to me about?" Emma asked slowly. "The spiders or how safe it is now?"

"Um . . . I um," Robert stammered.

"I knew it! Why do people try to lie to psychics?"

Robert took a deep breath. "Okay. The biggest spider I've ever seen may still be in the house, and it is scary big. But," he emphasized, "I left the exterminator there to work on it, so there's that at least."

"I will see what I can pick up from the outside of the house," Emma said. "Maybe I won't even have to go in."

"Oh, I do hope you will go inside. I want some answers about the shadow man and some other things I'll show and tell you about when we get there."

"I talk to spirits, but not all shadows are spirits. And I don't have a clue what giant spiders have to do with the paranormal or psychics or anything I know about. This may have been a bad idea," Emma said nervously.

"And here we are," Robert said as he came to a stop behind Rocky's van.

Rocky emerged from the van dressed in his full exterminator regalia. Emma gasped in surprise and fear.

"If he needs that to go inside this house, then why do you think I'm going in there?" Emma asked, looking sternly at Robert.

"Rocky and I are going in to find the spider. You are going to see what you can see or feel or hear from the door. Once we have determined the house is clear, then we will escort you in. Rocky even has an extra suit you can put on if it makes you feel more comfortable," Robert said, trying to calm her down.

Robert showed Emma over to the monitors he had set up earlier. "You can watch us from here if you'd like, Emma. Are you ready to go in, Rocky? And where is Cheryl? Her car is here."

Rocky indicated toward the side of the house. "She's looking through windows."

"Cheryl!" Robert called out. "Come around to the monitors, will you? We need you to watch us while we go in."

Cheryl strolled out of the kitchen with a cat carrier. "I caught it," she said nonchalantly, holding out the cat carrier for everyone to see. The problem was, the carrier was empty.

"Cheryl . . . that's an empty cage," Rocky said slowly.

"Are you blind? Just look at this big bo— Wait . . .. Where did he go? He was in here, I promise. I caught him. I tricked him. He was here," she said, shaking her head and looking like she was on the verge of tears.

"Yeah, I'm not going in there," Emma said with a sharp nod. "What did it do, squeeze through the air vents like an octopus? Nope. Not going in."

"Fine, just walk with me around the house and see if you pick up on anything. How about that?" Robert asked.

"Okay. That, I can do."

Robert and Emma walked toward the front of the house, stopping at each window. Emma seemed to relax into it. As they approached the bedroom in which they had seen the shadow man, Robert slowed the pace to a stop.

"Do you feel anything here?" he asked.

"I feel things all around this house. I'm not sure how to sort it all out."

"Can you hone in on this room?" Robert asked.

"I can try. Wait . . . .. There's a man in there."

Robert looked through the window. There was no one in the room. "I don't see anyone," he said.

"I don't mean a real man. It's a spirit, but he's not very happy. He doesn't like all these people in his house."

"What's his name?"

"I don't know. He's not talking . . . he's just scowling at me," Emma whispered.

"Could you describe him to Cheryl?" Robert asked.

"Yes, do you want to just leave him here or do you want to ask Cheryl to come around here?"

Robert signaled that he was going to get Cheryl and disappeared around the corner of the house.

He came back with her and when they approached the window, she gasped, "You found the giant spider!"

"No, we found the shadow man," Robert clarified.

"All I see is the spider."

"Uh oh," Emma said, "he's projecting images on her and you as well, most likely."

"We all saw the spider on Rocky's back," Robert said. "And it bit him bad enough to take him to a clinic."

"I'm sure there is a large spider. I'm just not sure it's as large as all of you think it is. Large enough to bite means it could be the size of a tarantula."

"It wasn't a tarantula!" Robert yelled and ran his hands through his hair. "It made a tarantula seem small."

"I understand." Emma put her hands up, trying to calm Robert down. "Let me spend a little time with the spirit and see what I can learn. Your team can look inside, just do me a favor . . . . Find a box with no vents or air holes, unless they are no larger than the hole a straw would make."

"Fine," Robert said with a nod. "We'll get started on that while you get to know the shadow man."

"Spirit," Emma called as Robert and Cheryl walked away, but he wasn't listening.

Emma was basically accusing them all of seeing things. He didn't like it one bit. He headed back around the house.

"I don't understand what's happening," Cheryl murmured. "I know I had that spider in the carrier. It was not an illusion, Robert. It was as real as any one of us. Why is she insisting it wasn't? Did you show her the bite marks on Rocky's neck? Who does she think she is?"

"A full-blown psychic provided by Madam Celeste and that is a strong referral. She has probably seen something similar to this, which could be why she's so sure. And think about it, Cheryl . . . . That spider bite could have been from something smaller than what we all saw. I think we need to investigate with that in mind. Maybe that spider wasn't as big as we remember it," he said as they walked up to the rest of the group assembled by the picnic table.

"I never saw it," Rocky said, "but from the look of the bite, I would say it would have to have been about the size of a tarantula."

"Tarantula? It was the size of a small chicken!" Cheryl yelled.

"Let's put the size on hold for a minute," Robert said. "Let's just go in and look for any spiders. How about we do that?"

"Buddy system," Cheryl said.

"Absolutely," Robert said.

Rocky nodded. "Agreed."

Emma stayed outside and watched the monitors while the three adventurous types went in to find any spiders. Rocky carried his tank of poison, while Cheryl carried an oversized box with small holes punched into it. Robert carried a recorder in his shirt pocket and a stick the size of a walking staff in his hand.

There were considerably fewer webs today.

"I know there are fewer spiderwebs, but shouldn't there be no webs at all? We bombed the house pretty thoroughly. I know some of them in my brother's room were still alive, but I just don't get it."

Rocky replied, "Some insects are more resistant than others, especially to those bombs you buy at the grocery store. They are nowhere near as effective as the chemicals I use. And I spray them where they live, not just a general spraying of the air. When I went in yesterday, there was an accumulation of them near and on the window because there was an air gap there. Or at least, that would be my guess."

"A spider the size you're talking about just doesn't exist. The closest thing would be the Theraphosa Blondi. It isn't poisonous, but its bite is big enough to draw blood. And it's a tremendously large spider, one of the top ten largest in the world. In fact, its common name is the Goliath Bird Eater. That name alone would scare a sane person."

"You sure know a lot about it," Cheryl said.

"It's my job," he said with a shrug.

"How big does the "Thera what's it" get?" Cheryl asked.

"Oh, they can grow to the size of your hand . . . and that's just the body part. Those can catch and eat rodents."

"Do they usually show up in the US?" Robert asked.

"Not really. But you know people keep some very strange pets these days."

"But no one has lived here for years," Cheryl said.

Rocky shrugged. "Makes it that much more attractive to an oversized spider. No one to mess with its webs, nor to spray poison at its food. Security lights at night to draw bugs and more. It's really the perfect environment for a former pet."

"Sounds like something my brother would have kept without telling Mom or Dad," Cheryl mumbled.

As they approached the spider bedroom as they had nicknamed it, they slowed down. It was as if no one really wanted to go in. Everyone knew it wasn't just a spider in there. There was some kind of spirit that could possibly make them see things that weren't there. Or at least, exaggerate the appearance of things.

"So, we're looking for a smaller spider than we thought, and we're on the lookout for any smaller spiders that are still alive," Cheryl said.

"That pretty much sums it up," Rocky said. "And don't forget we have a net." He pulled it out of somewhere on his highly pocketed pants.

They all took a deep breath and opened the door. Cheryl immediately started to spit. The doorway was almost blanketed in spider webs. Now she was covered and had gotten a mouthful.

"Don't bedroom doors usually open in?" she asked. "That was disgusting! What does it mean?"

"It means there is a huge spider in there and it's still very much alive, and so are a lot of its babies," Rocky said with a bit of a nervous pitch to his voice. "How long had this house been closed up?"

"Years."

"So, there could be dozens of large spiders in there," Rocky said.

"I guess so, but I'm hoping a lot of them were killed by the bug bombs yesterday," Cheryl murmured.

"Here, Cheryl, you take the net. Let's put the box in the middle of the room. Robert, you're going to brush down that web over the doorway. Everybody ready?"

"Ready," they chimed in.

"Go!" Rocky yelled.

"This web is strong! And very sticky," Robert yelled.

"Looks like you're getting it, though. Keep at it."

The drama of that first "Go!" yielded to something akin to waiting for the tub to drain. It took several minutes to eliminate the door covering. The room was better but still had excessive webs. They all entered.

CHAPTER 8

This was certainly not the room they had taken pictures of mere days ago. The spider webs were very thick in certain places.

"It almost looks like little forts made of thin rope," Cheryl remarked.

"That's as good a description of it as any," Rocky said. "There could be a good-sized spider inside each of those. Let's poke through one and see. Robert? You have the stick. Just poke it in and swirl it around."

"What if it's a thousand little spiders?" Robert asked. "Wouldn't that be worse?"

"Nah, it's not. Their young hatch out of a large egg-looking thing except it's not an egg at all, and it's light brown."

"Like this?" Cheryl pointed to a light brown ball in the corner."

"That would be it," Rocky said with a nod. "Let's deal with the adults first, okay?" After everyone nodded, Rocky explained further. "We're going to break into one of these webbed "houses" and I'm going to spray the inhabitant and see if there is any effect."

Robert stabbed the one closest to Rocky and started to jab it to open it up. Soon, a huge spider crawled out onto his stick.

"Rocky? Now would be a good time to test that poison."

"Oh, sorry. I was just fascinated by the size and beauty of it. Maybe we could catch it and sell it."

"No!" Robert yelled.

"No way in hell!" Cheryl shrank backward.

"Kill it **now**, Rocky!" Robert yelled again as the spider inched closer on the stick.

Rocky started to spray it lightly with his chemicals. It withdrew a few inches but very slowly. It teetered on its web line and then fell to the floor. Its legs started to curl, reminiscent of the dead witch scene in the Wizard of Oz.

Everyone breathed a loud sigh of relief almost in unison.

"Pick another one, Robert," Rocky said.

Robert picked the next closest one, and the same thing happened. Robert and Cheryl became a little more relaxed about the whole project as they continued to jab at the web houses. They were on the fifth one when what came out was unbelievable—the spider was as big as the one they had seen the other night.

Emma was watching from the monitors and realized instantly what was happening. They were being mind-controlled again. The spider was the same size as all the others they had killed, but this one was making them think he was much bigger. Emma decided to go in to tell them. She hurried into the room and saw not only the spider but also the shadow man.

"What do you want?" she shouted at the shadow man.

He stood there smiling in delight at the others' reaction to the spider.

"We want to kill this monstrosity of a spider," Cheryl yelled, never taking her eyes off the spider.

"The spider is an illusion," Emma said calmly. "It's the same size as all the others were. Just spray him, Rocky."

Rocky sprayed the spider and watched it change into just another very large spider. Seeing a spider as big as your hand is still a frightening thing, after all—just not quite as scary as the monster they had all seen.

The shadow man left. He seemed to be there for the show. And with Emma on the scene, the show was apparently over for now.

"Are you going to save one in the box?" Emma asked. "You may want proof as to just how big they were."

Rocky nodded. "That's a good idea. I'll mount it to a board and use it to demonstrate what happens when these kinds of pets get out of control."

"Seems cruel to me, but it *is* a big, old, hairy spider. I guess I don't mind," Cheryl said with a shrug.

Emma helped them capture one and then went back out to the monitors. She still felt uncomfortable in the house. She didn't trust the shadow man and wasn't sure the shadow man was what had caused the illusion. What if the spiders were capable of causing these hallucinations? It could have developed a defensive skill that would work very effectively as long as there was no one observing from a long distance.

Emma thought about what she had picked up from the shadow man. He seemed cruel standing there watching those people get scared out of their minds like that. What kind of sadist does that? He could have just as easily warned them that it was an illusion. Instead, he kept to himself, which was a good argument for him being the illusionist.

Emma also found it strange that no other spirits were showing themselves. Robert had told her the story of how the father and son had died together in a boating accident. She would normally expect to see one or both of them here. She wondered if the father was the shadow man. More information was needed.

Emma looked at the monitor and realized the room was empty. Had they gotten them all while she was deep in thought? She walked toward the door to the kitchen. There was no sign of them. Maybe they had gone to another room. She switched the monitor back to the four cameras at once. There they were walking toward the back door.

Emma wanted to ask Robert how long he thought it would take to clear out the spiders, wanting to come back when there were fewer people, but not interested in wandering around in the house with all those spiders and webs. She found it was sometimes easier to communicate with spirits when there were less people to distract her or the spirits. It was especially difficult to have a conversation with a spirit when people kept answering your questions like they didn't know you were *trying* to converse with a spirit.

"That was intense," Cheryl said as she walked out first. "How long do you want to wait until we go back in and get the rest of them?"

"I think we need to take a lunch break. Then try to get the rest of them after lunch," said Rocky, "but I'm just the hired help on this mission."

"Emma, do you have time to go to lunch and come back?" Robert asked.

"Actually, I was hoping you could get the spider situation under control and then have me back. I'm hopelessly worthless with all these spiders. But I want to explore the illusion of size and the shadow man."

"If the illusion is coming from the spiders themselves, then don't you need to be around them?" Cheryl asked.

"I sure hope not, but I need to talk to Madam Celeste about this, too. Maybe you could take me back to her house, and we can arrange another time for me to come back."

"If that's how you want to do it, we're glad to have you whenever we can. Does anyone want to go to Gloryville with me to drop Emma off and pick up some food? They have an Arby's."

"I'll go," Cheryl said.

"Me too," Rocky said.

"I can't wait to talk to Madam Celeste about this,"

CHAPTER 9

Robert dropped Emma at Madam Celeste's and headed toward Arby's.

Emma ran into Madam Celeste's.

"Celeste? Are you here? I have to talk to you about this case. I need your help."

"I'm in the kitchen, Emma. Come on back," Celeste answered.

Emma proceeded to get Celeste up-to-date on her first real case. She was obviously excited that it was something Celeste was letting her run solo, but also knew she needed advice.

"Did you ever see one of the spiders in its illusionary form?" Celeste asked.

"No, I only saw them in their real size and shape."

"But you were watching through a monitor?"

"Yes, but so were they when Rocky was bitten," Emma clarified. "They were all watching from outside and saw a spider as big as a . . . uh . . . Well, its body was at least twelve inches long according to them."

"Very curious," Celeste murmured.

Celeste was a well-known psychic in the area, who had even helped the FBI with a case or two. She wouldn't tell anyone when she was working with them, though. She had a large clientele and had taken Emma as an apprentice over a year ago. Emma had her own in-house reading clients now, and if you asked Celeste, Emma had stronger psychic abilities than Celeste but lacked training. She had come a long way in the last year, and Celeste couldn't be happier.

"You are certain there is a shadow spirit there, as well?" Celeste asked.

"Yes. I have seen it myself, but it wouldn't talk to me. It was like it was trying to scare us away by showing itself, but it wasn't nearly as scary as those spiders. Even seeing them in their natural size was disconcerting. And there were so many of them . . .." Emma shuddered.

"Do you need me to come with you and see if I can find some more clues?"

"Not yet. I really want to do this on my own." Emma blushed. "I know I'm asking for advice, but that's different. I want to do as much on my own as I can. Do you understand?"

"Absolutely," Celeste said with a smile. "My advice would be to get the shadow spirit's name. See if you can engage him when no one else is around. He may be more willing to talk to you then."

"That's exactly what I told Robert I wanted to do," Emma said proudly.

"You have good instincts, my dear."

"I'm going to let them take care of the spider situation first so it may be a few days before I go back."

"Excellent choice. Do you have any clients this afternoon?"

"I had one set for four, but she called and moved it to tomorrow," Emma said glumly. "Maybe I should go back with Robert to see if I can help them this afternoon."

"I need you here answering phones and taking care of your regular duties," Celeste said. "I can't really afford for you to spend a whole day on this case."

"I'm off the clock for this one. I know it's a freebie, and that's how it should be for my first one. Robert and his friends just got lucky this time, didn't they?" she said, winking at Celeste with a smile.

"I appreciate that probably more than they do. But, I'd still like you to stay here this afternoon. Call it a feeling."

"Okay, well, I have plenty to do here. You're right. I'll wait until tomorrow and give Cheryl a call to see how the spider situation is coming along."

"I have a feeling they won't get the spider situation under control until they get the spirit taken care of," Celeste murmured. "There is something unnatural about the spiders. I don't know exactly what, but I can feel it."

"Then you think I *should* go back over today?"

"No, they need time to try. The group needs to see for themselves that they cannot quite control it. Then they will listen to you and let you work on the spirit. If you just fix it, they will never know what the real problem was."

"That's what they're doing this afternoon—getting rid of *all* the spiders. You think the spiders will come back or never really be gone."

"I don't think they can truly be gone until the spirit is satisfied. But you will take care of the spirit in due time. Don't spend any time worrying about it. Go about your day and let it go for now. Your mind will work it out in the background, and by tomorrow, you may know exactly what you need to do."

"That is so much easier said than done, Celeste. But I'm going to try. It's difficult not thinking about what they are doing over there. You didn't see the size of these spiders, and there were so many of them . . .."

"Well, I have a client coming in ten minutes, and *you* have a lot of paperwork to catch up on. Concentrate on that for a while."

While Emma was trying not to think about spiders, the group was getting ready to go back in and capture the rest of them. They decided to use the same technique of puncturing the nest and putting the spider in a box they had rigged as a cage.

Rocky had a friend who would pay him wholesale prices for the spiders, then would sell them online. Cheryl thought that would be an excellent way to pay Rocky for his trouble. Robert was enjoying the whole investigation, so there was no need to worry about his remuneration.

"Shall we go back in and face the little demons?" Robert asked after they ate.

"Let's do it!" Rocky said.

"Ready," Cheryl said as she headed toward the room.

"Let's start where we left off," Rocky suggested. "We know that room is the most infested. Let's clear it out first."

"Guys! Uh . . .. *Guys*! Can you get in here? *Now!*" Cheryl screamed.

"What the hell?" Rocky whispered as he entered.

The three of them stood at the door to the room they had begun clearing that morning. It looked like a spider web had exploded in there.

"It's like we have to start all over," Cheryl pouted. "They've put it all back."

"I'm going to suggest we start clearing again and don't quit until we have them all," Rocky said as he glanced around the room. "I've never seen anything like this. The only consolation is that they're not poisonous."

"Well, let's get after it," Robert said.

They had worked out a system which seemed to provide the smoothest capture. Robert and Rocky kept at it for two hours. Progress was being made and the spiders were losing ground. And Rocky was amassing a small fortune in rare spiders to sell.

By four p.m., they had filled two boxes with the huge spiders. They were two-thirds of the way through the room and beginning to feel like they could pull this off.

"Let's take a quick break to make some more boxes," Rocky said. He didn't want anyone getting any ideas about killing them off.

No one argued. Everyone was ready to be outside for a few minutes. But they didn't want to lose their advantage, so they worked quickly to put together two more boxes with ample air holes.

As they walked back in, they were relieved to see the spiders had not been busy at all.

"It looks like we might make it through all of them," Rocky said excitedly.

They continued using the stick to make holes in the nests, driving the spiders out and into the box.

Before nightfall, Rocky let out a sigh. "I think we've done it. Does anyone see any nests we might have missed?"

"I don't see any more of them," Cheryl said after looking around the room. "But I think we should clean up the spider webs. You know, a fresh start."

The guys grabbed brooms and started to sweep the ceiling and walls. Cheryl found an old rag and started to wipe off the furniture and knick-knacks.

They made quick work of it and were more than satisfied with the results.

"I think we have it ready for Emma now," Robert said with a nod. "I'll call her tonight and see if she can come tomorrow. I'm anxious to find out if she senses anything here now that the spiders are cleared out."

"While there's still some daylight, maybe we should clear out the webs from some of the other rooms, too," Cheryl suggested.

"Good idea. That will make her feel more comfortable wandering through the house."

"I can't believe my brother had spiders for pets in this room. I wonder if my mother knew they were in here . . .."

"I don't know about that, but I know we're going to need a flashlight in the den. That room is dark!" Robert said.

"I have more flashlights in the truck," Rocky said as he made his way toward the door. "I'll go get them."

"Robert, can I ask you a question?" Cheryl asked.

"Of course."

"Do you think the shadow man has anything to do with the spiders? I mean, it just feels so unnatural to have all these spiders and to see them larger than they are at first, but this afternoon they haven't done that. What does it mean? Is this house just infested with spiders or is there something else at work here, too?"

"That's a big question, Cheryl. And honestly, I'm not sure how to answer it, yet. I think there is something paranormal going on here, but it's just not possible to tell what it is until the psychic is willing to come inside. Hopefully, that's what we're doing now." "I still just get a bad feeling, and I don't think it's the spiders. It's like my dad is hanging out in this room."

CHAPTER 10

Cheryl, Robert, and Rocky spent the rest of the daylight cleaning up spider webs from around the house. When they were satisfied, Robert called Emma.

"Emma, this is Robert, from the house full of spiders?" he asked as if she might not remember him.

"Yes, I vaguely remember," Emma said with a chuckle. "Did you get the spiders cleared out?"

"For the time being, yes. We were wondering what time you could come over tomorrow?"

"Let's shoot for ten a.m., and I'll drive myself," Emma said. "That should make it easier on everyone."

"I thought you couldn't drive, or at least that you didn't drive."

"That's Madam Celeste, who is subject to start channeling without warning, which can be dangerous if you're driving on public streets. I don't channel like that, so I'm fairly safe to drive. I can be there by ten. Who will be meeting me there?"

"Well, it's Cheryl's house, so she'll want to be there." Cheryl silently nodded. "And I'm the one who brought you in, so I'll want to be there. Is that too many people?"

"No, not at all. The more, the merrier. Just don't freak out if I start talking to people you can't see." Emma laughed.

"We'll try not to, but no guarantees."

"See you in the morning, then." Robert slid his phone back into his pocket.

"This just gets better. She'll be here at ten, and I don't have to go get her!" Robert said.

"If it makes you feel better, you can swing by and pick me up," Cheryl said.

"Can I be here?" Rocky asked. "You know . . . just to make sure the spiders are still under control, of course."

"This is Cheryl's gig. It's up to her," Robert said sincerely.

"That's fine with me," Cheryl said with a smile.

Robert's phone rang. It was Jeremy. "Did you ever find out what was going on in that house?" he asked.

"Not completely, but we're just finishing up cleaning out the spider webs. You're not going to believe how many spiders the size of your hand we found in one room. We have four boxes full of them. Rocky is going to sell them to a wholesaler he knows."

"Well, that's more interesting than the chicken tracks. Mind if I come by one day this week and have a look?"

Robert turned to Cheryl. "Cheryl, Jeremy wants to come by and have a look now that the spiders are gone. Is that okay?"

"Doesn't matter to me. He can come by tomorrow since we're going to be here anyway," Cheryl offered.

"Cheryl said to come on by tomorrow. We'll be here around ten a.m."

"See you then. Bye," Jeremy said before hanging up.

Emma arrived about fifteen minutes early the next morning. She didn't like being late and wanted some time alone with the house. It was locked up tight, but she didn't mind spending time outside of the house.

She walked to Pete's room where all the giant spiders had been. She didn't walk up to the windows, just wanted to get a feeling of the space. There was a feeling of someone watching her. It was a little cold, but not threatening and allowed her to embrace it, though no one showed themselves. She walked on. Passing the outside of the den, there was a feeling of malice emanating from the exterior walls.

She walked on around the house. Near the back, there was a path worn into the grass and weeds. She started to follow it, but after a few yards, it sounded like a car pulled up. She turned and headed back to the house.

They would want her inside, but she would be sure to mention the path which had obviously been well-used and recently judging by how little growth there was.

"Emma!" Robert yelled. "Are you here?"

"Just walking around the house," Emma replied. "I found a path back at the other end of the house. I was about to follow it and see what was back there. It looks pretty well worn like it's been used lately."

"We would use that to get to a lake on the other side of the trees when I was young," Cheryl said. "I imagine today it would look more like a pond, but when we were kids, we thought it was a big lake." She smiled at this forgotten memory.

"But you say it looks like it's been used recently?" Robert asked.

"Yes. Very recently. Maybe some animal travels between here and the pond."

"We'll check that out today," Robert said.

Cheryl noticed Robert had a special voice reserved only for Emma. She thought it was sweet. "Emma, do you want the house to yourself or do you want someone to be in there with you? Will it make a difference?"

"I'm not afraid to be alone in a house with paranormal activity, but I have to admit that spiders and wild animals do scare me a bit. I would probably feel better if someone went in with me."

"I'll stay with her. You and Jeremy can go look for tracks to the pond. Sound okay?" Robert said.

"Sounds like a good plan," Jeremy said as he walked up to the three of them from the driveway. "What are we tracking?"

"We don't know," Cheryl said. "Emma says there is a path from the house and it may go back to an old pond. But it seems recently used. Want to track it?"

Jeremy nodded. "Sure. That's what I do."

"Emma? Are you ready?" Robert asked.

"Ready as I'll ever be."

The two of them walked to the back door which was locked. Cheryl joined them to unlock it before she took a key off her key ring and gave it to Robert. "This is the spare key. You keep it for the time being."

Robert stopped long enough to put it on his key fob then opened the door for Emma. "Here we go," he said in a soft voice meant to give the moment a supernatural feel.

"I want to go to Cheryl's brother's room first," Emma said.

"That's the one that had all the spiders," Robert reminded her.

"Yes, I know. I want to see if they're connected to the haunting. I've been advised that they might be."

"Do you need me to do anything in particular or just be quiet?"

"It doesn't matter," Emma said.

"May I film and record?"

"Certainly," she responded. "Do you need me to wait for you to set up?"

"No, no. Go ahead and start," Robert said.

"I guess I already have," Emma whispered. "There is a man in the corner. He seems to be hiding. I'll try to get him to talk to me."

Robert got the camera set up faster than he had ever done. He wanted this recorded. "Where is he exactly?"

"He's just there," Emma said, pointing to the corner near the window.

"That's the window we saw him standing in," Robert confirmed.

"Was this your room?" Emma asked.

The figure shook its head no.

"Was this your house?"

Again, she was told no.

"Why are you here, then?"

The figure started to become less shadowy and more solid. It looked like someone trapped with no place to run.

"Please talk to me," Emma said. "I'm here to help you if I can. What can I do to help you? Do you want to be here?"

The figure shook his head again. "I have no place to go," he said. "I am here because she wants me here."

"She who? Who wants you here? Do you know her?"

"My friend's mother. He died in a boating accident with his father when we were twenty. She wanted me around after he died. It gave her comfort. I don't remember how I ended up here."

"I have no idea what to do with this," Emma said. "I'm going to need to talk with Madam Celeste. I don't know what to do with someone who doesn't remember how they got here, much less why."

"You'll figure it out," Robert said. "Ask him if he remembers dying."

"Do you rem—"

"I can hear him," the figure interrupted. "I was in a car accident when I was in New York . . .. I was nowhere near here."

Emma relayed the info to Robert.

"What's your name?" Robert asked.

"Andrew."

"Andrew what?" Emma asked.

"Andrew Bell."

"We can look for that in the newspapers. They would have put an obit in a hometown paper," Robert said.

"Or we can just ask Cheryl," Emma suggested. "He was her brother's friend, right?"

Robert nodded. "That would make sense."

"You seem afraid," Emma said to Andrew. "What are you afraid of? Is it something in this house or something outside this house?"

"Something outside this room. I can't leave this room. The door is always locked."

"The door is open," Emma said in confusion. "We came in through the door."

"You walked right through it like ghosts," Andrew said. "There have been many people doing that lately. They act like there isn't even a door there."

"There isn't one for us. It's just an open door."

"How can that be?" Andrew asked.

"I don't know. I will ask my mentor, but I would guess you are trapped in this place at a certain time in history. The problem is you don't know when or why," Emma said. "We will try to find some answers from our side, but it would be good for you to try to remember from your side, too. We're going to go now. We're not leaving the house; we're only leaving the room."

"I saw you outside," Andrew said. "I saw you look in the window, but you didn't see me. Are you a ghost, too?"

"No, I'm very much alive right now. But I see ghosts often. I'll see you later."

Robert and Emma went to the study. It was dark and creepy as ever. Robert turned on two flashlights and Emma gasped.

"Why are you here?" she asked.

"Because Cheryl wanted some help clearing this house," Robert said slowly.

"I'm not talking to you. There is a child in the chair in the corner. He is about fifteen. He's just staring at the desk, but I don't see anyone at the desk. Wait! He's standing by the desk. He's walking over to the boy. He's yelling, but I can't hear what he's saying. It's like a movie playing in a loop with no sound."

"It must be what we, in the field, call a residual. There's no intelligence to it," Robert said.

Emma moved to stand near the boy. The man walked right through her as if he didn't see her. It was unnerving. The boy looked terrified.

"I can't do anything with this," Emma said. "It's just a memory etched into the fabric of the room. I don't know how to erase it."

"Is there anything else or anyone else in the room?" As the words left Robert's mouth, a man materialized in front of Emma, though Robert couldn't see him.

"There is a man here. He just showed up."

"Of all the things I regret, this scene you are witnessing is my deepest regret. I terrified my children and for what? My son is dead, and my daughter is afraid to come inside this house, much less this room. It haunts me." The man looked around sadly. "Can you tell my daughter I'm sorry?"

"That I can do! And I can do it today. She is here with us, just outside following a trail to the lake."

"She always did enjoy going to that old pond. All the kids called it a lake but it's nothing but a watering hole. She got in trouble every time," he said disappearing with the last word.

"I wonder who else is hiding in this house," Emma whispered. "They just seem to come out of the woodwork."

"I can't wait to review the video and audio to see if we picked up any of it. This could be some of my best evidence ever. I've never had such a powerful psychic with me on an investigation. This is awesome!"

"Shall we try another room? We don't know how many more there may be lurking in the different rooms. But I'd like to find out while I'm here."

"You say that like you won't be coming back," Robert said. "You have to come back. You promised that one man you would consult with your mentor."

"True." Emma nodded. "And I am a woman of my word. But it may be a few days before my schedule opens up."

"Maybe next weekend," he said.

"I have to help Madam Celeste with a gallery reading on Sunday, but maybe Saturday?"

"We'll plan on Saturday then," Robert said. "For now, let's see what else is in this place."

Emma walked through the house while Robert followed filming. Every now and then she would stop. There seemed to be several spirits, but not all of them were attached to the house. They seemed to wander in just to talk to Emma.

Reaching the door to the basement, she stepped back. "There is something ominous down there," she said. "I don't think I can go down there just yet. Let's go check the dining room."

"If that's what you want," Robert said, but he was extremely curious about what was downstairs.

They toured the rest of the house together. Emma stopped in the dining room for almost half an hour. There were at least three spirits there she conversed with. The first one was a great-grandmother of the family.

"Are you here all the time?" Emma asked her.

"Most of the time, yes. This is where most of the talking was done. We would sit here after the meal was finished, just talking and sharing what was going on in our lives. I wish they would come back . . . .."

The second one was a child who seemed to be dressed like you would expect from the 1920s. "This is my favorite place. There are so many people here. And the older ones talk to me and tell me stories and give me hugs."

The third one was a young woman. "I missed out on having my own family here, but I stay here. It's the only place that gives me comfort. I died before I could even start a family. So, this is my family now."

"They just seem so sad and lonely," Emma said softly. "I would stay and ask them questions all day."

"Let's find out if Cheryl's father hangs out in the living room. Doesn't that sound good?" Robert asked, trying to convince her the dining room wasn't really haunted, but she knew better.

As they moved into the living room, Emma pulled away. She did not want to enter this room.

"It has the same feeling as the basement," she argued.

Robert hurriedly set up the camera and voice recorder. Something was going to happen in here, he just knew it.

"There is a spirit here. It feels so heavy and terrifying. It's scaring me to death, and I haven't even seen it or heard it yet. We really don't need to stay here. It's not like the spirit wants us here. We're only making it angry."

"Let's stay for a few minutes, at least . . .. I have all my equipment set up." Then he saw a red glow come from the corner of the room. "D-do you see that?!" he called out to Emma.

"Does it look like something from the bowels of hell?" she answered.

"No, I see something glowing red over in the corner."

"Be happy you don't see it in its full form," Emma screamed. "It has a horn, and it's red and very tall and thick. I've not seen anything like it before."

"What's it doing?" Robert whispered.

"It seems to be growing."

"Growing?"

"Yes, it's getting larger. And the larger it gets, the meaner it looks. I don't think we need to be here," Emma screamed. "We can't stay here, Robert. Leave your equipment if you like, but we need to leave *now*!"

Emma ran toward the back door with Robert right behind her. He would retrieve his equipment later. He had never seen anything more than the red glow, but it had been getting larger and seemed to be pulsing. No one would blame him for leaving.

They ran outside to find Cheryl and Jeremy were running from the trees behind the house. They looked like they, too, had a story to tell.

.

CHAPTER 11

When Cheryl and Jeremy went to track the trail Emma had found, Jeremy was trying hard to impress Cheryl with his tracking skills. He pointed out where Emma had turned back, but then he saw a set of tracks that seemed to bother him.

"This is unusual to see in this area," he said pointing to a track Cheryl couldn't see, even with him pointing to it.

"What's so unusual about it?" Cheryl asked, more as a courtesy. She was far more anxious to see the old lake and how small it would look to her now after so many years.

"It's not an unusual animal. It's just unusual to see it around here. It's a gray wolf. Have you ever seen a wolf around here?"

"No, but I haven't lived here in years. Aren't wolves more inclined to live in the woods?"

"Yes," Jeremy said. "Especially a wolf this size, it's larger than any I've ever seen."

"How do you know it's not just a big dog?" Cheryl asked.

Jeremy stopped. He turned to Cheryl as if she had just slapped his face with an iron. "I'm a tracker. It's what I do. I take it very seriously. I thought you realized you were dealing with a leading expert, but you have the audacity to ask how I know the difference between a wolf and a dog? Really? Do you take me for a hack? Do you think I am just some amateur that mistakes a chicken for an extinct animal?"

"I didn't mean to hurt your feelings. I truly thought the tracks would be the same. I thought there would be no way to know the difference."

"I'm sorry," Jeremy said. "I shouldn't have gone off on you like that. I have a temper. I keep it buttoned up most of the time, but you just hit the right button at the right time."

"Sounded like the wrong button to me," Cheryl said, trying to lighten the moment.

"The point is there is a wolf. Its tracks are very distinct. He doesn't seem to stray from this path, either. It's as if he's worn the path himself. He is not hunting here. He is just traveling back and forth, almost as if he were in a cage."

"Let's see if it changes near the tree line," Cheryl said, trying to hurry him along. She was so anxious to see the old pond, and the excitement made her feel like a young girl again. She and her brother used to pretend to track animals here, but certainly, it never took them this long to get to the 'lake'.

He sped up only slightly, not wanting to miss any sign an animal had crossed or joined the wolf. There was no sign until they reached the tree line itself.

"Look at this," Jeremy said as he pointed to something virtually invisible to Cheryl. "The wolf does not stick to the path as he enters the trees. The tracks are all the same, but they take off in tens of different directions. What was he hiding from?"

"Or hunting," Cheryl offered.

"True. This may have been a small hunting ground for him. There are a few cat tracks, and even a rabbit or two that may have lived here."

As they passed into the trees, Cheryl realized she could see the pond ahead through the trees almost immediately. What had been an adventure as a child was just a walk in the trees as an adult.

Jeremy interrupted her thoughts. "Some of these tracks are fresh from the last few days. There is evidence that one of the cats made for a meal probably in the last twenty-four hours or so."

"The wolf is still here?" Cheryl squeaked.

"Yes, he's at least in the area. We need to be careful."

"Should we go back and get guns?"

"I always carry one. We will be fine. Look here. A human has walked on this side of the tree line recently. The tracks lead down to the water."

"I'm suddenly not feeling as comfortable out here. Maybe we should go back . . . ." She turned to leave and stopped. "Jeremy," she whispered, "look behind you."

Jeremy turned and saw the over-sized gray wolf standing on the path in the trees. He drew his weapon from its holster hidden on his right hip.

The wolf stood on the path for a few more seconds before it turned and disappeared into the trees.

Cheryl began to run for the path back to the house. Jeremy was right behind her.

"Cheryl, stay with me!" he called. "We don't know what else is out there. I can protect you."

But Cheryl didn't want to hear it. She ran, not following the path, making a beeline for the cars by the side of the house. Meanwhile, Jeremy wanted to find where the tracks started near the house. He followed them to a sidewalk, but lost the animal there. He walked all around the house but could not find any sign of fresh tracks.

There had been a gray wolf very close, and now there was no trace of where it had gone. How could that have happened? He doubled back to the trees to look for the latest tracks from where he had seen the wolf standing. Once he found the tracks, he proceeded cautiously to follow them.

"Jeremy!" Robert called from the car. "It's time to leave for the day. Come on back to the house."

Jeremy looked at Robert and put his finger to his lips using the universal signal of quiet.

Robert walked out to the trees to talk with Jeremy. Robert had had enough adventure for one day but was not willing to leave Jeremy here alone when there may be a demon in the house.

When he caught up with Jeremy, he said, "We need to leave. There was something very evil in the house. Emma believes she saw a demon. What are you doing out here?"

"I saw a gray wolf. I'm tracking it. I don't believe in demons, but a gray wolf is pretty close. I need to find out where it went. It didn't go back to the house. It's out here in the trees."

"And what will you do if you find it?"

"At the very least, I'll report it to the game warden. There shouldn't be any gray wolves in this area. He needs to be made aware of it."

"What's so special about a gray wolf?" Robert asked.

"It's the biggest wolf on the planet, and *this* is not its habitat. You think those spiders are an anomaly? They are nothing compared to a gray wolf. The one I saw on the path was the biggest I've ever seen or heard of, by the way. This is a big deal."

"Okay, fine. We'll wait for you. I'll even come with you to back you up. Just let me tell the others."

Robert returned to the cars to tell Cheryl and Emma what was going on. Before he had a chance to return to Jeremy, he saw him walk through the trees toward them. He walked to meet him.

"What happened?" Robert asked.

"I lost the track," Jeremy said. "I feel like an idiot. How could I lose such a fresh track?"

"Nothing around this place makes sense," Robert said. "Let's go share evidence and see what we have so far."

"That's just it . . . . I have nothing but tracks, and they don't make sense. They come here to this house and disappear at the sidewalk. They go to the woods and scatter like there's a pack, but there isn't. This is just crazy."

"Well, wait 'til you hear what happened to Emma and me! Talk about not making sense. She thinks she saw a demon, and I know I saw a glowing red light in the corner of the room. And it was growing!"

At this point, neither Jeremy nor Robert were actually listening to the other. They were still too wrapped up in their own personal phenomenon. Jeremy had only come to see what happened with the spiders. He hadn't anticipated an adventure in his area of expertise.

As they approached the cars, Emma and Cheryl were in a tense discussion about Emma staying to deal with whatever this was.

"I need to go and talk this over with my mentor," Emma said. "I know she has dealt with this kind of thing before, but I'm not sure what she did about it. It was on my first day, and a lot was happening very quickly."

"I think we all need a break," Robert said. "I think Jeremy wants to do a little research. Emma wants to discuss how to handle what she and I saw, and I don't blame her. I sure don't know what to do. Cheryl, this is going to take a little more time than we had anticipated, but we will get to the bottom of everything."

"You got rid of the spiders and Emma saw the shadow man, so I'm happy so far. I just don't want to walk away yet."

"I know you want answers right now, but I don't have them. Maybe I should bring Madam Celeste in on this, but I don't think it will be free anymore."

"I'm not as concerned about the cost as I am about getting some answers," Cheryl said firmly. "But, if you're not ready to give up trying, then I'm with you."

Emma smiled. "Thank you. I really do want to solve my first real case without having to hand it over to Celeste."

"Then go get her input and call me when you're ready to come back." Cheryl then turned and looked at Jeremy. "I ought to call Texas wildlife about this wolf. You claim it's not indigenous. Does that make it a "no-kill"? Do I want a gray wolf staking out my property as its own? I have more questions than you have answers. Do you want to continue?"

"Yes. I'd at least like to spend some more time researching and tracking. And I'd like to do it today while I still have daylight," Jeremy said.

"Then have at it," Cheryl said. "You won't have access to the house because we're going to be leaving to do our own research. Is that okay with you?"

Jeremy nodded. "That's fine. All my tracks are outside anyway. Do you want me to call you if I find anything?"

"Of course," Cheryl said emphatically. "I want to know anything you find out that affects this house or this land. Something is going on here, and I don't like not knowing what it is. But only share with our little group, please. I don't want any "lookie-loos" showing up here. This is still going to be my house one day, and I'd like for there to be no legends hanging over its head."

Emma drove back up just as Cheryl finished speaking. "I just realized what Madam Celeste is going to tell me to do. I'd like to go ahead and do it. Can we stay a little longer?"

"Well, Jeremy was staying anyway . . . . I don't mind. Robert, do you want to stay and help?"

"Count me in," Robert said with a grin.

"Okay, we're going to go back into that same room and see if we can contact the spirit that was transforming before my eyes. Anyone who goes in with me has to stay calm and not show any fear. Can we all do that?"

"I'm going tracking in the woods out back, so you won't have to worry about me. I'll go ahead and head back there now," Jeremy said.

"You two understand? No fear," Emma said sternly to Cheryl and Robert.

"No problem for me unless the spiders came back," Cheryl said.

They walked slowly into the house and through the kitchen to the room where Emma had seen what—to her—looked like a demon. There was no sign of it now.

Emma called out to it. "Show yourself, please. If there is anyone here that wants to be recognized and heard, we are here to help you."

The figure slowly started to appear. It was a young man. He looked around the room noticing who was there.

"Do you see him?" Emma whispered.

"No," Robert and Cheryl answered. "Let me get my camera out." Robert pulled out his camera and focused on where Emma was looking. Nothing showed up on the camera, either.

"Well, there's a young man here. He could be about twenty, if that. He's looking right at me, but he's not talking," Emma said. "It's not often you encounter one that won't talk at least a little. It's like he's really shy. I think this isn't who we encountered earlier."

"You mean there are *two* here?" Cheryl whisper-yelled

"Honey, there are usually quite a few. This house is pretty quiet, spirit wise. However, the spiders are another matter altogether."

With that, the figure started to wave his arms wildly and jump as if to get Emma's attention.

"Why don't you just tell me what you want?" she said to the ghost. "I'm right here looking at you. If you talk, I'll be able to hear you and make some sense of this."
The figure continued to flail his arms and jump wildly. Then, he disappeared in an instant.

"Now he's gone," Emma moaned in frustration. "What the hell was that? He was jumping and acting as if he wanted my attention. How could he not know he was all I was paying attention to? This is so frustrating. It was like he was trying to warn me about something, but what?"

Cheryl screamed. Robert turned to see what was wrong. He dropped his camera. Emma didn't see what they were upset about. Cheryl ran for the back door, with Robert right behind her. Emma just stood there. Then she saw it. They had missed one of the spiders, and it was crawling across the wall towards her. It was pretty big, but she didn't see that it was any bigger than any of the others they had captured.

Emma walked over to it. "What were they so afraid of," she whispered to the hand-sized spider. "They don't frighten this easily from what I've seen. I'm the one that should have gone running."

Emma went out to the car where Robert and Cheryl were hiding. "What was your problem?" she asked.

"Did you not see the size of that spider?" Cheryl's voice trembled. "It was as big as the one we saw the second day. It was at least a foot long, and that was just the body."

"No, it wasn't. It was only the size of my hand," Emma calmly replied. "You must have been hallucinating, but what would have caused you both to hallucinate? And why didn't it affect me? Are we dealing with a spirit that can cause mass hallucinations? Is that even possible? It must be. But why not me? Unless . . . .. Maybe the man I saw was a hallucination. Maybe that's why I couldn't hear him. That would explain so much. Okay, I have to look for the real spirit and get into communication with them."

"Sounds like a very powerful spirit if it can manipulate three people's minds simultaneously," Robert said. "I've never heard of such a scenario, but what if it happens all the time and people just don't realize it?"

"I wouldn't go that far. I only know what might be going on now. I've never heard of it before, either. I think we have to ask or discover why the spirit is doing it. It might be that they are all capable of such things, but they just don't usually have a need. What is going on in this house that causes this particular spirit to use this particular skill?"

"Maybe it would help to know who it is," Cheryl said. "It could be my dad or my brother, or it could be someone who just wandered in and has been enjoying the solitude."

"True. I may need to do a séance to get in touch with the ones we know could be here and determine if they have been here at all."

"Can you do a séance? Have you done one before?" Robert asked. "Those are pretty powerful and can invite some things we may not want."

"Séances, I've studied. I help Madam Celeste with them. It's just a matter of keeping control of the space, which I can definitely do."

"How many people do we need?" Cheryl asked.

"At least four. We could do it with who we have here, or you could bring a couple more."

"Let's do it," Robert said. "We'll do it one night this week. How about Wednesday? I'll make the calls if that night works for you two."

Both Cheryl and Emma nodded in agreement.

"Wednesday it is." Robert smiled. "This is going to be awesome. I'll set up cameras and recorders, too. We're going to document this. I can't wait! I'm going to go collect that spider and make sure I have all my equipment."

Emma laughed. "He sure turned on a dime, didn't he? Guess I convinced him it would be safe. You, on the other hand, do not look convinced. Does the idea scare you, Cheryl?"

"It makes me a little nervous because of all that is going on in this house. How can we trust our eyes and ears in here?"

"Great idea! We'll do it someplace else first. Grab something of your father's and something of your brother's, and we'll do the séance at . . .. Hmm, where can we do it?"

"Robert is pretty excited. I'm sure he'll volunteer his place," Cheryl offered.

"Robert, oh Robert," she called out to him as Emma chuckled.

.

CHAPTER 12

"A séance? By yourself? With a group who've also never done one before? What were you thinking?" Madam Celeste was not as happy as Emma had hoped. In fact, she seemed to be as upset as the time Emma arranged for a gallery at the last minute on a Sunday. "You're dealing with an entity you don't understand yet. One that is possibly causing mass hallucinations, and you expect me to let you go into a séance alone?"

"No, the séance won't be held at that house, and we want to contact the father and brother of the client."

"Have I taught you nothing? You have no control over who shows up to a séance. How will you know that you are not talking to this entity that you're hoping to avoid?"

"I-I-I'm not sure . . .." Emma was now truly upset over having set up the séance in the first place. She had not expected this reaction, hoping for support and guidance. Instead, she was met with anger and disappointment. Celeste was not usually like this. She was usually calm and protective. "I'll call it off," Emma said softly.

"No, you've already set it in motion. We must follow through. The universe is now acting to bring it together. Let me think. I will want to be there as your back up. But you will run the actual séance. I will ask Paul to come with us. As a spirit himself, he will be able to see if we are dealing with who we think we are. It will work. We will invoke protection for everyone. We will do that part together, and then you will take charge."

"Thank you, Celeste. I knew you would be able to figure it out. I'm sorry I upset you so much."

Paul popped in. "Did I hear my name mentioned?"

"Paul, I'm so glad you're here. We would like for you to attend a séance with us. There is a being that seems to be able to cause hallucinations, and we want you to be able to tell us if we're talking to the spirits we think we're talking to. Will you help?" Celeste asked.

"Sounds like fun," Paul said. "When do we start?"

"It's Wednesday evening at Robert's house. I will come by to pick up Celeste. Can you just meet us here?" Emma asked.

"Sure thing. What time? Who am I kidding? I have no sense of time. I'll just hang out all afternoon. We know how time gets away from me." Paul was laughing as he said it.

Both Celeste and Emma could see Paul clearly, though Emma was the only one who could hear him. He had to project his thoughts for Celeste to hear him, which was part of how Celeste knew that Emma had more natural talent than she did. He had been very helpful to them with the first case Emma worked on as Celeste's apprentice. It was also the first time Celeste had met or worked with Paul. In fact, he was a big part of the case, but that's a different story.

He had been around when needed—and sometimes when *not* needed—ever since. He was a likable sort and didn't seem to have a mean thought in his head.

"So, you will invoke the protection? Will I help with that at all?" Emma asked Celeste.

"Considering what we are dealing with, I think it might be more powerful if I did it solo, that way I won't need to restrain myself in any way."

Emma's eyebrows rose. "You restrain yourself when I'm helping?"

"Only to let you develop your power, Emma. You are far more powerful than you realize, but you haven't owned it yet. Once you do, you will be more powerful than I am. But you have not embraced that yet."

"It's a little scary," Emma said softly. "What if I mess up? I have so much still to learn."

"Like when to have a séance?" Celeste smiled.

"So, will you do the invocation before we form our circle or after?" Emma asked, ignoring the remark.

"I will not be sitting within the circle, but I think everyone should be ready, and in their place first. Then I will do the invocation, and when I nod, you will take charge of the event."

"What about me?" Paul asked. "What am I supposed to be doing during all of this?"

"Should we tell our guests about Paul?" Celeste asked.

"I don't think so . . . .. They are nervous about the spirits we've encountered at the house. I don't know how they would react to having a friendly one sitting in, even though it's to help. Do you agree?"

"You know them better than I do," Celeste said with a nod.

"Let's play it by ear, but I think it would be okay for Paul to show up after we've started the séance. That way they can just accept it as part of the event."

"Very well," Celeste nodded. "Now should we go over what to do to conduct a proper séance?"

"Great idea!" Emma said.

"So, what will you do first?"

"I'll place the items belonging to the men we are trying to contact into the middle of the circle. Then, I will call out for them to please come to us and give us a sign that they are with us."

"Of course, you and I will be able to see them without any sign, but I hope they would do something to show the others they are there," Celeste said.

"I'll talk to them," Paul offered. "Maybe they could just pick up their personal items and shake them around a bit?"

"That would be perfect! And you will tell me if you think they are imposters?" Emma asked.

"Like puppets?"

"Yes," Emma said. "I hope that if they are real, they will be able to answer some questions. The one I saw at the house was acting like he was mute or had been put on mute."

"I can imagine that happening. Newcomers are easier to manipulate," Paul said.

"Oh, they have been dead for years. They are not newcomers."

"Years are like days here, sweetie. Trust me, they're newcomers."

"I had no idea," Emma said.

"That's part of why you need help still. You have so much to learn. But you will get there, and this will be a great learning experience for you," Celeste said and squeezed her arm. "So, once you have made contact, what are you going to do?"

Emma blushed. "You mean *if* I make contact."

"No, I mean when. You *will* make contact with someone or something. Paul and I are just there to help determine exactly with what or whom you've made contact."

"And to make sure I don't release a demon or something," Emma pouted.

"Not at all, dear. Now stop trying to play the victim card. What happens next?"

"I ask them if they know of anyone else in the house. Then see what they know about the spiders."

"What will you do when the participants start blurting out questions of their own?" Celeste asked with a raised brow.

"I will take control and calmly ask them to please ask their questions through me so we don't scare the spirits away."

"Perfect!"

"What do I do if we're dealing with imposters? Will you need to step in?"

"If it's an imposter, we will still want to determine what they are up to. I may help with the questions at that point, but you will still be in control of the séance."

"I'm afraid I won't know what to do then," Emma said.

"You'll be fine. I will not leave you floundering or let you get into trouble you can't get out of."

"Please tell me you're joking. I don't need to get into trouble with an imposter. This isn't going to be the place for that kind of lessons, is it?"

"No. You're correct. If anyone gets into trouble, it will be me."

"I really wish I hadn't set this in motion," Emma said, shuffling her feet.

"You will be fine, and we will get some kind of answers. Don't worry. The experience will be worthwhile. And it might prove to be fun."

"I guess it could be. This may be a little bit of stage fright. But, you're right, it should be fun."

.

CHAPTER 13

As everyone finished their pizza and took a seat in a circle on the floor, Madam Celeste gave each participant a crystal. "These are to absorb any negative energy that tries to enter the circle. Keep them in your lap or directly in front of you." Then she moved to take a seat on an overstuffed chair behind the circle, being sure to be in a position to be seen by Emma.

"Please, may I have your attention," she started. "We have come together here to contact the spirits of Pete and Mr. Ray Brently. We call on angels and spirits, friendly to anyone and everyone in this room, to protect us during this venture. Guard us against imposters or anyone with harmful intentions. Keep us safe from those who would try to trick us or lie to us about the facts involving the house in question or the boating accident. Thank you. Let the séance begin." Madam Celeste extended her hand in a grand gesture toward Emma.

Emma cleared her throat, seeming quite calm. "Thank you, Madam Celeste. That was wonderful." Emma turned to the others. "We have personal belongings from both Pete and Mr. Brently here in the middle of the circle. We ask them to join us to clear up some misunderstandings and to help us determine what is going on in the house."

Nothing happened. Not even for Celeste or Emma. The room was still. Emma looked at Celeste for help, but Celeste nodded for her to continue.

"If you would join us here to answer a few questions, we promise to be quiet and respectful," Emma said. "It's very important to Cheryl. She needs some answers, and we think you may have them."

"Maybe you should be quiet for a bit and give them a chance to answer," Robert offered. "They could be here waiting for a chance to communicate."

"If they were here, I would know it, Robert. It's my gift."

As Emma was speaking, someone began to materialize in the circle. Emma was hopeful until she saw it was Paul.

"You want me to shake these things so they'll know someone is here?" he asked.

Emma shook her head slightly.

"Who are you shaking you're head at?" Cheryl asked wide-eyed.

"I saw it, too," Mia whispered.

"There is a spirit here that I know personally. He was trying to be helpful, but we don't need that kind of help. We need help contacting Pete or Mr. Brently. Paul was going to shake the items to put on a show for you."

Everyone gasped as Paul raised the pen and the key fob that had been placed in the center of the circle. "See? Now they believe you." Paul smirked.

"They already believed me, Paul. We need to make contact with Pete or Mr. Brently. Can you find them? Maybe they're at the house."

Cheryl was trying to decide if Emma was for real or just crazy. "You're talking to a ghost right now?" she asked.

"His name is Paul. He helps Madam Celeste from time to time. He's very nice, but sometimes his idea of help is to trick people, which is not what we're trying to do."

"There's a bona fide ghost here, and you're worried about tricking us because it's not the ghost you asked for?" Robert said with a chuckle. "Can he help find who we're looking for?"

"He's gone. I'm hoping to find them or at least one of them. He can be pretty persuasive with spirits when he wants to be," Emma said. "Let's all concentrate on the people associated with the pen and the key fob. Maybe we can call them to us by thinking about them. Think about the room that was your father's, Cheryl. Call him in your mind. Let him know you need him here."

There was a long silence while everyone concentrated on Cheryl's father. Though some of them had never met him, they had seen pictures and heard stories. A tear welled in Cheryl's eye as she thought of him and with that, he appeared to Emma.

"He's here," Emma said in a hushed voice.

"Where?" Cheryl asked, wiping a tear from her eye.

"Most of the people here cannot see you, Mr. Brently. Will you pick up the object that was yours to show them where you are?"

The next thing they saw was the pen floating in the air. Cheryl's father had been most attached to that particular pen and considered it his lucky pen for signing contracts and other important papers.

"I'm going to ask you some questions for Cheryl and the others. If you answer me, I will relay your answer to the group. Does that sound acceptable to you?" Emma asked.

The apparition nodded as if he couldn't speak.

"If you speak to me, I can hear you. It will make the process a lot quicker," Emma said. "Do you spend most of your time at the old house?"

"Not usually," Mr. Brently said softly. "I have better places to be, but lately I have been drawn to the house more frequently. There is something wrong there."

Emma repeated what he had said, and the room erupted with questions. Emma raised her hands and lowered them slowly to quiet her new friends. They complied.

"What do you feel is wrong?" Emma asked.

"They can't hear me, but you can? Really? Are you a witch or something?" Mr. Brently asked.

"Not exactly, I just have a gift that allows me to see and hear spirits. Madam Celeste over there has a similar gift. She can see you but can't always hear you. Now, what doesn't seem right at the house?"

"Recently I've noticed another spirit around. It's not my son, who I recognize when he's around. This one seems to be both spirit and physical, but not . . .."

"Not what?" Emma asked after allowing plenty of time for him to think.

"I don't know. It's not right. It's not what it appears to be when it appears at all. Most of the time I can feel it, but I can't see it. Yet, I can see things I've learned are not actually there. The house has become confusing. I try to avoid it, but something keeps drawing me back."

Emma explained what she had just heard.

"Can he see the spiders?" Cheryl asked.

Emma looked at Mr. Brently knowing he had heard the question.

"There are a lot of them. I don't know why your brother wanted those. To me, they're just creepy, and there are so many of them now. I don't like it one bit. I think it was a good idea exterminating as many as possible. You tell Cheryl that was the right decision." He waited for her to fill everyone in. "I saw what you were seeing, yet I knew it was an illusion. I don't know how I knew. I just did."

"Is something coming in from the woods and stalking the house?" Robert asked next.

"I don't know. I don't look beyond the house."

"Were you there when I saw the demonic-looking entity?" Emma asked.

He looked her directly in the eyes. "That was not me. I had nothing to do with it. That's part of what is wrong with the house. I don't know what it was or where it came from. I am not responsible for everything that happens in that house. It is not my fault. None of this is my fault. I was not responsible for the boating accident or the spiders or the tracks or the red entity. You think it's entirely my fault, but it's not!"

He was speaking too fast, and Emma could not keep up relaying every word. She could feel the emotions pouring from him, and it was not pleasant.

"No one has accused you of anything, Mr. Brently. We are looking for clues and answers to some questions. If we find them, then maybe it will help you, as well," Emma said.

"What makes you think you will find answers where I have not?" Mr. Brently sneered.

"Think about why we didn't just do this at the house. Why do you think we wanted you far away from that house?"

"I guess it has frightened you," he answered.

"What frightens us is that we don't see things clearly when we are there. The spiders seem ten times bigger than they really are, and a small red light appears to be a vicious creature. Things don't look the way they really are when we are there."

"That's ridiculous! What would cause something like that to happen?"

"That's exactly what we're trying to find out. Did you see us at the house the other day?" Emma asked.

"Yes."

"Did you try to communicate with any of us?"

"I tried to talk to you. I approached you, and you ran out screaming. I saw Cheryl when she was there without all the extras. I could have sworn she at least felt me, but never acknowledged it. And then came back with all those people and their weapons."

"Weapons?" Emma cocked her head to the side. "What kind of weapons did they have?"

"They were all carrying some form of a lightsaber, and they had boxes for capturing spirits."

"I think I get it now. Those were a kind of controlled hallucination. That's what happened to us, too. We saw things that weren't really there or that were there, just not what they appeared to be. It seems you have had a similar experience. Those weren't lightsabers . . . they were flashlights, and the boxes were for trapping the spiders."

"Someone or something doesn't want us in that house or speaking with my father," Cheryl said. "Daddy, have you seen Pete? Does he come around the house like you?"

"I see him from time to time in lots of different places. We never plan to meet, though; we just bump into each other. He is very attracted to the house. I think he spends a lot of time there."

"I wonder why he hasn't come here," Emma whispered almost to herself. Then she turned to Mr. Brently. "Where else do you see him? What other places does he hang out?"

"There are places you wouldn't understand. I won't even try to explain them to you. But, in your plane of existence, Pete is mostly, as I said, at the house. Sometimes I will see him at the soda fountain, in the jewelry store, and I've seen him at the gym at the old high school. And I often see him at the lake where the accident happened. I go there a lot myself. I'm not sure why, but sometimes I'm drawn there and can't leave."

"Why do you think he's not here now?" Emma asked.

"He and I rarely speak. He blames me for the accident. He doesn't understand there was nothing for me to do. He has a lot of anger issues. He had them when he died, and he has them worse now."

"You would say that, you old coot," Pete arrived screaming. "It's entirely your fault. Don't lie to these people, especially to Cheryl. She deserves to know what a coward you are. I stayed for you and how did you repay me? You tell lies. I have every reason to be angry. Every reason."

CHAPTER 14

Pete was acting like a spoiled teenager. He was little more than a teenager when he died, but did spirits stop maturing after death? One would think he would have gotten over some of these things. One would think the mere act of becoming spirit would impart a certain level of knowledge. Perhaps Pete was an exception to that.

Madam Celeste stood. "We will get no further information tonight. Pete needs help from Emma and me and his father, if Mr. Brently will stay for a time?" Mr. Brently nodded.

"What are we supposed to do?" Cheryl asked.

"You might want to go home and get some rest. Once we get this sorted out, there will be a lot of work to be done."

"What about Robert? This is his place. You can't ask him to leave," Cheryl protested.

"Of course, Robert can stay in his home. He just won't be participating in what happens next," Celeste said firmly. She looked at Robert, and he nodded in agreement. "Everyone please, leave my crystals on the table before you go."

Cheryl wanted to stay. This was her family they were interviewing. She should be able to stay and participate. How would just being here slow the process down? Even now, Paul was teaching father and son how to throw their thoughts into Celeste's mind so the conversation would be very one-sided to anyone listening. Celeste intended to help get the two spirits unstuck from the incident of their death, which seemed to have them both trapped at least part-time and strangely tangled together. It had occurred to Celeste that Pete might be the one causing the hallucinations at the house, so she knew they needed to proceed very cautiously.

"I'm going to ask you to do some things that may seem odd, but I assure you they are important for each of you more than anyone else. Mr. Brently, I'm going to ask Pete to describe the accident from the beginning, and I want you to go to the boat and experience the whole incident from Pete's point of view. Don't interrupt or argue . . . just try to see what he sees. Will you do that?"

"Yes."

"Pete, what were you doing right before the accident?"

Pete smiled softly. "I was playing around with a spinnerbait. I thought maybe I should switch up and use that."

"Then what happened?" Celeste asked.

"Well then the boat hit us and we died." He glared at his father.

"Did you see the boat coming?" Celeste asked gently.

"Yeah, we could see it from across the lake. It was headed straight for us. My dad should have moved the boat," Pete spat.

"I see." Celeste nodded. "How long do you think it took the boat to cross the lake?"

"I don't know . . . .." He shrugged. "Maybe five or ten minutes, long enough for Dad to move us out of the way."

"Did you say anything to your dad about moving?"

"I don't remember. It all happened so fast. But maybe I yelled at the boat. Yeah, Dad was yelling and flagging them with our lantern. He kept yelling, 'You're headed for shore!' because they were. We were fishing the bank in a cove. Why were they going all out toward the shore? Wait . . .! The driver was drunk. They were all drunk."

"Thank you, Pete. I know how hard that was for you. Will you go back to the moment you were playing with the spinnerbait and just look at the whole scene again, please?"

"Yeah, that's a little different from how I've remembered it. It might not have just been Dad's fault."

"Well, let's go back to the moment you were playing with the spinnerbait and look at the whole incident again, but this time, I want you to be where your father was. Look at it from his viewpoint. What did he see?"

"He was casting, and he saw the boat across the lake. It seemed to be headed our way, but boats change directions on the lake, you know. He kept an eye on it and moved his lantern up to the highest rung at the front of the boat—that way they would see us better. When they were about halfway to us and hadn't turned, he started holding his lantern above his head and told me to do the same. Then he started swinging it from side to side to get their attention. But they kept coming, and they didn't slow down . . .. He tried to fire up the motor, but it wouldn't turn over." Pete paused and looked at his father. He shuddered before he said, "Then my dad looked at me and said, 'I'm sorry.' Then, he pushed me overboard. About that time, the boat hit us square in the middle. Dad died instantly, while I was disoriented and later drowned." He got very quiet for a moment. "None of this was Dad's fault . . . "Pete and Mr. Brently both began to cry. Paul looked like he was going to join them. Madam Celeste looked at them and said, "There is more work to be done, but not today. Today you have made a breakthrough I want you both to enjoy. Do you feel differently toward your father now?"

"I don't feel as angry now. I understand what happened and why. I might have survived if I hadn't gotten disoriented. But on the boat, I didn't have a chance."

"You'll probably realize a few more things in the next few days, that is if you count days where you are. Just acknowledge the realizations and enjoy it," Celeste said. "We can work together some more when you are ready." She then turned. "Emma, do you want to take your séance back and wrap it up?"

"Yes, of course. First, I want to thank Pete and Mr. Brently for joining us. We look forward to talking to you again. We ask you not to follow anyone here or anyone who was here earlier, but we want you to know you may reach out to Madam Celeste or myself if anything else occurs to you. I want to thank everyone for helping us hold this safe space and sharing the experience. The séance has ended."

CHAPTER 15

Robert was curious about the technique Madam Celeste had just used. "Where did those questions come from?" he asked. "Are you a psychiatrist or something?"

"Not quite. Don't tell everyone, but I am a licensed psychotherapist," Celeste said. "Sometimes spirits, especially the ones who have had a traumatic exit, will have some unresolved issues which can keep them stuck here. I just use my skills to help them."

"But you didn't pray or invoke any magic or hoodoo or any of that. You just talked to them."

"You're the paranormal enthusiast in the group, aren't you?" Celeste asked.

"Yes, ma'am. I do some investigating."

"Spirits are more powerful than many of them know and certainly more powerful than you know. Be careful. They can be tricky, and they don't always have your best interest at heart."

"So, I should invoke protection . . .?" Robert seemed a little confused as to the message Madam Celeste was trying to convey.

"You don't see and hear like Emma and I do. You have to be more careful. You're relying on recorded responses and talking board type of activities. You don't have a lot of clues as to who is on the other side of the conversation. Is it an ordinary spirit? Is it a vengeful one? Is it truthful? Is it trying to get you to do something it thinks it can't? There are many things to consider when you don't have the gift. Do you understand?"

"Yes, ma'am. I think I do. You think I need to be more careful."

"Do you?" Celeste asked.

"Well, it never seemed so real to me before this . . .. I will be changing a lot of my routine, so I guess the fair answer would be that I haven't taken it as seriously as I should. But I promise I will from now on. You could actually see and hear the ghosts you were asking those questions?"

"Yes, we could." Celeste nodded to Emma.

"See, I never met anyone who could do that. I've known people who claim to, but I never saw anyone stand there and have a conversation with anything the way you did. It changes your whole outlook on it."

"I'm sure we'll meet again, Robert. This case isn't solved yet. In fact, I believe there is a lot more to this than we yet know. It's been a pleasure to meet you, and I will see you again soon. Thank you for letting us use your apartment for this," Madam Celeste said as she walked out the door.

"Can you stay, Emma?" he asked. "I have so many questions."

"I guess I can stay for a little while," she replied. "It's hard to switch gears after an experience like we just had."

"*You* just had. The rest of us watched you and Madam Celeste talk to thin air." He hadn't meant any harm by the comment, but Emma's face belied her disappointment.

"Do you doubt they were here?" she asked. "Because they were. They even moved the trigger objects like you wanted."

"No, no . . .. You took me wrong. I know it happened. I guess I'm just a little jealous that both of you can carry on conversations with ghosts and I can barely get a good EVP."

"She prefers that we call them spirits. It's only semantics, but it's a sign of respect. At least that's how Celeste feels."

"She lets you call her Celeste? Wonder if I could get away with that. Madam Celeste seems a little hokey once you know her."

"Well, we don't want you feeling hokey," Emma chuckled. "You said you had a lot of questions."

"I do. Like how did you meet Paul? And what was the glowing red light and what did it have to do with Cheryl's father and —"

"Maybe we should take one question at a time." Emma smiled and Robert nodded. "Celeste met Paul when she was working on a case that ended up involving the FBI, but that's a story for another time. What you saw as a glowing light and what I saw as something more demonic was Mr. Brently. As evidenced by his statement that he came toward me and I ran out. It's all part of what we suspected — there is something there that can cause hallucinations. What's scary though, is that it can cause them for spirits, too."

"What could cause that kind of hallucination? Is it necessarily a demon?"

"We don't know yet, though I suspect Celeste has some ideas. She has a lot more experience with these kinds of things than I do. I've seen a spirit look like a demon before, but when Celeste was finished, they were back to looking like a spirit. It was pretty scary," Emma admitted.

"Maybe the longer you're dead, the more powerful you get," Robert murmured.

"I think if that were true, Pete would have been more powerful than he was. He acted like he didn't understand anything that was going on, almost like a child. But I'm sure Celeste will be able to help him."

"How did you get connected with Madam Celeste?"

"I needed someone to help me learn to use my abilities. Madam Celeste is very well-known and well thought of in the area. So, I called to see if she would take me as an apprentice. It took some convincing, but eventually, she said yes."

"How long have you been her student?" Robert asked as he gestured for Emma to have a seat on the sofa.

Emma sat down. "I've been with her for almost a year. I can't believe how much I've learned and how much more there is to learn."

"She's lucky to have you," Robert said. He gently took Emma's hand. "Would you have dinner with me one night?"

"I don't know if that's such a good idea," Emma said slowly. "At least while we're working on a case together, we should probably keep things on a more professional level."

"I like you . . . and I get the feeling that you like me, too. Or did I misunderstand?"

Emma did like him. There was a spark there. Energy was her business, but the energy flowing between her and Robert felt different. She had been in love before, more than once, and this could definitely lead there. But, did she need or want to mix business with pleasure? What would Celeste say? Of course, he was interested in the paranormal. He was actively investigating and looking for ways to prove what she already knew. Maybe this was the kind of person she should get to know better. Maybe this was the kind of person who would not be threatened by her gift. It would be nice to have a friend who appreciated what she did.

"I do like you," she said hesitantly. "There has to be a line, though. I can't afford to get physically involved with anyone right now. My focus has to be on my studies. I'm taking college courses, you know. I want to do what Celeste did—get a degree in psychology or social work or something that will help the people that come to me for guidance."

"I didn't know, but when has that ever stopped someone from having a friend with benefits?" Robert knew as the words flew across his tongue that it should never have been spoken. He watched the look on her face change from warm and friendly and willing to listen, to an icy fortress no words would melt—at least, not tonight anyway. He tried to salvage it anyway. Before she could speak, he put his hands up. "I didn't mean that. I'm not looking for a friend with benefits. That just came out. I have no idea from where. Please, erase it from your mind and let me start over."

"I have a lot of studying to do. I should get home." She

gathered her things and headed for the door. Robert beat her to it, and she wished she had taken that karate class last semester.

"Can't you read my mind and know how I feel?" he asked, blocking the door.

"I don't have to read your mind. You made it pretty clear," Emma said with a frown.

"You have the wrong impression of me," he said grabbing her shoulders ever so lightly. "I'm not like that. I just chose the wrong words. Please, look in my mind and see who I really am."

"It doesn't work that way. I don't read minds. I see spirits. It's completely different."

"Let me take you to dinner," Robert pleaded. "No funny stuff, just dinner and conversation. We can meet at the restaurant so you feel safe. I'm a good guy. Ask Cheryl or any of the others. I screwed up a couple of words tonight but please, don't hold that against me. Please, Emma."

"I have class tomorrow, but we could eat the next night," she said after a moment. The truth was that Emma was about as socially skilled as Robert. Her gift had always made things awkward, and she had learned not to talk about it with anyone. The evening so far had been really enjoyable, being able to open up with Robert and his friends. She felt like part of the group for the first time ever. However, she was not ready to get serious with anyone. She had a lot to learn and not all of it could be taught by Celeste or at school.

"Do you want me to pick you up or meet you there?" Robert asked.

"Let's meet there," Emma said with a nod.

"Do you like Italian?"

"I do."

Let's meet at Flora's at seven then," he said.

Emma nodded and squeezed past Robert to get to the door. She felt oddly calm about him and didn't sense any deception on his part, and while she could not read minds, she could read emotions and intentions. His intentions seemed good. It was decided that she still liked him and would enjoy dinner with him.

CHAPTER 16

Madam Celeste was expectedly unhappy with the turn of events. Emma probably should have left out the part about friends with benefits, but Celeste would have guessed it anyway. It wasn't easy to slip anything past her. Celeste actually liked Robert. She hadn't interacted with him much, but he had volunteered the use of his home and had kept the mood relaxed but serious. Celeste had a good feeling about him—that is, until she heard he had accosted Emma.

"He didn't really accost me, Celeste. He just kept me from leaving before he had a chance to plead his case. He's a good guy, and I do like him."

"It's Helsinki syndrome!" Celeste yelled.

"I think you mean Stockholm Syndrome and no, it's not. I was not held hostage. I was not held at all. Maybe if we had skipped the talking and gone straight to the holding, this would have turned out better. I know I would have enjoyed it more."

"You're a grown woman, Emma. If this is what you want to do, I have no place to try to stop you. I see some dark things down the road for you, but I suspect that they have little to do with Robert or your relationship with him."

"What kind of dark things? What do you see?"

"I cannot make out details, just dark areas here and there. No more so than I have. We have given ourselves to helping people, and that often comes at a cost. These things I see are not devastating and nothing more than we have already been through. We might look at them as adventures."

"Does that include this house I'm investigating now?"

"You know the answer to that already, Emma. You have not begun to scratch the surface of what's going on out there. Neither of those men I met last night seems capable of causing mass hallucination, so there must be something else at that house that does not want to be discovered. What is your plan to determine what is going on there?" Celeste asked.

"I don't really have a plan. I'm not really keen on going back there given the idea of hallucinations. But Cheryl does need help if she's ever going to reclaim the house. What would you do?" Emma asked.

"Let's see . . ... First, I would do some research on what kind of being would be capable of such a thing. Could it be someone who could hypnotize people when they were alive? Could it be some kind of creature we've never encountered before? Are there any myths or legends of such things happening even to one person? What we have already learned is the more powerful the person, the more powerful the hallucination. This could be very tricky for you and for me."

"So, I can start doing some online research. I'll get on it this morning. I only have one client who won't be here until eleven, and I'm pretty much caught up on your paperwork. You have two appointments this morning and three this afternoon. Maybe you could ask Paul if he's ever heard of anything like this?" Emma said.

"Great idea. I'll try to get hold of Paul now. We'll touch base again this afternoon before you leave for class."

They were in Celeste's home which was also her place of business. There was a nice little room where Celeste did readings and then an office for paperwork and phone calls. Emma rarely was able to use the reading room because Celeste had a pretty full schedule most days. She had only let Emma have a few clients of her own while she was in training, but Emma was happy to have them.

Emma went to the office and brought out her laptop. "Let the research begin," she said to no one in particular. The research was not Emma's favorite thing, preferring the readings and exploring in person, but college was teaching her how important it was to be able to research. After only a few searches on Google, she found the area was ripe with paranormal activity. Most references to hallucinations attributed them to drugs or stress-induced delirium. She was about to find another search engine when she stumbled on a reference to the Djinn on the supernatural Wikipedia page. "Djinn - *Monsters* which are able to infect humans by touch which *cause* the victim to experience incredibly realistic *hallucinations*, *capable* of convincing them that they are in a perfect world or confronting their worst fears."

"Hmmm. This warrants further research," she mumbled to herself. "I wonder what a Djinn is . . .."

Opening what she thought was a Wiki site, Emma found a site created by the show Supernatural, hence the name Supernatural Wikipedia. There were half a dozen supernatural explanations for hallucinations. There was even a hellhound who caused people to hallucinate just by being in the vicinity. They used this to terrify their prey, causing them to leave a safe hiding place and come out into the open. *What if Jeremy is tracking a hellhound and doesn't realize it?* she thought to herself.

Looking further, she found something called a buru-buru which can cause 'ghost sickness', which includes hysteria, hallucinations, and sometimes death of the human victim. Maybe there was a buru-buru at the house. She wrote down all the information under "TV theories" and went on to more serious research. There was an article which posited that macular degeneration has caused some very strange hallucinations which fringe elements claim are not hallucinations, but in reality, they are crossovers to other dimensions. The disease is called Charles Bonnett syndrome, named after the man who discovered it. This article was followed by many more. Who knew how much information there was on hallucinations? It was all starting to put

Emma to sleep. She looked for her notes on her eleven am. client. Finding them, she proceeded to straighten the room and prepare for her session.

Emma's eleven o'clock was a man with his own business. He came in once a week to "have his fortune told." Emma had told him she wasn't really a fortune teller, but that's what he insisted on calling it. He liked to hear if any problems were coming up in the week ahead, anything he should or could prepare for. Emma would tell him what she could see and it wasn't always pleasant, but he always took it well, claiming he would rather see a problem coming than have it sneak up on him. Emma couldn't argue with that, and he was always happy with the reading. She used a standard oracle deck which suited him perfectly.

She welcomed this break from the research today. She always welcomed being able to do a live reading. It was getting easier and easier to tell people what she could see without scaring the begeeses out of them. Madam Celeste was an excellent teacher and made a real impression on Emma about how important the delivery of the message is. You could be spot on and say it wrong and take away any benefit the client might have. So, she had learned to pay attention to her wording and her demeanor when telling clients what she perceived.

The session went well, and Emma went back to researching hallucinations. "This is crazy!" she finally said out loud. "How am I going to get around the hallucinations? How can I shield myself from them when I don't know what's causing them? And there are only a few potential causes, but none of them seem plausible." She sat back in her chair and wished she had more of Celeste's knowledge. Looking up she saw a book in Celeste's collection, *Hallucination Spells*. If it contained hallucination spells, then maybe it also contained anti-hallucination spells. Opening the book, there was an immediate warning. "Not to be used in solitary circumstances." She had opened to a section toward the back, but it was what was needed. *Overcoming a Hallucination Spell of unknown origin*. Now this was more like it.

"Solitary circumstances. Does that mean alone or does it

mean without another practitioner?" she murmured

"Another practitioner of what?" Paul said, appearing without warning.

"I'm not sure yet," Emma answered, barely glancing up from the book. "I need to ask Celeste. This is one of her private books. I only just started reading. It may be a witchcraft book, or it may be some other form of magic, but it has spells."

"Probably witchcraft," Paul agreed. "You better not mess with that without her help."

"Tell me something I don't know," Emma said sarcastically.

"Richard thinks about you a lot," Paul said nonchalantly.

"What?"

"That boy you were with last night."

"That was Robert, but why are you telling me this?"

"You said to tell you something you didn't know. So, I did."

"That wasn't a real statement. It was rhetorical."

"Oh . . .."

"But since you brought it up . . .. How do you know he thinks about me a lot? Do you read minds?"

"Not always. But sometimes I do," Paul said.

"He really seems like a nice guy, doesn't he, Paul?"

"I'd have dinner with him, if I was a girl, and if I was alive."

"Thanks, Paul. I'm going to go find Celeste and see what she can tell me about this spell."

Emma found Celeste in the kitchen preparing her lunch. "May I talk with you about what I found out about hallucinations?" she asked.

"Of course."

Emma explained what she had found online and then showed her the book she had found. Celeste was silent for a bit. Emma couldn't tell if the woman was angry or upset or just thinking—but she hoped it was the latter. The silence between them felt heavy.

"First, this is my private book, Emma. When a book is handwritten, you should ask before delving into it. Second, the spell you have marked is labeled not for solitary use."

"That's why I stopped and brought it to you. I'm not even sure what it means exactly. If I have Cheryl or one of the others with me, does that make it not solitary?" Emma asked.

"No, this is for practitioners of witchcraft. It is meant to be done with at least two practitioners."

"So, this is what people call the dark arts?" Emma asked.

"No, this is not the dark arts."

"So, you can work this spell with me?"

"You have more to learn about many things before we begin studying the magic of nature," Celeste said.

"But this is the best thing I could find to deal with whatever is causing the hallucinations. The other possibilities are a djinn and a buru-buru and other things more absurd than that. If I need to learn about the natural ways, I will gladly do it and the sooner the better. Are there books I can study to speed things up?"

"I do have a book or two for you to read. When you have finished reading them, we will talk about working together to perform a spell. You must not attempt to rush this by practicing it by yourself. Are we clear?"

"Yes, ma'am. Which books do I need to study? I'll get started right away."

"You may spend one hour a day on the clock studying. More than that, you will have to do on your own," Celeste said sternly.

"I don't mind that at all," Emma said with a nod. "What must I complete before we can begin the anti-hallucination spell?"

"Read *White Magic* first. You don't have to memorize the spells, herbs, or stones. But you must be familiar with them. Then read *Shadow Work*. You're going to be surprised by how similar the two books are. But that is part of the lesson—look for the similarities in all things. That is where the magic exists. Now I must eat quickly to be ready for my one o'clock."

"Thank you, Madam Celeste. I will begin studying immediately," Emma said with full respect.

"Leave that one with me, dear," Celeste said, pointing to the hallucination book. "You needn't be looking at that one yet, but I must brush up on it for the days to come."

"So, we will work it together?"

"If you study properly."

Emma beamed as she turned to leave the room. "Challenge accepted."

CHAPTER 17

Emma's next task was to inform the team there would be a delay. She called Cheryl and explained that she would need about a week to study what was going on and do some research. She told Cheryl it was not a good idea for anyone to go in until Emma or Celeste could join them. Even Jeremy could be affected, so he needed to spend his time on research as well. Emma asked Cheryl if she would tell everyone to stay away from the house until they were contacted.

"Even Robert? Don't you want to call him yourself?"

"Why would you say that?" Emma asked slowly.

"You two seem to be hitting it off pretty well," Cheryl said.

"Just play the liaison for now? Please?"

"Okay, okay. I'll call everyone. What happened with my dad and Pete last night?" Cheryl asked.

"Your dad was pretty easy, but Pete has some work to do. We'll be doing sessions with him in the next few days. We learned a little more than we knew already, but a few mysteries are still lingering. That's why we need more time. Cheryl, sometimes spirits have answers . . . they just don't realize they have them. They have to be questioned one way and then another to find out what is ultimately true. They are not usually lying, but their perspective is so different from ours that it can appear like they are lying. We will get to the bottom of this, and we will help your brother."

"Thanks, Emma. I appreciate it."

"Good. Now I have a great deal of studying to do. It seems I've taken on a new course and it's very important I get caught up by this weekend. I will call you when I have news and hope you will do the same."

After she hung up with Cheryl, Emma spotted both of the books Celeste had asked her to read and study. *White Magic* was a paperback print book. There must be thousands of copies. It was a very inviting book. She imagined if she saw it in a store, she would buy it. It was added to her study books. The next book was called *Shadow Work*. Much of the hardbound book was handwritten. It had been created with room for exactly that, plenty of typed pages, but an equal amount of blank lined pages which had since been filled in. She wondered how old the book was and how much, if any, of the book had been handwritten by Celeste. Just when Emma was beginning to think she understood Celeste, some newer deeper part of her would be revealed.

Emma was tempted to start with the Shadow book but did as instructed and opened the White book. It was very informative and bright. Any thought of using magic for something bad was deflected with all the reasons such as a spell would backfire, but mostly the book talked about all the good that could be accomplished with natural white magic. There was a section on stones and some of the mystical qualities contained in each of the various stones. Emma had seen most of these stones in Madam Celeste's personal collection, and now she understood why they were there.

Another section of the book was devoted to herbs, weeds, and flowers. Each was said to have properties to help soothe, refresh, console, or a myriad of other things. And most could be found in apothecary jars in Celeste's kitchen.

There was also a section on spells and incantations. On the surface, they seemed to be only silly little poems a child could have written, but perhaps in natural magic simplicity is the key. She had not really thought of Celeste as a magician or witch, and it seemed odd to do so now. What would her new friends think if they thought she was a witch? Would they drop the whole thing rather than associate with such women?

Celeste had hinted before Emma was a witch, but Emma hadn't taken it seriously or even thought about what it meant. Reading all these spells—ones that she could have easily written—caused her to wonder if she could learn to be a witch, and if so, would she. The idea of belonging to a coven didn't appeal to her, but the book had talked about solitaries. Could she be that? A solitary who maintained a friendship with another witch, but not a coven or anything so organized? Could this be her future? There was a great deal to learn. She dove into her studies and forgot about everything else. When Celeste found her, she was slumped over the white magic book, which was turned to the page for curing insomnia. It had worked—she was fast asleep.

"Emma," Celeste whispered, "you've fallen asleep, dear. You need to wake up."

"What are you doing in my house?" Emma asked, still confused from sleep.

Celeste chuckled. "You've fallen asleep in my office. It looks like you were reading a cure for insomnia and put yourself out."

"Oh, no!" Emma yelled. "What have I done? What time is it? I have a class this afternoon. Please don't fire me. I don't know what happened."

"You're fine, Emma. Calm down. You have plenty of time before class. We'll just call it your lunch hour."

"I wasn't even sleepy. I don't understand . . .."

"Look at the spell you were studying."

"Do they all work that well?" Emma asked.

"They do when performed correctly by a powerful witch. And you have proven once again how very powerful you are. You need more training, but that is being handled. You need practice, and that will come in time. You are truly gifted. We need to speed up your training."

"So, I'm a witch? Like Samantha or Sabrina on TV?"

"TV isn't what I would call accurate, dear. There is no twitch-your-nose type magic that I know of. And you are only a witch if you choose to call yourself one. I do not. There is too much negative associated with that name. I call myself a solitary. No one else has the exact same beliefs I have, so solitary is a good description, and I'm fine with that. You may learn from me, but you will have your own beliefs. Never let anyone shove you in a box and tell you what you have to believe, not even me."

"Hmmm, you're saying it's okay for me to disagree with you," Emma said.

"I'm saying you will disagree with me. There will be times when that will be a problem, and there will be times when we will agree to disagree."

"But you are my instructor. How will I know when to believe what you're teaching me?"

"That's a good question. We all carry our own truth. We have gut reactions to information—listen to that. If you don't have a strong certainty of your own, then listen to me. Or ask. Ask me how certain I am. We can always discuss things."

"So, if we're both solitaries working together, are we still solitaries? I mean, how can we be?"

"I will always be a solitary. You are my apprentice. You don't have to name what you are yet. You don't have all the information yet," Celeste said.

"But, just to be clear, I am studying witchcraft?"

"You may call it that."

"What do you call it?"

"I call it nature's gift, among other things."

"Well, then. What would be the best book for me to start with? Maybe not one full of spells."

"You're going to have to learn to control your gift if you're going to try to study it. We don't want you reading a spell for causing harm to someone and having it work just because you read it. Perhaps we can write a charm to be read at the beginning of a study session and another at the end of the study session. That can be your first assignment. Write a charm, prayer, or spell asking that your magic not work while you are studying and then write another one to be read when you are finished, to restore your natural abilities."

"Now?"

"I would suggest doing it before you read anything else. In the meantime, I will find the perfect book with which to begin."

CHAPTER 18

Emma met Robert for dinner. It was a little awkward at first, but by the time the main course was served, they were discussing cases they had been on, and planning for Emma to accompany Robert on his next investigation. Emma had been right—he was someone she could talk to. He was fascinated by everything she did that others were afraid of. He either enjoyed her company or was a great actor. It was the best date she could remember. They sat in Flora's until they were ready to close. Robert wanted to know all about her new study of witchcraft. Emma felt no need to sugarcoat it. She called it witchcraft, and Robert was fine with it. He wanted to know if he could help her study. He thought he'd like to learn about it, too.

"It might help me in the field," he said. "And maybe I could be some help to you."

"It would certainly make studying more fun, but I don't see myself getting as much done," Emma said smiling.

"We could try it one night and see how it goes," Robert offered.

"Okay."

"Do you want to come over to my place?"

"Not tonight, Robert. I should get home. Thank you for dinner, though. Next time I'll make something at my place, and you can come over. How's that?"

They were by Emma's car now. Robert leaned in and kissed her for a long lingering moment. *Don't do this!* Emma's thoughts screamed. But the flesh was weak and enjoyed the activity far too much to listen to reason. They slipped into her car and enjoyed the chemistry for a while. The next night they found they were actually good study partners. Robert was truly interested in the subject, so they were both quite serious about the lessons.

Emma was a natural at writing spells, and Celeste seemed quite pleased with her progress. There had been no more mishaps with unintentional spell casting. Emma was becoming comfortable with knowing she had special gifts and was beginning to be at ease with the term witch. Paul insisted that both Emma and Celeste were witches. In fact, he had been convinced for some time Celeste was what he called a weather witch. Her neighborhood was in a floodplain, but since Celeste moved in, there had not been one flood that came inside anyone's house. It would come to the steps, but not into the house. He had seen her both stop a storm and start it up again. Who knew what would be Emma's specialty?

Celeste pushed Emma hard that first week. She needed Emma to understand the basics and be able to apply them as needed. Celeste had a feeling about what was waiting for them at Cheryl's house. She wanted to be prepared for it, hoping that Emma would be able to cast a spell the second they needed it. She had even thought about getting Pete away from the house for more talks before tackling whatever was using the house as a refuge. There might be more he could tell them if they asked the right questions, but they would have to do it away from the house. They could not trust any answers they received while in the house.

Jeremy was pursuing any facts he could find about the buru-buru, and the other leads Emma had come across. A month ago, he would have said hogwash to the whole idea, but he had been taken in by the illusions, too. He was determined to find out if what he was tracking was real and if it was, was there a possibility it was supernatural? The idea made him chuckle, but it was possible, and he knew it. He had no idea how the ladies intended to prove what it was, but he had seen some pretty amazing things these last few weeks and knew if anyone could do it, it would be those two women.

He had been studying the buru-buru since Emma had told him about it and it made some sense, but there were holes in the logic. He thought surely there must be something that made more sense, though he hadn't found it yet.

"Emma, let's have another séance with only you, me, Paul, and Pete. I think you're ready. We'll do it here in the reading room. We can do it in the evening or this Friday afternoon. What do you think?" Celeste asked.

"I'm ready to get back on the case and find out what tricked me so easily," Emma responded.

"Do you want to wait until Friday or do it one evening? I'm free any night this week except Friday. Joe will be coming over Friday," she said, almost blushing.

"I wondered what happened to him. I haven't seen him for weeks."

"Well, we had a difference of opinion about something important to me. We've cleared it up, and hopefully, I'll be seeing Joe more often."

"I can't believe you had a fight."

"It wasn't a fight. It was a misunderstanding about my desire to see other people. It's an option I prefer to keep open."

"Well, I've got nothing going on, so we could do it any night you want. My one-night class is over for now. How about tomorrow?"

"Okay. Let's plan on tomorrow after our last client."

"Are you sure you want to do it here? Isn't that like inviting the monster in?"

"We're inviting Pete in. I don't believe Pete is a monster," Celeste said.

"Alright. Is there anything special I need to bring? Should I stop off at Cheryl's and pick up Pete's key fob? Or would you like to try something different this time? Maybe I could pick up one of those spiders." Emma laughed.

"It didn't seem to be the keys that delivered him last time, did it? If I remember correctly, it was his father that got him riled up enough to show up. And getting his father to show up took Cheryl getting emotional."

"You want me to invite Cheryl?"

"I think that might be a good idea as long as the girl knows she's the bait and won't actually be participating in the séance."

"She calls me like every two days to see what we've learned. She'd be happy to help."

"I'll let you arrange it. Shall we go for dinner and meet back here at six-thirty?" Celeste asked.

"Sounds good to me. I'll tell Cheryl to grab some food and meet us here at six-thirty. She doesn't need to bring anything, right?"

"Nothing I can think of."

"I have a good feeling about tomorrow night," Emma said. "Something exciting is going to happen."

"As long as we get some answers . . ." Celeste murmured.

CHAPTER 19

Robert was disappointed when he found out he was not invited to the séance, but he understood. He thought Emma would do a great job and made one last pitch to be there for documentation. Emma didn't think Celeste would buy it, so Robert finally dropped it.

Cheryl was on board immediately. This whole thing was just dragging on from what she could see, and she still wanted answers and soon would be good.

"Cheryl, you're getting this for free at this point because it's part of my training. If Celeste has to take over, it's going to cost you more than you think. Celeste is a really nice lady, but she's a businesswoman and as such, not in the habit of giving these sessions for free. Cool your jets, and enjoy the show," Emma said.

"I know, I know. But eventually, I'm going to reach a point where I say screw the money. Do what you have to do to get it solved. It's not that I don't trust you, Emma, but I really want this solved and we don't seem to be moving on it at all," Cheryl said.

"Tonight is going to change all that. I can feel it. We're going to learn something that changes everything. I know it."

Emma and Cheryl arrived at Madam Celeste's promptly at six-thirty. Paul had been there off and on all day. Emma had the trigger objects, and of course, the biggest trigger object of all was Cheryl.

Madam Celeste and Cheryl did the protection invocation together, and Emma called for Pete to join them. Surprisingly, he showed up instantly, as if he'd been waiting.

"I thought you were starting at six-thirty," he said. "You're late."

"It's been our experience that most spirits don't keep track of time very well," Emma replied. "How did you know we were starting at six-thirty?"

"Your friend, Paul, found me. He told me what you think is going on and it seems pretty crazy to me. A buru-buru? Or ghost sickness? Can a ghost get ghost sickness? And don't you think the ghosts are hallucinating things, too?"

"Celeste, does this feel right to you?" Emma asked.

"He doesn't sound like the same boy we met last time," Celeste said.

"You helped me work through a lot of things last time we were together. I've got my bearings now. What did you want to ask me about?"

"We want to know what is going on at the house," Emma said. "Why are people hallucinating? Have you seen or felt anything sinister there? Does it have anything to do with your spiders? We know they can cause hallucinations if they bite, but no one has been bitten except for Rocky."

"I've seen Dad there. He can be pretty mean. I've seen a lot of my spiders. They were doing great until sis decided to bomb them. Why did you have to do that, sis?"

"She can't hear you, you know," Emma said. Celeste was leaving this to Emma unless she needed help. It was great practice, and Pete was pretty harmless.

"Oh yeah, I forgot," Pete said sheepishly.

"Has there been anything happen at the house which would frighten you?" Emma asked.

"Sometimes I will hear someone talking, but there is no one there. Or I can see things moving around or the lights will come on when no one is there but me or me and Dad. Me and Dad don't talk to each other much when we're both there, but I think we both get drawn back to the place a lot, though not as much since our session with you, Madam Celeste. You really helped."

"I'm glad to have helped, Pete. What would you say is the scariest thing that has happened at the house or around the house?" Celeste asked.

"That's hard to say. It's pretty scary when people are talking around you, but you can't see them. And then there's this red light that comes on out on the back patio. That's kinda creepy. We never had a red light back there that I can remember, and it moves. It goes out to the woods. I don't like being there when that happens, but sometimes I can't leave no matter how bad I want to."

"Does the red light ever have a shape?" Emma asked.

"Not that I've ever noticed, but I don't go looking at it. It's already too creepy," Pete said.

"I wonder if that ties into what Jeremy has found?" Emma said to Celeste.

"Who's Jeremy?" Pete asked.

"He's a tracker who's been looking around in the backyard and in the woods. He thinks he saw a gray wolf out there, which would be a rare find. Do you know anything about that?" Emma asked.

"No, I don't know much about wolves. Never saw one around the house."

"Did you ever see anyone that seemed bigger than they should?"

"Like have I ever had a hallucination? How would I know? If it was, would I know it?"

"Have you ever seen a live person act like they were having a hallucination?" Emma asked. "Maybe they were running away from something, but you didn't see anything there, or maybe they were swatting at something you didn't see?"

"Maybe, it's all kinda confusing from this side."

"Wait! You saw the ghost hunters carrying lightsabers when they were only flashlights, right?" Emma rushed out, feeling like she'd accomplished something.

"No, I think that was my dad. I never saw that."

"Oh yeah, it was your dad." Emma nodded. "Tell us about Andrew. Why do you think he shows up at the house?"

"Who's Andrew?" Pete asked.

"Your friend, the one that died in a car crash. You don't remember him?"

"Oh, Andrew . . .. He seems stuck in the den, doesn't he?"

"Yes, he does. Do you have any idea why someone who died so far away would be stuck in your father's den?" Emma asked.

"Well, I don't think it's because he wants to be close to Dad. They were never great friends. He didn't like Dad any more than I did. I wonder if he's been stuck there since he died?"

"Good question. Andrew? Can you join us here for a while?" Emma asked. They waited for him to appear, but nothing happened. "Maybe he really is stuck? We'll have to deal with that after we clear up the hallucination situation."

Celeste nodded in agreement.

"What do you think, Celeste. What else can we ask Pete that we don't already know?"

"Where is Paul? Have either of you seen him?" Celeste asked.

Pete disappeared.

"What the hell?" Emma said, glancing around confused.

"We're going to have to be very careful," Celeste said slowly. "I don't think that was Pete . . .."

"What do you mean that wasn't Pete? It had to be," Emma said. "Who else could it have been?"

"I don't know, but I'm worried about Paul. He obviously went to the house to get Pete. Why didn't he come back?"

Emma paused, looking thoughtful in the distance. Softly, she said, "He didn't know who Andrew was . . .. It wasn't Pete." Her eyes were wide as she glanced at Celeste and Cheryl.

"What does Andrew have to do with any of this?" Cheryl asked. She had been so quiet they had almost forgotten about her.

"He was a friend of your brother, wasn't he?" Emma asked.

"He wanted to be. He even told people he was, but Pete didn't like him that much. He thought he was a dork," Cheryl said with a frown.

"Hmmm. He seemed so timid when I met him, certainly not capable of all of this. He seemed as afraid as anyone."

Out of thin air, Paul and Pete showed up. At least it looked like Pete.

"Where have you been?" Celeste asked. "And why did you disappear so quickly?"

"He came to get me," Paul said. "He knew I could vouch for him. I sent him over here earlier. I didn't think you needed me, too. I was checking out something strange back at that house."

"I panicked," Pete said softly. "You sounded like I was in trouble. So, I took off to find Paul."

"So, we were really talking to Pete, not an illusion of Pete. And it makes sense you didn't know who Andrew was. And it makes sense he would be attracted to your house, but why the den?" Emma asked.

"Yes, every answer seems to bring more questions with it," Celeste added. "I'm afraid we're going to have to go to the house."

"I don't know," Paul said warily. "We need to know more about what's going on over there, it's true. But can any of us trust what we see or hear? I would suggest investigating from a distance as much as possible. There are beings at that place that don't belong, and not just at the house—they don't belong on this plane. It's creepy, even for me."

"Maybe Andrew knows more? If it's so creepy, then what is he doing there all the time?" Emma asked. "Pete, will you stay with us for a while and see if you can help us get Andrew to come here? Or maybe go to him there and ask him to join us here?"

Pete nodded. "I can do that. He should be pretty easy to find in the den. I'll be back as soon as I can." With that, he disappeared.

Paul gave Celeste a look. She nodded, and Paul disappeared, too.

There was a long silence. Then Cheryl said, "Pete, why did you let all those spiders loose in the house? Didn't you know they were dangerous?"

"Pete isn't here right now," Emma said. "We're waiting for him to convince Andrew to join us here."

"I thought you said you were going to go there?" Cheryl asked, understandably confused.

"Paul thought it would be better to find out as much as we could from here," Emma explained.

"Do you still need me here?" Cheryl asked.

"You were the bait for Pete, but he seems very cooperative now, so, I guess not." Emma looked at Celeste for confirmation, and Celeste nodded in agreement.

"I think I'll get in touch with Jeremy and see what he's uncovered," Cheryl said. "Will it bother you if I'm doing that while I wait?"

"No, that's great. It will be interesting to see if what he's found ties in with what's going on inside the house," Emma said.

"Cheryl, Pete mentioned the lights coming on by themselves. Did you have the power restored at the house?" Celeste asked.

"Yes, I had it done last week. I thought since we're kind of using it right now it would be nice to have electricity."

Pete popped back in. "Andrew has tried to leave, but before he gets here, he gets snapped back to the house. He's pretty well stuck. Looks like you might have to go to him if you want to know what he's seen. He's such a weenie. He's actually happy most of my spiders are gone. Little dork . . . .."

"Have you found any solutions for the various possibilities that await us over there, Emma?" Celeste asked.

"Not much, but enough to cast a spell or two to keep us safe, and possibly to ward off hallucinations," Emma said.

"Then we must continue at the house," Celeste said as she packed her bag to leave. "Andrew seems to be attached to something there. Cheryl, we can't let you come with us this time. I know it's your house, but it would be safer for you to stay away until we better understand what's going on."

"Do you want to go tonight?" Emma asked.

"I have a full schedule tomorrow, dear. If we're going to pursue this, I think we should do it now. You're driving, of course."

"Of course," Emma said, running after Celeste and out of the house. "What about the things we need for the protection spell?"

Celeste stopped. "Do I have what you need here in my house?"

"I think so . . .. It's pretty straightforward. Sage, of course."

"Of course." Celeste nodded.

"Spearmint, fresh ground coffee beans, dragon's blood leaves dried, smelling salts, and plantain."

"I think I have all that. Let's go mix it up," Celeste said.

.

CHAPTER 20

Meanwhile, Cheryl was able to contact Jeremy. He wanted to get together at the local pancake house to show her what he'd found. She was already in Gloryville, so she agreed.

He had a booth for them when she arrived. "I've spoken with a local wildlife rep, and it looks like there was a gray wolf reported here over fifty years ago. There had been a circus in this town back in the early 1900s. They may have had a foreign wolf or two."

"But that's been over a hundred years," Cheryl said in disbelief. "There would either be a lot more of them or none at all."

"That's what I thought, but if one was seen fifty years ago, then maybe there is a small pack out in the woods in Bella View. I saw it with my own eyes and saw its tracks."

"But it could have been a hallucination. You know that," Cheryl said.

"I know. But I need to get back out there to see what other signs I can find. I'll stay well away from the house. I'll park at the entry and walk around as far away from the house as possible."

"I wish I could go with you, but I'm not risking the house or a wolf. Would you go during the day?"

"It would be better at night. They are more likely to be out at night."

"So, you're talking about going now?"

"I thought I'd wait until tomorrow. I'll go set up some night cameras in the woods during the day, then camp in one spot with night vision goggles tomorrow night. Maybe I can see something while I'm filming it. This has become very important to me, Cheryl."

"I can't imagine anyone having any objections to what you've described. Go ahead and do it. I'll back you up if anyone says anything. So . . . what else is going on for you?" Cheryl asked, trying to prolong the get-together. She enjoyed being around Jeremy, but he didn't seem to notice.

"Like what else am I tracking? Nothing really. This is my only project right now, and I'm so lucky you called me in about the chicken scratches. If not for that, I would never have suspected anything this exciting was happening practically in my backyard." His eyes lit up as he talked about the wolf. Cheryl didn't hear him, though. Her mind was imagining more interesting things she'd like to be doing with Jeremy.

" . . . don't you think?" Jeremy asked.

"Hmm. What? My mind was distracted for a minute. What were you saying?"

"I said it would be nice to have lunch in a couple of days so I could share what I find. We could watch the video together. Will you have lunch with me here on Friday or Saturday?"

"Really?" she said. "I think that would be awesome! What time? Which day?"

"Why don't I call you Friday morning? If I have anything ready, we can meet here on Friday, or I'll let you know we need to wait until Saturday."

Cheryl beamed. "Perfect. I hope you catch some interesting footage. What will you do if there is a gray wolf here?"

"I'll turn the footage over to the Texas wildlife commission, I guess. Then I'll write a paper for the Trackers Guild. Maybe they'll ask me to speak at a conference and show my slides and videos."

"Oh, I'd like to see that," Cheryl said.

"Well, I'm getting ahead of myself. I don't have any footage yet, just a questionable sighting."

"Is there any danger to anyone going in those woods if the wolf is there?"

"There haven't been any reports of attacks or missing pets or the like, so I'm going to say it's fairly safe. But I won't be going back there without my pistol handy, that's for sure."

"Then I'll tell Robert to keep his people close to the house when they start going in again, just to be safe."

"This has been great. Hopefully, I'll have something to share with you on Friday," Jeremy said as he walked Cheryl to her car.

Cheryl was sure the only thing on Jeremy's mind was that wolf. However, she was more interested in Jeremy. So, it came as a surprise when Jeremy pulled her close to him and pressed his lips to hers. She enjoyed it all the same, and they lingered for a time before leaving the parking lot.

As all this was happening, Madam Celeste and Emma were headed over to Cheryl's house to confront Andrew. Emma was unusually quiet. The sun had set, and she seemed focused on driving.

"Are you afraid, Emma?"

"I'm a bit anxious," Emma admitted. "What if there really is a buru-buru or something worse like a djinn?"

"I don't know much about djinns, but I've never heard stories about them around here. I think there would be some legends about them at least if there were any in the area," Celeste replied.

"What if it's a demon?" Emma asked softly.

"Then we will need more than your spell, and we will leave and find someone who specializes in such things. I have a few friends who could be called in if needed. Why do you think it might be a demon, though?"

"You've never seen anything like it. There's very little on it in the research tools. But I didn't look up demons. It's like I didn't want to know. I still don't, to be honest. I don't want to be in a house with a demon. The idea terrifies me."

"Well, we have learned you are not meant to be a demon hunter and I'm just as happy to know it. Just remember, we are not going to this place to find a demon. We are going to find an explanation that makes sense and a situation we can solve."

"You make it sound so easy. Aren't you the least bit afraid?"

"Not yet," Celeste said with a half-smile. "I try to wait until there's something to be afraid of before I become afraid."

"You don't find an unknown entity that can cause mass hallucinations something to be afraid of?"

"I might when I find it, but I haven't found it yet."

"Well, I have! I've already experienced this thing, and it scares the living daylights out of me."

"I didn't mean to make light of your experiences here," Celeste said gently as they pulled up to the property. "But we came prepared. You have created a good spell, and we are a powerful pair of solitaries, like two aces in a hand. We'll be fine."

"Thanks, Celeste. That actually helped. Shall we go in?"

Cheryl had given Emma and Robert keys to the house. Emma parked toward the back of the house so they could enter through the kitchen. She didn't want to walk into the living room first. Feeling her way around cobwebs in the dark for the light switch led Emma to decide to find her flashlight. No need to bump into a leftover spider with her hand, was there? There were some webs, but not as many as the group described from the first time. Emma was grateful for that. The switch was on the wrong side of the door, but she found it with the flashlight.

There was only one bulb working in the ceiling fan, which was set on high speed and sent a good deal of dust flying. Celeste reached up and pulled the chain to lower the speed, but ended up turning it off, so had to start over. She found low speed and walked toward the living room to get some light in there. There was no overhead light, so she looked for lamps. Again, most of the bulbs were gone or not working, but there was one that came on. Emma went via the dining room and turned a light on there. Then, she found the hall switch and then the entry.

It was not bright, but there was light throughout the living area. Emma would light the rooms as they reached them.

"Let's recite your prayer and spritz the place," Celeste suggested.

"Prayer? You said it was a spell. I wrote a spell."

"Prayer. Spell. Incantation. Mantra. It's all semantics, nothing more. Shall we read it together?"

"Gather here together, spirits, good and true,
Protect now your servants, the brave, though the few.
Who seek now to solve this strange mystery,
And finally, uncover its dark history.

Keep us safe from visions that tell us only lies,
Making us forget what we see with our eyes.
Let our minds remain clear ne'er succumbing to fright,
Let us walk in the bubble of your truthful light."

As they repeated the spell, they walked through the house spraying the liquid mixture they had prepared together in Celeste's kitchen. With every step, Emma felt calmer and more confident that the evening would go well. They finished off back in the living room.

"Now what?" Emma asked.

"Now we look for Andrew."

They walked toward the den and encountered a spider, but it was no larger than a large hand. It was progress. They went into the den which was where Andrew was supposed to be stuck. Even with the light on, the room was dark. There was a faint light emanating from one corner of the room, almost like a small night light hidden behind a chair. Emma gasped to see it, and all the fear came rushing back to her.

Celeste, seeing what was happening, called out to Andrew, "Andrew, is that you? We'd like to talk to you. Can you show yourself?" Drifting up from the corner came a wispy figure less like a man than a column of smoke. Ever so slowly, Andrew materialized, but he was faded and translucent.

"Thank you," Celeste murmured. "Are you here all the time?"

Andrew nodded, and Celeste had the distinct feeling he wouldn't be doing much talking. He seemed to have so little energy it was a wonder he could manifest at all.

"Emma? Tell me what you see."

"I, uh . . . I see a very faint figure in the corner. It's barely there," Emma whispered.

"Then we see the same thing, and it is not intimidating or overwhelming."

"So, it worked?" Emma asked, coming back to full awareness. "We're not hallucinating?"

Celeste nodded. "That's my thought."

"Andrew?" Emma asked.

Andrew nodded timidly.

"What are you afraid of, Andrew?"

Andrew raised a long, withered finger and directed their eyes to the large desk in the center of the room. The look on his face was less of fear than desperate acceptance. He had apparently given up hope long ago, and all that remained was despair.

But neither Celeste nor Emma could see anything or anyone at or near the desk that might cause such a reaction. If Andrew was being compelled to stay here, it was the result of either an illusion or something they were not capable of seeing. Either way, they had no clue what he was trying to show them.

"This isn't the spirit I met here last week. It is, but it isn't. He's less," Emma said.

"Less what?"

"Just less. Literally and figuratively there is less Andrew here," Emma clarified.

"I don't know what to make of that," Celeste murmured. "Does it mean he's losing his essence? Does it mean part of him is here and part of him is elsewhere? What would cause such a thing?"

"You're asking me?" Emma drawled somewhat sarcastically.

"Not really, dear. I was just putting the idea out there to look at, though I'm open to your ideas."

"What if it's an illusion," Emma blurted.

"Hmm . . .. This doesn't feel as outlandish as the other illusions were. I think we must consider that Andrew is being drained somehow."

"Then we should look at the desk he's pointing to. Maybe there's a clue in it or on it." She began to shuffle papers around on the desk. There was a picture of Mr. Brently and Andrew standing next to a car in a very busy downtown area. It was big enough to be Dallas, but she didn't recognize the area.

"Why would Mr. Brently have taken his picture with Andrew, and why would he have kept it on his desk?" Emma continued to inspect the picture before she glanced at Celeste. "Andrew!" Emma screamed. "What are you doing? Let go of her!"

"Emma? What are you talking about? Andrew isn't doing anything but pointing," Celeste said.

"He has his other hand around your neck!" Emma screamed. "Let her go, Andrew. She has done nothing to you. Let her go."

Celeste looked at Andrew and saw the same thing she had seen earlier and had no idea what Emma was talking about. Andrew was standing there pointing at the desk. Then she started to feel it. It was as if someone had a hand wrapped around her neck and had started to squeeze. It didn't seem to be Andrew, but it did seem to be happening. Instinctively, she grabbed for her neck. This fed into Emma's vision of Andrew strangling Celeste.

"Let her go!" she screamed again and repeated her chant from earlier. She found the mister and sprayed him with the special blend they had mixed for this house, continuing to chant until Andrew let go.

Celeste was coughing, partly from the perceived strangling but also from being sprayed with the magical mix. It was not a mixture conducive to breathing.

"Celeste, are you okay? I couldn't think of what to do to get him to let go, but the spell seemed to work, didn't it? I'm so sorry it took me as long as it did. I couldn't think clearly. It was all very upsetting. Can you speak? Are you okay?" Emma finally stopped for a second to draw breath and Celeste jumped in.

"Emma, when you started screaming, there was nothing strangling me and even when there was, it was not Andrew. It was coming from somewhere else. It's possible you were hallucinating."

"Or maybe we were both hallucinating," Emma said quietly.

"We can't trust much of what we see here, but you have to promise not to react to anything that seems horrific until we have both verified that we've seen or heard it, okay?"

"I'm sorry," Emma said. "I couldn't help it. It was just so real. Do you think reciting the spell periodically would be helpful?"

"It couldn't hurt," Celeste said.

Emma repeated it again just for good measure. Then, she looked at Andrew. He seemed more 'there' now. He was no longer pointing at the desk. In fact, he seemed to be pointing at Emma. Looking down to where he was pointing, she realized the picture was still in her hand.

"Celeste, it's something about this picture he wants us to see."

"Let me carry it," Celeste said. "We'll take it back to the house where we can study it without the threat of hallucinatory shenanigans."

Andrew's arm stretched across the room to Emma's side. He grabbed the picture and his arm snapped back to its original position. Emma and Celeste turned to each other and paused for a second. Then both nodded as if to say, "Yes, I saw it, too."

Celeste crossed the room like a bolt of lightning, and before anyone knew it, she had the picture in her pocket and was at the door motioning for Emma to come along. She led them to the dining room. She had not heard of anything ghastly happening in that room.

"We will go to the car together and place this picture in the glove box," Celeste said. "Then we will come back in and see what, if anything, we can find out from Andrew. But I want that picture out of this house. I have a theory."

They walked together toward the back door. Immediately, a red glowing apparition appeared in the door. It seemed to be a man, but not quite. Its shape was changing from one second to the next.

"Repeat the spell," Celeste whispered.

Emma complied, even though she did not see the apparition.

"Did you feel something?"

Celeste turned to her, wide-eyed. "Did you not see the red object in the doorway?"

"I saw the reflection of the phone light off the glass in the storm door," Emma said.

"Oh, this thing is devious. Start repeating the spell and do not stop until we are in the car."

"Are we leaving?"

"Just for a few minutes," Celeste replied. "We must secure this picture outside the house to see if we can determine a range. There is obviously something about the photo that's important to someone. I think we should find out whom that someone is."

Emma began to chant the spell and continued until Celeste raised her finger to her lips. The photo was now in the glove box, and the duo proceeded to re-enter the house. They were allowed to enter with no interruptions. They crept cautiously back to the den. Andrew was still there, but he looked different—he was more solid and less wispy.

"Andrew, will you please talk to us?" Emma pleaded. "We have a few questions that need your help. And Celeste is starting to disbelieve me that you even can talk? Will you please say something?"

"What do you want to know?" Andrew asked, whose mannerisms were now those of a very awkward, timid boy. It was as if he'd been caught doing something naughty.

"Was that picture taken in Dallas?" Emma knew the answer would not help them in the least.

"No," Andrew said softly.

"Where was it taken?" Celeste asked.

"It was in—"

There was a loud crash from the living room.

"Start chanting," Celeste yelled as they both ran toward the sound. Neither Celeste nor Emma could see any sign of damage or even anything out of place. There was nothing that could have made the noise they heard.

"Wait," Celeste said slowly as she turned to Emma, "what did you hear?"

Emma stopped chanting. "It was a loud crash . . . like a lamp had fallen over or something."

"That's what I heard, too."

At that moment there was another noise, but this time it seemed to come from one of the bedrooms or possibly the den. This new noise was quieter and more like paper or boxes being disturbed.

"Keep chanting," Celeste whispered as she began to chant along.

They moved slowly, checking each room for an intruder or any sign of a disturbance, but they found nothing. There was no trace of any person, creature, or spirit. Then they heard a moan come from the den. "Andrew?" they said in unison. The moaning continued.

As they entered the den, they both started to chant automatically. In the corner next to Andrew was a large red apparition both of the psychics could see. It had Andrew by the neck. Andrew was reacting as if he had a body and could be hurt in this way. Celeste was fairly certain that was not the case, but to be safe, she started to talk to the creature before her that looked like an overgrown man but with less chiseled features. It glowed red with black eyes and what appeared to be steam escaped its ears and nostrils. "If we leave, will you let Andrew go? Will you stop torturing him?" The creature nodded. "Then we will leave for now," Celeste said as she started to back away toward the door.

She and Emma walked briskly to the car. In their haste, they left every light in the house on—not that there were many.

When they were a few miles down the road, Emma pulled over. She was shaking. Celeste reached into the glove box to retrieve the photo. It was not there. Had it been an illusion? Had the spirit taken it while keeping them distracted with Andrew? What was so important about that picture?

CHAPTER 21

"Should we go back?" Emma asked, hoping that Celeste would say no.

"We disturbed something massive tonight. It had already been disturbed by all the activity around this house in the last week or two. And I think we have managed to make it worse. I have to consider this and do some more research before we go back. You will want to continue your own digging. Maybe there is some connection between Andrew and Mr. Brently which we are not aware of."

"And maybe there is some connection between the mystery in the woods and the mystery in the house," Emma said. "I'm still looking into the buru-buru and other legends that could explain both the strange happenings."

"I have a full schedule tomorrow so I won't be much help. We may have to wait until Saturday to go back. Will that work for you?"

"That should give me enough time to do my studies, get my work for you finished, and make some phone calls about the buru-buru."

"Don't get behind on your school work. That is most important in the long run," Celeste said.

"I'll keep up with it. I've been working on a paper that is really easy. It's about some of the first things you taught me to spot when people are lying. I think I learned more from you than in the class."

"Keep in mind that not everything you learn from me is in the books. There will be times when the books will disagree with me. You must give them the answers they are looking for," Celeste said.

"I know." Emma nodded. "What a waste. I might get together with Cheryl, too. I can see what Jeremy has found out about his wolf in the woods. I really hope he doesn't think there's some kind of wolfman."

Emma dropped Celeste off at her house and drove home. It was dark tonight, and she looked up and saw the moon was almost new, offering little to no light. It made the drive a bit creepier. It didn't help that she was still shaking a little over what had happened earlier. And the idea that the photo had been in this car and then disappeared rattled her more. Was her car now haunted and if so, by whom? She slept uneasily that night.

Emma was at Celeste's with time to make coffee in the morning. She had not slept well but felt rested. She didn't speak with Cheryl the night before as it had been late, and she was exhausted. The call would wait for today.

Madam Celeste had an appointment at nine, so she was up and getting the reading room ready. Emma couldn't help but notice the lingering scent of bacon and eggs. Celeste loved a good breakfast.

"I'm going to do some research on the gray wolf and the buru-buru this morning if you don't have something else you'd prefer I do," she said to Celeste.

"That sounds fine. Did you talk to Cheryl?"

"No, I'm going to give her a call later today."

"Good. Let's have a strategy meeting this afternoon. I'm booked all morning, but my one p.m. is still open," Celeste said.

"I'll get as much information as I can by then."

Neither woman mentioned the mysterious disappearance of the photo last night. Were they avoiding it? Or was there just nothing to be said about it?

As Madam Celeste's first client arrived, it no longer mattered. She took off for the reading room, and Emma sat down at the computer. The research was tedious with occasional spurts of interesting. Learning about real two-foot long spiders, for example, left her shivering. The fact that some of them slipped into the U.S. with bananas, presumably when they were young and small, made her glance at the fruit bowl cautiously. Emma was not a spider person and didn't understand how anyone could be. There had to be some level of mental illness in that.

Emma wished she had someone to bounce around the hallucination theories with when it hit her—Robert would be just the person. She took a chance and texted him to see if he could talk. He called immediately.

"Sup?" he asked.

"Hi," Emma said. "I'm looking into possible causes of the hallucinations we're having at Cheryl's house, and I was hoping you could be a sounding board. Celeste is pretty much tied up until this afternoon."

"Do you have something in mind?" Robert asked.

"Well," Emma started, "I have several things that could at least partially explain it, but they are all paranormal or the stuff of myths and legends. Have you ever heard of a buru-buru?"

"Sounds familiar," Robert said. "I think they might have used that on a fiction paranormal TV show. Uhm, *Supernatural* . . . that was the show! They are born of fear when someone dies very frightened, and they use fear to control people. That does sound a lot like what we're dealing with. I mean, they magnify what we're already facing and make it more terrifying. To tell you the truth, I thought they just made that one up for the show."

"That's what I thought at first, but I dug a little deeper and found that the legend exists in several cultures. That show's writers did their homework. So, what if a buru-buru formed during the boating accident? Or when Andrew died? I mean, Andrew seems afraid of his own shadow. Well, I guess he doesn't cast a shadow now . . . .."

"How would you prove it?"

"Well, there's nothing to prove. If it doesn't cast a shadow, it isn't physical," Emma said.

"I was talking about the buru-buru. How would you prove it? And have you found a defense against it? Or a cure or whatever you want to call it. You know, a way to get rid of it?"

"Not yet. I'm not even sure that's what it is yet. There are other things it could be."

"Like?" Robert asked, coaxing an answer.

"Like a genie," Emma rushed out.

"Like the girl in the bottle TV show from the 70s?" Robert asked in disbelief.

"That's a very twisted version of the original, which was called a djinn in Islam and a shedim in Hebrew. They are older than man, but more like a man than angels or demons. And they can do all kinds of things if a magician controls them. They can't be seen by humans, but they're not technically spirits and—"

Robert cut her off, "I'm more inclined to believe in the buru-buru theory on the face of it, but we have to be able to prove it, and we have to find a way to deal with it."

"Well, there has to be something, and it definitely isn't normal . . . .. I guess it must be paranormal because what happened last night cannot be explained by anything physical."

"Did you go over to the house alone last night?" Robert asked sternly.

"Of course not," Emma said. "Madam Celeste and I went over together. We took a protective spray and a specially written spell with us."

"And did it protect you?"

"Maybe. It could have been a lot worse. We did have some bazaar hallucinations, though. There was a picture we don't know why it was there, but we put it in the car and then it disappeared as if it had never been there in the first place. We're going to go back when it's daylight to look for it. If it's back in the house, then we're dealing with a creature that can move objects from a closed glove box in a closed car back into a house. And if it can do that, what else can it do?"

"I don't know. But I know I don't want you going back there without me," Robert said.

"You think you could do something we couldn't? It's not human and it's not an animal. It's supernatural. What do you think you can do about that?"

"I can be there for you," Robert murmured. "I don't like the idea of you putting yourself at that kind of risk. I'd rather you not go back there at all, but I know how likely that is. At least agree to let me go with you. Three is better than two. It has to be."

"You're going to make me think you care about me," Emma said softly.

"I do," Robert said, matching her tone. "I thought you knew that. You're psychic, right?"

"It doesn't work like that. I can't read your mind, only your emotions."

"Then . . .."

"Flirting on my dime, are we?" Madam Celeste said as she entered the room.

"I'd better go," Emma whispered and hung up abruptly. "Robert was helping me sort through some of the information I've dug up about our possible villain at the house."

"That's not what it sounded like to me." Celeste chuckled. "I'm teasing you, dear. I know how these things go. Did you come up with any ideas?"

"Yes, but I'll save them for one o'clock. Your next client will be here any minute."

"Yes, they will. I'd better get ready. I can't wait to hear what you've learned. Will we have time to run over there while it's still daylight today? Move my last appointment of the day if you have to." Celeste scurried off to her next client before Emma could answer.

145

Emma was surprised Celeste would move an appointment just to go during daylight hours. "I guess she's a little spooked, too," she said to herself. "Or maybe just curious and doesn't want to wait until Saturday. That could be it."

Emma pulled out her phone and called Cheryl.

CHAPTER 22

"Hi, Emma," Cheryl said. "How did it go last night? I see you're still alive." Cheryl laughed to herself.

"Hi, Cheryl. It was a little unnerving actually. Even with protection, something managed to confuse us about what was real and what was not. We're going to go back over this afternoon while the sun is still up. Though, to be honest, I don't see that making a difference."

"I doubt it will, too. It didn't work for us the day we went to bug bomb the place. Just be careful, please. Jeremy and I are going over tonight to look for his wolf. I don't believe it's really a gray wolf. What I saw looked more like a man, but we're going to check it out. I hope he isn't some crazy werewolf fan or something because I kind of like him, you know?"

"I get it," Emma said. "I'm in a similar situation with Robert. I really like him, but he thinks we're dealing with a ghost and I can usually see ghosts."

"You and Robert? Really? To each his own, I guess. He and I have been friends since he moved here from New York years ago."

"New York? I wouldn't have guessed New York, but I guess it makes sense. I knew he wasn't from around here."

"Well," Cheryl said, "maybe we will run into each other tonight . . .."

"Wait. There's a reason I called you. I wanted to find out more about Andrew and how he died, and how he knew your father."

"He didn't really know my father. He stalked my brother, following him everywhere and acting like they were friends. But they weren't friends, my brother couldn't stand him. He thought he was too much of a geek."

"But we found a picture last night of your father and Andrew in a downtown area, like Dallas or Houston," Emma said, confused.

"I don't know how that happened, unless he followed Pete there on a sports trip and convinced Dad that he was a friend of Pete's. My dad never hung out with my brother's friends, though. He was never a "one of the boys" kind of father."

"We tried to bring the picture out with us last night, but it vanished out of the glove box."

"Are you sure it was ever there?"

"I guess not," Emma whispered. "Why would it show us that kind of picture though? And one that wasn't true. What is this entity up to?"

"That's the real question, isn't it?" Cheryl murmured. "That and why Andrew is in the house at all?"

"Well, he acted like it had something to do with the picture," Emma said.

"The picture that disappeared?" Cheryl asked, who sounded convinced that there never had been a picture and she wasn't too sure Andrew was there, either.

"I still think it was real and I know Andrew is real . . .. I think he's tied to the picture," Emma said.

"We'll see," Cheryl said. "Did anything else interesting happen last night?"

"Besides getting the begeeses scared out of us? No, I guess that was it."

"I'm ready to get the rest of those spiders out of there before they start multiplying again. Do you think it's safe to do that?"

"If I had to guess, I'd say no, not yet. I think whatever we're dealing with wants those spiders there to scare people off. You got rid of most of them, but I think the last few will be a lot harder to catch. Do you still have the bug guy on standby?"

"Sort of. Rocky knows we didn't get them all, but he doesn't need any more yet. He's still marketing the ones we captured—he'd rather keep them alive to sell. But if we want to pay him, he'll kill them, I'm sure."

"I guess maybe we'll see you out there later today. Gotta' go," Emma said as Madam Celeste's line started to ring.

"Madam Celeste's. How can we help you fulfill your destiny today?" Emma said in a professional voice.

"I've never been to a psychic before, but I'm at my wit's end. Can you get me in today?" the caller asked frantically.

"I'm not the head psychic, I'm the assistant. Madam Celeste likes to meet clients herself before letting me work with them, and she's booked all day. I could get you on her schedule for tomorrow at eleven. How would that work? It's her last appointment of the day."

"I guess it will have to do. Is Madam Celeste with a client now?"

"Yes. May I ask what this is about?"

"My daughter is coming in from school tomorrow for spring break. I think there's something wrong, but she won't tell me. I heard Madam Celeste is the best in town. I'm hoping for her help. It's very important to me to be able to help Sharon with whatever is troubling her."

"Eleven tomorrow is the best I can do," Emma said with all the sympathy she could muster.

"Then I'll take it."

"Good, let me get all your information, and we'll get you set up."

Emma scheduled the appointment as Celeste walked in from her eleven o'clock.

"Emma, why don't you go get some sandwiches and we'll start our meeting while we eat? Sound good?"

"Yes, ma'am," Emma said as she took Celeste's credit card and headed for the door. "Your usual from Schlotzski's?"

Celeste nodded. "That sounds wonderful."

Emma took off while Celeste did a little straightening up in the reading room, then freshened her makeup for the afternoon. Emma wasn't gone long enough for her to do much more.

When she returned, they enjoyed their sandwiches and Emma filled Celeste in on the fact that she had a new client coming in.

"That will be an easy one," Celeste said. "Her daughter doesn't want to go back to school but can't find the right time or means to tell her mother. She's going to be fine."

"But, Celeste, you always advocate for going to school."

"No, Emma, I do not. It depends on the career and the potential. Some people need to explore life for a time before they choose what to study in depth. This girl is one of those people. Though it may be a bumpy ride for her."

"How do you know all this without having even talked with either of them?" Emma asked.

"I see possibilities, probabilities, and potentialities. I don't see details. That would be nice, wouldn't it? But that is how it is for me. You probably have it, too. You're just not experienced enough to recognize it yet."

"Do you ever see your own future?" Emma asked softly.

"Oh yes," Celeste said with a far-off look in her eyes. "I can't always change it, though. People will always be who they are."

"I don't know that I want that gift," Emma said. "It seems to make you sad."

"Nonsense!" Celeste said, snapping out of it. "What have you learned about the spider house?"

"Robert thinks it's more likely to be a buru-buru than anything else. I'm not through exploring possibilities, though. There has to be an explanation that makes sense, at least in some supernatural way. What do you think?"

"There is apparently something there that can cause us to see what it wants us to see and even feel what it wants us to physically feel. Can your buru-buru do that?"

"Yes, it's within the realm of possibility. But so could a djinn," Emma said.

"A djinn would be out of place here in Texas, wouldn't it? Don't they live in the Far East and the Middle East?"

"Now that you say it out loud, yes, they do. But the buru-buru isn't exactly native to our continent, either."

"Have you looked into Native American legends?" Celeste asked.

"Nothing came up in my search, but I wasn't looking for Native American legends."

"Native Americans like to think they were the first ones here, but they were not. There were tribal Americans that pre-date any of the tribes that existed when the Pilgrims landed by thousands of years. Looks like you have a lot more research to do, indeed. Though it may or may not be relevant to the case, it is a fascinating part of ancient American history," Celeste said.

"I may need to go to an actual school library to find something. I'll do some more digging. Will you be ready for our daylight visit after your three o'clock today?"

"Yes, I'm quite excited to see what tricks this little devil can pull off in the daylight."

"Are you saying you think it's a demon?" Emma asked with wide eyes.

Celeste shook her head. "Highly unlikely. I suspect we're looking for a prankster. It's having a bit of fun at our expense, but no real harm has been done yet—unless you count the spider bite on Rocky's back, which could be a coincidence."

"Yet . . ." Emma repeated.

Celeste and Emma both had two o'clock clients. It was time to prepare for work. Emma's client was a member of a local church. Madam Celeste and Emma, by default, were quite popular for doing angel card readings for them. Most of them would allow nothing else to be used for their readings, and today's client,

Maggie, was no exception. Emma was ready for her with angel cards out. It was not her favorite type of reading as she found it very restrictive. The angel cards did not allow much wiggle room for intuitive knowledge that would come in.

None the less, Maggie was pleased with the reading and scheduled for next week. Emma was happy to add a client to her six regulars and was proud to have each one.

After Maggie left, Emma sat down to the notepad and typed in Native American legends and mythical creatures. There were dozens. She read about each of them. Some were duplicates from different tribes. The only thing that came close was what they called a 'Skin-walker.' It's supposed to be an animal that could change or morph into other creatures and practically hypnotizes a human into thinking it was someone they knew or something familiar like a dog or a coyote. It was close, but not close enough. It didn't explain the mass hallucinations and everyone seeing all the spiders as many times their actual size. Nor did it explain the picture Emma was no longer sure even existed.

She ran out of time as Madam Celeste showed her last client out at two-forty-five. She was ready to go as soon as the client was gone.

"Let's not waste any daylight, dear. We'll talk on our way," Celeste said as she grabbed her bag and they left.

CHAPTER 23

During the twenty or so minute drive, Celeste wanted to hear all about the angel reading Emma had done this afternoon. Emma relayed all the details of the reading and Celeste seemed pleased.

"So, did you have any more time for research on what we may be facing in a few minutes?" Celeste asked.

"I did a little," Emma said. "The native tribes have similar legends, but most are meant to scare the children from wandering off near the water or at night. The chupacabra is interesting and can make a person see what it wants them to see, but there are not many stories that include mass hallucinations. There was one that included two people who saw the same thing, but the nature of it really doesn't fit our case."

"So, we are agreed there is mass hallucination taking place," Celeste said. "And that it is most likely being caused by something supernatural or paranormal. Any other possibilities we should keep in mind?"

"I still am not happy with anything I have found," Emma admitted. "I was starting to learn about an interesting belief that Natives have about spirits and a thing called ghost sickness, but I had to put the research away. It was time to leave."

"So, this could be as simple as a spirit?"

"Yes and no," Emma answered. "The Native Americans believe there are three kinds of spirits. There are positive spirits, negative spirits, and incomplete life cycle spirits."

"So, this could be what they call a negative spirit?"

"No, this would be more like an incomplete cycle kind of spirit. Negative spirits are part of the natural life cycle and part of the balance between positive and negative forces, and they serve a purpose. Incomplete spirits are those who were not buried properly or whose bones have been disturbed. They are angry or disoriented and want to take it out on humans. They can cause a lot of havoc and ghost sickness. That would be the kind of spirit the Natives would call it."

"Hmmm. That would mean there was a Native American involved somehow. There needs to be someone who believes the legend for it to work. But this gives me something to work with. Let's see what we can do with it."

"What should we do first?" Emma asked as she pulled into the driveway.

"Let's look for the picture that disappeared. I want to know if it ever even existed."

"So, should we look for it on the desk? Where it was initially?"

"Yes, and let's not forget to sage and spritz and recite the chant. Oh, and I think we would do well to stay in the same room together at all times."

"No problem," Emma said with a nod.

They walked into the kitchen to see the lights were still on as they had left them. There was a disappointing number of spider webs that had been attracted by those lights. Emma found the broom and started to sweep her way to the den.

"There it is!" Emma reached across the desk only to have it disappear as she watched. "Wait! You saw it, right? I didn't imagine that. It was there on the desk."

"I'm sorry, dear. I didn't see it. You were between me and the desk. I never saw it."

"Oh, no you don't!" Emma screamed. "Put it back! Put it back *right now*!" She began to spray the potion that had worked for a little while last night.

Slowly the picture began to materialize on the desk as if it had only been rendered invisible. "That's better," Emma nodded to herself. "You see it now, don't you?" she asked Celeste.

"I don't," Celeste said calmly. "Maybe we imagined it all along."

Emma reached to pick it up but it disappeared again. Emma screamed again—not in fright, but in aggravation.

"Why is this happening? Is it really here and being blocked from us or was it always our imagination?" she said.

"Since Cheryl doesn't believe her father and Andrew were ever in a picture together, logic says there was no picture. It was a ruse by a naughty spirit to keep us from seeing something real. I want you to douse this whole room in 'sage plus,' then we'll recite the spell a few dozen times. Then you'll spray it again. Then we'll see what we see."

Emma followed her instructions, and when they had finished chanting and she had re-sprayed the room, they started to look around the room with fresh eyes. There was a photograph on the desk, but it was of Pete and his father. Pete was much younger, and the picture was actually printed by a photo lab.

"Why do you suppose a spirit would not want us to see this?" Emma asked.

"It's a strange thing to do. We would not have paid any attention to this picture, so if he wanted it hidden, he should have just left it there as it was."

"What if he was trying to bring attention to this very picture?" Emma countered. "Do you see anything abnormal about it? They seem happy to be together. Is there something unusual about the car or the city?"

"Not that I can see," Celeste said after a brief pause. "It's just a picture of a boy with his father somewhere downtown."

"Where? Where do you think they are? What are they doing there? Maybe they were doing something they shouldn't have been? We'll have to get Cheryl to take a look at it. She might see something we're overlooking, something we don't know about the situation," Emma said. "Should we try to contact Andrew while we're here?"

"Yes. Let's do it, especially since it's still early and we have electricity to light the place. Be on your guard for the trickster, though."

"Andrew? Are you here? Can you talk with us today?" Emma called out.

Andrew appeared, but he was barely visible. Daylight is not easy to see spirits that aren't putting in maximum effort, and even then, it's difficult for them to look solid in daylight—or any light for that matter.

"I thought you were gone for good," Andrew said. "You seemed pretty freaked out."

"We were, but we need to find out what is going on in this house."

Andrew glanced around nervously before he whispered, "We're not alone."

"Are you saying that there is another spirit here?" Celeste asked in a hushed voice. "A spirit we can't see."

"Well, of course, there are other spirits here," Andrew whined. "There are spirits everywhere! What makes you think you can see them all?"

At that, Paul showed up. "Who do you think you are talking to my friends like that? They're probably trying to help you."

"Hello, Paul," Celeste said with a smile. "Andrew, is this who you were referring to?"

"No," Andrew said softly. "There are people here . . . I can feel them. They're outside for now, but they were really close. Now they're moving away."

"That must be Cheryl and Jeremy. They're supposed to set up some infrared cameras out in the woods today and maybe do a little tracking," Emma offered.

Paul disappeared and came back. "Yep, they're hauling equipment out to the woods. No cause for alarm."

"I wasn't alarmed. I was just warning the ladies," Andrew said sheepishly, who was becoming less and less visible, like a flashlight dimming as the batteries ran out.

"Don't trust him," Paul whispered. "There's something not right here. Better ask him what he knows pretty quick—he's fading fast."

"Andrew, did you ever travel with Mr. Brently? Maybe to a bigger city?" Celeste asked.

"You mean like Oklahoma City?" Andrew asked.

"Yes, like that."

"One time I went with him and Pete—something our moms had arranged. They were just giving me a ride to my cousin's house. I sat in the back the whole way while they ignored me. Pete is sorta weird, but he's my best friend. He was just goofin' around."

She started to shuffle through the papers on the desk and opened drawers looking for . . .. She stopped. "What am I looking for? I don't think this is about a picture. There is something else . . .. Something we will need to connect the dots between it and the non-existent picture. I need to think." She sat down in the chair. There was an object under the sheet—small but big enough to be felt. Lifting the sheet cautiously revealed a notepad in a leather case, bearing the initials RRB.

Emma looked at Celeste as if to verify she saw it, too. Celeste nodded as Emma picked it up. It was an appointment notebook, not elaborate like a day planner, just a year's worth of dates and a few blank pages. This one was for the year of the boating accident.

Upon opening the datebook, it revealed itself assumingly about the day it was opened to. Emma and Celeste began to share the vision. There were clouds in the sky and rain in the distance. There was one part of the clouds that looked especially angry and green. It was a good way off, but they both knew that was a warning sign of a tornado. Apparently, Mr. Brently knew it, too. He was moving his car to a covered parking area and headed for the basement of the building he was in. But curiosity got the better of him, and he walked back to watch.

Never having seen a tornado up close made him brave. This was an opportunity to witness what so many of his colleagues already had. He would gain bragging rights and have a story to tell. The tip of the thin tornado descended quickly from the sky. Two blocks from where he stood, a tree toppled over, and the tornado died as quickly as it had begun. Ray Brently beamed with pride. He had seen a tornado, witnessed Mother Nature's fury unleashed. It was over so quickly that he felt let down. He wanted more. He went back to the parking garage and pulled Andrew from the car while he grabbed his camera. He had Andrew take his picture. A passerby took the camera and directed Andrew to get in the picture. Ray Brently protested, but the stranger insisted.

He would have pictures of the very spot where the tornado had touched down and where he had been standing. It started to rain, and the two thanked the cameraman for his help before they hurried back into the garage.

"Your aunt should be here by now," Mr. Brently said. "Perhaps she's been delayed by the tornado activity. I'm going to have to leave soon for my meeting. Will you be okay here until she arrives?"

"Yes, Mr. Brently, I'll be fine," Andrew said. "I'll make sure the car is locked up before I leave, too."

"It's a pity you missed that tornado," Mr. Brently said. "It was a sight to see. Just like you've heard it described, right down to the train noise. Remarkable!"

"Maybe next time," Andrew responded, hoping there would be no next time for him. He was mortally afraid of tornadoes and didn't care who knew it. They killed people more often than not or left whole towns in a pile of rubble. He wanted nothing to do with them. Had he been on the street with Mr. Brently, there was no doubt that he would have kept his eyes closed the whole time.

Emma and Celeste put the datebook down and looked at Andrew. "You were with Mr. Brently during a twister in OKC? That's what you're hiding?" Celeste asked with her brows drawn.

"No, not hiding. Just forgot. Not hiding." With that said, Andrew disappeared.

'Where did he go?" Emma asked, frustrated. "We were just getting to the good part. We could have asked him some questions about that day, like where was Pete when the tornado was going on? And why was Mr. Brently there, and why was Andrew there and—" Celeste raised her hand to quiet Emma.

"There will be time to ask these things. There will be many more visions from that book, for instance. We must give Andrew time to refuel. He has expended a great deal of energy today. This story may have been no more than a distraction from what we really need to find here. Do you fervently believe Andrew is involved in whatever is being hidden from us?"

"I don't know anymore . . .." Emma slowly shook her head. "There are so few clues and Andrew seemed to be in a lot of them. And there was a picture!" Emma yelled. "I knew it. I knew it. I knew it! Right now, isn't he our best suspect?"

"That may appear to be the case," Celeste said, "but I would be surprised if he is involved in the real matter at all."

"Then why are we pursuing him?" Emma asked, no longer trying to hide her frustration.

"He has information that will prove vital at some point. Keep that in mind. In the end, we will be glad he chose to talk with us. We'd best head out. It's beginning to get dark out."

CHAPTER 24

While Emma and Celeste were working inside the house, Cheryl and Jeremy had been setting up nature cameras and working in the woods behind the house. There were eight cameras to set up, which had to be attached to a belt-like thing latched around a tree. Fortunately, there were plenty of trees so no need to set up tripods.

There was other equipment Cheryl didn't recognize, but Jeremy was giving her a rundown as he set them up. She found it mostly boring. Everything seemed to be motion activated, and they were not going to stick around to watch. But that was the whole point—to find out what happened when no one was around.

They had parked at the entrance to the driveway not wanting to come barreling up to the woods in a noisy car. As they carried the equipment into the woods, Cheryl asked, "How often do you do a setup like this?"

"Not too often really. It's rare to have tracks and activity that I can't identify. So, this is a fun challenge. I can't wait to see what we capture on the footage."

"Will it happen the first night, do you think?" Emma asked.

"I suspect so. These animals are creatures of habit. It will have a territory and a path. These woods are not that big. Of course, there are places on the highway that it could cross into the forest or even the Mesquite brush if it were desperate. How often it visits here will tell us a lot. We'll just have to observe the footage and see what we get."

Jeremy made short work of setting everything up. The sun was just setting when they finished and walked back to the car. Jeremy pulled out a computer and loaded up the software to observe remotely for a little while. Cheryl was not familiar with surveillance and felt they should be entertaining one another instead. She would try to start a conversation only to have Jeremy let it die.

"Are we meant to just sit here in silence?" she asked.

"Exactly," Jeremy said, not glancing up from the screen. "We watch the screen and look for anything moving. The odds are we won't be here watching when it comes, but we can always hope."

Cheryl took out her phone and started looking at shoes instead. Several new styles looked good. Then she saw a blouse that appealed to her and started shopping for real. Her cart was looking pretty good when Jeremy closed the laptop.

"I thought you wanted to hunt with me," he said.

"This part is too boring," Cheryl said. "I thought there would be something to watch. This is like watching leaves fall in the spring."

"I tried to tell you that, but you insisted it would be okay."

"And it is okay. I've found a pair of shoes and three new tops. It's great."

"You're okay with just shopping in my car while I watch for whatever we're watching for?"

"Absolutely," Cheryl said with a smile. "If something happens, I'm right here to watch it in real time, but I don't have to just watch the screen. It's the best of both worlds."

Jeremy was amazed. Most of the people he knew would be bored and complaining by now. Cheryl was just as happy to sit there shopping, keeping him company without saying a word. This was too cool for words. He opened the computer again.

"Are you ready to go to the coffee house?" he asked.

"Not unless you are," Cheryl said. "I thought you wanted to sit out here for the evening and watch."

"I did, but now I think I'd rather go get a coffee and visit with you."

"Aww, that's so sweet," Cheryl cooed. "Will you still be able to watch the cameras from the coffee shop?"

"No. These are only for close range. I'll have to wait until tomorrow to come back and switch out the— Wait. Did you see that?"

They both turned to watch the screen. There was something in the woods.

"What did you see?" Cheryl whispered.

"I'm not sure. Something moved though because it triggered the recorder," Jeremy said.

"Where do you think it went? How did it go through just fast enough to trigger the recorder and then it's gone? Will it come out here? Are we in danger?"

"Shhh," Jeremy said. "Calm down. It could have been a rabbit or a bird or any number of things. We'll just have to keep watching to see if it's still in the area. The trick now is to watch all the cameras. If it's still in the area, it may set off another recorder. With eight cameras, we're bound to catch a lot of movement tonight."

"There!" Cheryl pointed to screen three. "It was like a wolf, a really large wolf." The cameras were night vision, so they didn't show colors.

"That's a gray wolf alright. Wow! Has it wandered way outside its range, or has it been here all along and no one spotted it before? That's the next question."

It looked directly at the camera and growled. Cheryl drew back and Jeremy whistled softly.

"Well," he said, "that was unusual. It was like he knew we were watching, but that's impossible."

"Maybe it smelled us," Cheryl whispered. "You know, we were touching the equipment and the trees. Maybe he was just staring at the smell."

"He looked into the camera like he knew what it was, and that he was looking at someone," Jeremy said. "I think there's more to this wolf than meets the eye. We might have a skin-walker here."

"What's that?"

"It's a tribal myth. Skin-walkers can change into different shapes, including human, wolf, or other monsters. This is not the answer I was hoping to find. No one wants to be noticed by a skin-walker . . . there are few who live to tell about it."

"Well, we didn't see it change into anything. It could have been a coincidence that it growled at the camera. There might have been something behind the camera that it saw and growled at."

"That's true." Jeremy nodded. "No sense jumping to conclusions. You're a good partner at this. You keep your cool under pressure. I like that."

"It's what I do." Cheryl grinned. And it was. Cheryl had never been the one to run away from the unknown or the scary. She was the first to offer a logical explanation for implausible things.

They kept watching the camera screens. Cheryl was into it now. She couldn't wait to see something else move. Would the wolf turn into some beast called a skin-walker? Would it show up again as a wolf? This was as good as reality tv. But it turned out the show was over for now—there was no more movement for now.

They would have to wait. Cheryl went back to shopping and Jeremy went back to watching. After some time, Cheryl did become bored with her phone. She watched the screens with Jeremy for a while and then she conceded that she was done.

"This has been fun, but I'm ready to get back to civilization," she said.

Jeremy closed the computer and stretched his arms as much as he could in the vehicle. "Do you want to go for coffee or do you just want to go home?"

"Coffee sounds good," Cheryl said.

They rode in silence back into town, entranced from watching the footage for so long. Cheryl started to come out of it first, having only been watching for fifteen or twenty minutes. "I found some very good bargains online tonight. I can't wait for them to come in. Now I'll just need someplace to wear them," she said.

Jeremy was still lost in the footage and took a minute to respond. "What kind of place?" he asked.

"Well, there was one outfit that is going to need a nice dinner, maybe someplace in Denton or Sherman or one of the yacht clubs."

"That would be nice," Jeremy said, obviously not taking the hint.

"Of course, that kind of an evening is better spent with a partner . . .."

Finally, Jeremy got it. "Oh! I would love to take you to dinner," he said. "But do we have to wait for your new outfit to come in?"

Cheryl smiled. "Not at all."

LINDA ANTHONY HILL

CHAPTER 25

Robert called Emma on Friday to see how the encounter at Cheryl's had gone. He was surprised by how little they had learned. "We need to have a team meeting and compare notes," he said.

"Really, Robert? What have you found out?" Emma lashed out.

"Whoa! Not making accusations. Just want to get everyone on the same page and brainstorm. This thing is driving all of us a little nutty. If we sit down together at my place and just see what everyone knows, I think it could help."

"I'm sorry. I didn't mean to snap your head off. Whatever we're dealing with is a trickster, and it's wearing my patience thin," Emma said. "That's a great idea to get everyone together. When did you have in mind?"

"I didn't. I mean, I just thought of it so . . . I wasn't thinking of when, but how about tomorrow afternoon? We can—"

"Pick up a couple of pizza pies?" She laughed at his New York reference to what most people would just call a pizza.

"Exactly!" Robert said. "Let's say four or five. I'll call Cheryl, and she can contact Jeremy to see if he's available. I haven't heard from Brooke or Mia. I'll call them to see if they're still involved or want to be, and see if either of them is free tomorrow afternoon."

"I guess I'll see you then," Emma said while trying to leave the door open for Robert to ask her to do something tonight. It was Friday, after all . . . he could ask her to go to a movie or something. But he didn't. Emma hung up a little miffed at the whole situation.

Madam Celeste was with her 'emergency' eleven o'clock. She had a date with Joe tonight. Emma didn't see anything getting in the way of that so, she assumed Madam Celeste would handle the emergency with plenty of time to spare.

As they came out of the reading room, Madam Celeste was patting the woman's hand and reassuring her things would turn out for the best.

"Emma, will you set Nita up with an appointment for next Wednesday or Thursday, please. We'll be seeing each other on a weekly basis until this matter sorts itself out."

"Yes, ma'am," Emma said as she pulled up Celeste's appointments. It was unusual for Celeste to pass off appointment setting to Emma when the client was there in person. She couldn't wait to hear this story. She made an appointment for Nita and gave her a card before sending her on her way.

"What was that all about?" Emma asked as soon as she heard the car pull away.

"That was Nita Combs. As I suspected, her daughter is arriving home from school today. Nita did not yet realize that her daughter wants to quit school and travel for a year. I have informed her and she took it rather well, all things considered. But I also think she's going to put up a fight. I tried to let her see through the tarot cards that it would be a good thing for her daughter to take a small break, but I don't think she wanted to hear that yet. Time and tide," Celeste murmured. "Time and tide."

"There will be nothing to do here this afternoon," Emma said. "Do you want me to stay and answer phones?"

"That would be perfect as long as you have no classes or plans," Celeste said, knowing full well that Emma never had class on Friday.

"I'm good," Emma said. "I'll go get some lunch then come back and cover the office."

The phone rang and Emma answered, "Madam Celeste's, how can we help you fulfill your destiny today?"

"This is Dori. I know it's her afternoon off, but this won't take long, and this headache is going to be the death of me. I really need her help."

"Well, Ms. Dori, let me check with her and call you right back."

"I'll wait. Or you can let me talk to Madam Celeste herself . . .. In case she needs convincing."

Celeste had been standing there waving her arms no, but Emma could feel the headache emanating from Dori and knew how this was going to end.

"Alright, dear. Get here as quickly as you can."

Three minutes later the doorbell rang. Emma answered to find Dori on the step. "I was in my car when I made the call." She gave a half-hearted smile. "I just can't go on like this. It's the worst headache I've had since the first time Celeste fixed me up."

Celeste had already fetched a clean and energized crystal. Dori knew what to do. She grabbed the crystal and held it to her temple. She relaxed almost instantly. After a few minutes, she opened her eyes and said, "That's always a surprise. How does that work so well? Someday, I'll find out what kind of magic you put on those stones. For now, here is your fee. I need to get going." And just like that, she was gone.

Emma was astonished. "How did you do that so fast?" she asked.

"I've told her that she can do it herself. I'll sell her a crystal and teach her the cleansing routine, but she believes it's my personal magic, so I've stopped disagreeing. As long as she feels better, then no harm was done. Now I have a hair and nail appointment. I'll see you later. I do hope you can handle anything else that comes up."

"Have fun. I'm sure I can," Emma called as Celeste bustled out the door.

The phone rang again, and this time it was for Emma. "Do you have anything planned tonight?" Robert asked.

"Not much, what's up?"

"I thought we could get together over dinner and kind of, you know, go over our notes. How does that sound to you?"

She laughed. "It sounds to me like you want to ask me on a date, but you're afraid to, so you're asking me out to work on a quasi-date."

"It's easier this way," Robert said with a chuckle. "This way you're more likely to say yes."

Emma smiled and touched her heated cheek. "Pick me up at my place around seven."

"If I pick you up, it's really a date," said Robert.

"Mm-hmm," Emma answered. "Can you handle it?"

"Of course, I can handle it. I'm looking forward to it."

"Then I'll see you at seven," Emma said with a grin from ear to ear. *Now, what am I going to wear?* she thought to herself, *and why was Robert playing so shy?*

He was a strange character indeed. Emma never knew what to expect from him. He was always nice, but sometimes he was overtly nice, and other times it seemed more covert. Was she reading him wrong?

"Reading who wrong?" Paul asked as he appeared in front of her.

Emma screamed and threw her hands up. "I've asked you not to do that."

"Oh, did I surprise you? I'm sorry," Paul said sincerely.

"No, you listened to my thoughts. I don't like that, and you know it!"

"How do you think I find you people? Do you think I fly around looking for you?"

"I hadn't thought about it . . .."

"I listen. I listen for your thoughts."

"And there's no other way to do it?"

"Sure, there is, but why waste time looking when you can just follow a thought?"

"Paul, you're exasperating!" Emma sighed. "Did you find out anything more about Andrew? You said last night there was something wrong there."

"I did. And there was. I just don't know what it was yet. Andrew is hiding something, though. But my thoughts get all foggy when I get around him. I don't know what's going on there, but I will," Paul said.

"Thanks, Paul. I can feel it in my gut he just doesn't add up. And what is up with the disappearing picture?"

"I missed that. What disappearing picture?"

There's a picture of Mr. Brently with Andrew. We know they didn't hang out together, but the picture disappeared right in front of our eyes."

"That's pretty peculiar," Paul slowly agreed.

"I think we're dealing with something supernatural here," Emma said.

"Hello," Paul said, waving his hand in front of Emma's face. "What am I? What is Andrew? Of course, you're dealing with something supernatural."

"No, I mean something more. Something like a chupacabra or a spirit with superpowers. I mean, they're making pictures disappear and making us think we see gigantic spiders and other things."

"You don't think I can do that?" Paul scoffed.

Emma slowed and glanced at Paul. "Why would I think you could do that?"

"You wouldn't because I don't. But I could if I wanted to. The question is why would I want to? Why would anyone want to?"

"You mean any spirit could do this?"

"Well, not every spirit. Most spirits don't know what they're capable of. I only know because of Celeste. She helped me to understand not by explaining, because she didn't know these things herself. But it was her who pushed me to find out more about my situation. Most of us stumble onto most of our abilities, but I believe we all have them."

"This changes everything!" Emma yelled. "I've been looking for some super being when these things could have all been done by a spirit!"

"That's quite true. I didn't know you didn't know."

"I feel like I've been chasing my tail," Emma huffed. "I've combed the internet looking for any kind of supernatural being that could have caused so many people to see huge spiders and everything else that's been going on. Nothing came close, but this . . . this begins to make sense. We could be looking for a spirit who doesn't want anyone around the house. We still need to find out who and why, but the how is as simple as being a smart spirit or at least, an experienced one."

"Well, it's been a pleasure helping you out," Paul said before he faded from sight. "I guess I'll be moving along now." And with that, he disappeared.

Emma was left to wonder what else Paul knew but wasn't mentioning. Spirits, even Paul, could be very tricky with their information. So, who had a reason to keep people away from investigating the house? Was it the same being Jeremy had run into in the woods? Or were there two separate adventures happening so close to one another? That seemed highly unlikely. Emma could sense the two were related, she just needed to find that connection. Andrew was certainly an anomaly in all of this. He had no reason to be there, but there he was, smack in the middle of it. Ray Brently seemed to be the most likely person to want to keep people away from his home, but what reason would he have? Then there was Pete, who had a lot of issues with his dad. Maybe something there could explain the goings-on.

Andrew truly did not seem capable of doing what had happened thus far. He couldn't even leave the den. Unless he was just acting like he couldn't leave the den. What if it was all a smokescreen? But it was Ray Brently's house. Wouldn't Ray be more likely to be the one who was scaring people away? And he was older, so he would probably be better at using his powers.

CHAPTER 26

"What is it doing that scares you?" Emma asked.

The line was quiet before the stranger whispered, "You believe me?"

"Of course, I do. This is what we do."

"Wouldn't you be scared if a ghost was following you around?" the caller asked.

"Let's start over," Emma offered. "What is your name?"

"I'm sorry. My name is Charlie Tanner."

"Charlie, I'm Emma. Now tell me what this spirit is doing to scare you."

"Isn't following me around enough?" Charlie said.

"It could be, but there is usually more. How do you know it's following you? Do you see it or is it more of a feeling? Does it speak to you?"

"You really do believe me," Charlie said. "Finally, someone is taking me seriously. I see it out of the corner of my eye, but when I turn, it's gone. It feels like someone is watching me most of the time, and I hear voices coming from the next room occasionally. I can rarely make out what anyone is saying, but, when I can, they will call my name."

"Sounds like you have a spirit following you around," Emma said.

"Can you get rid of it?"

"Does it follow you everywhere?" Emma asked.

"It feels like it."

"Can you live with it for a few more days?"

"I guess I can. I've lived with it this long. But I'm at my wit's end. I just can't take it much longer. Are you going to help me?" Charlie asked.

"I'll certainly try," Emma said. "The problem is, that I can't get you in until Monday afternoon." She didn't want to take any chances of having to disturb Celeste. "Can you make it around two?"

"I'll be at work at two. How late can you see me?"

"I could see you at five. Would that work better?"

"Yes, I'll leave work early. I'll tell the boss it's a doctor's appointment."

"Then I'll see you Monday afternoon at five," Emma said before she gave him the address, in case he needed it.

Maybe Celeste would let her take this one. It should be a slam dunk. Spirits don't linger without reason. Emma should be able to determine that reason and either send it on its way or make Charlie feel more comfortable that it's there. Maybe it was a relative or a friend? Moments like this helped Emma remember just how much she loved her job.

Her personal phone rang, and it was Robert again.

"I hate to bother you again, but I've set up an informal meeting for Sunday at my place around two. Can you make it for that?"

"Sure," Emma said. "Are we still on for tonight?"

"Of course," Robert answered. "That was never about a meeting anyway."

"I like the sound of that." Emma smiled to herself. "Anything I need to know or bring for Sunday?"

"Well . . . you could ask Madam Celeste if she'd like to join us. I know everyone would love to hear her input."

176

"I'll mention it to her, but don't hold your breath. She doesn't work on weekends unless it's a gallery. You're lucky she's helping on this case in the first place."

"I'm pretty sure Cheryl is paying her, although I don't know if she'd pay for her to come to one of our meetings. It doesn't matter, though. I would be forever grateful if you would ask her."

"Consider it done," Emma said.

"Thanks. I guess I'll let you get back to work."

"See you tonight," Emma said.

The rest of the afternoon flew by like a hummingbird in October. There were a couple of appointment confirmations for Monday, and someone wanted their cards to be read for free. But there was nothing Emma couldn't handle with ease. Madam Celeste made it back around four-thirty. She had a date with Joe and looked fabulous. Emma asked her about Sunday afternoon.

"Aren't these people all about your age," Celeste asked.

"Pretty much."

"Why would they want to waste their Sunday afternoon hanging out with me?"

"You're a psychic for one," Emma said with a knowing look. "You're officially in charge of the case they're working on. They want to know if anything new has happened and they want to bounce ideas off of you. Psychics are like rock stars to paranormal people, especially if they're really psychic like you are."

Celeste was a little embarrassed by the flattery. It didn't show because she was already glowing in anticipation of her date. "Will you give me a ride?"

"Sure," Emma said. "I'll pick you up around a quarter 'til two."

"Then I'll be happy to go. It's almost five, why don't you go ahead and take off for the weekend?"

"Great! I have a date tonight myself." Emma blushed as she packed away her things.

"Have a good time," Celeste called as Emma made her way to the door.

Celeste and Joe were going to one of the fancy restaurants at the casino. It had been a while since Celeste was able to dress formally for an evening out and was looking forward to it. She had met Joe on a case involving a haunted warehouse. He had worked night shift since they first met, but now he was preparing to make the switch to day shift. She had secretly enjoyed having her nights free. How would Joe react to her wanting to keep it that way?

Well, no need to think about it tonight. It was going to be a wonderful evening, and Celeste always enjoyed spending time with Joe. He was, by far, her favorite boyfriend.

She took her time preparing for the date. Chaos came in to offer her opinions on makeup and gown. She seemed to approve of both until she lay down on the green gown and wallowed in it for a few minutes. It would take a miracle to get all the fur off of it. Apparently, Celeste would be wearing the blue cocktail dress. "Chaos! You're lucky I'm in a mellow mood. You could have ruined my gown!"

Chaos looked away as if to say, *look at me not caring.*

"We're going to have to work on your communication skills. There has to be a better way to tell me you don't like something," Celeste said.

Chaos got up, walked across the bed, and laid down next to the blue dress. She gently placed her paw on it, all while looking Celeste in the eye as she did it.

"I see," Celeste said with a nod. "If I had asked for your opinion, you wouldn't have had to be so aggressive with it. I will keep that in mind in the future." Chaos leaped into Celeste's arms and began purring her loudest purr. "So, I guess it's my communication skills that need work?" Celeste laughed and stroked her friend behind the ears. "You're such a good cat, Chaos."

The phone rang, and Celeste debated whether to let it go to voicemail. At the last second, she picked up, still holding Chaos firmly.

"Hello?"

"Hello? Is this Madam Celeste, the psychic?" the caller asked.

"How did you get this number?" Celeste asked in return.

"A friend gave it to me. They said you were looking for information about the old Brently house."

"And you are . . .?"

"My name is Darla Weatheral. I've lived in the area near that house for years. In fact, I live in a house my grandfather built. So, we go back generations here. I may have some info that could be helpful to you. When can we get together?"

"This is rather sudden, and I'm preparing to leave for the evening. How would tomorrow afternoon suit you?"

"What time?" Darla asked.

"It would need to be late in the afternoon, say around four or four-thirty?"

"I could meet you at the coffee house at four-thirty," Darla said.

"The one on Nevada St?"

"Yes."

"I'll meet you there at four-thirty, then," Celeste said before hanging up.

"This should be an interesting weekend," Celeste murmured to Chaos. "This woman may have just the information we're looking for to solve this puzzle. I wonder who her friend is and why she chose today to call. She seems closed to me for some reason. That can't be good . . .." She wrote herself a note about tomorrow at four-thirty. Then, she returned to the matter at hand—getting ready for her date—but her thoughts kept drifting back to what this woman had to share.

.

CHAPTER 27

Celeste and Joe made some blissful memories Friday night and Saturday morning, and then again Saturday afternoon. Joe truly was an amazing man. But, in truth, he had to work Saturday night and spent most of Saturday sleeping. Turning his body clock right side up was going to take some work. He left for home long before Celeste's appointment with Darla. Celeste even had time for a short nap before she got ready.

It was a typical Saturday afternoon at the coffee shop with more than half the seats taken. Celeste ordered a coffee and found a seat wondering how she would recognize Darla, but was surprised when Darla walked in and came straight to Celeste.

"I found your picture on the internet," Darla said. "It pulled you up on the first try. Let me go order some coffee, and I'll be right back."

Darla was a lot like Celeste had expected her to be. She was average height with a small build, mid-fifties, shoulder-length auburn hair, confident, and comfortable in her own skin.

"So, Teresa tells me you think there may be ghosts or worse at that house," Darla said.

"Teresa?" asked Celeste.

"Teresa Brently. The woman who's paying you to clear out that house. Teresa Brently, my neighbor. I thought you were supposed to be a psychic," Darla said.

Celeste paused before answering. She was being baited and knew it, but she also knew she could share some information and get some in exchange.

"We know there are spirits. We've spoken with some of them. But we also have some phenomena going on that can't be explained by the spirits we have talked with. Either one or all of them are deceiving us, or there is another entity causing things to happen on the property. Now, spirits are not the most reliable witnesses. They have a terrible sense of time, and they're not always sure of where they are. But they're better than nothing," Celeste said.

"Has anyone told you that was Indian land back in the day?" Darla asked.

"We thought it was a possibility." Celeste nodded. "But are you saying it definitely had Indians?"

"Oh, yes. There are several stories of Indians dying near the pond. One's body was never found. Everyone says it ended up in the pond. Some stories even talk of a skin-walker in those woods."

"A Skin-walker?" Celeste asked, hoping to gain more insight into the phenomena.

"They can change shapes. Mostly they change to wolves—extremely large wolves that can walk on two legs. Or maybe it's the wolves that change to look like men. People who get a good look at them don't live to talk about it," Darla said in a low, secretive voice.

"Who told you about this?"

"My family is part Chickasaw. These legends have been passed down."

"Who told you about the activity at the pond and the Brently house?" Celeste asked.

"Just rumors," Darla said with a shrug. "Just small-town rumors. It is close enough to my home to be important to me. What if the activity begins to spill over to my family's land? Teresa has told me a few of the unbelievable things that are happening. I've never heard a legend that involved so many spiders or such large spiders. Perhaps this is some new kind of evil."

"My team has come to believe that the spiders are being caused by a spirit of one of the men in the family or possibly a close friend," Celeste said.

"I heard that the close friend," Darla said, using air quotes, "was neither close nor a friend. It is whispered he was a stalker who continues to stalk them even now. How frightening it must be to be stalked when you're alive, but after you're dead . . .? That must be completely un-nerving."

"We don't know that he's capable of doing some of the things that are happening. There are still many viable theories."

Paul appeared to Celeste signaling for her not to talk or acknowledge him. He proceeded to make fun of Darla, mocking her speech and hand movements. He was playing the clown, and no one could see him except Celeste, who wasn't amused. She thought in his direction, *what are you doing? She has been kind enough to come to me with a great deal of new information about this case. Why would you mock her so?*

"When a woman volunteers that much information, there is a motive, one that is being hidden. What is the motive and why is it being hidden from you? Don't you think you should be looking for those answers and not just the ones that are being laid in your lap?" Paul said.

"Is something wrong, dear?" Darla asked, who had noticed she no longer held Celeste's attention.

Paul shook his head and hands to indicate no, and then disappeared as quickly and quietly as he had appeared.

"There was a spirit here trying to get my attention, but he didn't stay long enough to communicate anything that made any sense." Celeste found it much easier to tell the truth than to try to keep up with lies.

"Really? There was a ghost right here? And it was talking to you?"

"Well, it was trying. Spirits don't always make sense. They get disoriented and then leave when it doesn't work out the way they expected it to. I'm sure he'll be back if it was important."

"Could it have been one of the ghosts from the house?" Darla asked, her eyes wide as she glanced around the shop.

"No, this is one that visits me often."

"So, you have a stalker ghost, too?"

"I wouldn't call him a stalker. He just visits a lot, but he also assists me with investigations. It would feel empty not to have him around." She hadn't really thought about how much a part of her life Paul had become. He could be irritating, but she did count on his help frequently. Maybe he was right. This woman had a lot of information. Was it all true?

"Darla, has anything happened to you or anyone in your house? Anything that would make you think there was some spillover from the Brently house?" Celeste asked as she picked up her cup of coffee.

"Well, not that I can think of, but if there's a skin-walker, I definitely want to know about that. In fact, everyone in the area should know about it."

"But we haven't established there is a skin-walker, yet," Celeste reminded her.

"Yet," Darla said with dramatic emphasis.

"I have a meeting tomorrow afternoon with the young investigators that are helping track down what is going on over there. Maybe I will learn more then. I just don't see the possibility of finding evidence of a skin-walker. There has to be a more logical explanation," Celeste said.

"Well, I hope you'll keep me informed of your findings."

"I'll keep Cheryl informed," Celeste said firmly.

CHAPTER 28

Everyone gathered at Robert's apartment on Sunday afternoon. They sat in silence for what felt like an eternity while Robert went to pick up the pizza. No one wanted to share information without him there. It was awkward until Emma suggested she could read someone's cards if there were a volunteer. Everyone volunteered, so they drew a name. Cheryl won, and Emma laid out a simple past, present, and future pattern. The cards correctly called her past and present as everyone in the room knew them to be. For the future, Cheryl had drawn the High Priestess card. It said long kept secrets would be revealed. The whole group nodded in approval as it was the one thing they all hoped for Cheryl.

Emma drew another name. This proved to be an excellent way to pass the time. When Robert returned, Emma had only one person left to read. She read them quickly while the others readied the plates and drinks.

Madam Celeste saw no need to intrude and was quiet throughout. Emma needed the practice, and it was good to see her developing friends while maintaining her position as a psychic. There was a fine line to be walked between friendship and client status, and Emma seemed to be managing it very well. Celeste was pleased. These all seemed to be true friends, most valuable assets when one can read the future.

Everyone settled with their food, and it was quiet for a time. Even Celeste took a slice. With no warning, Robert began the discussion. "Several of us have made some headway in the last few days, and I felt it would be best to share what we know and what we suspect. Who wants to go first?"

"We've eliminated some of the more far-fetched theories that we or, at least I, started with," Emma said, who had already finished her small piece of pizza. "As it turns out, any spirit can cause the hallucinations to which we were subjected. Well, maybe not every spirit knows how to do it, but they are all capable of it."

"That puts us no closer to a solution," Cheryl mumbled.

"Actually, it puts us much closer to a solution," Celeste said. "We now know what it most likely isn't and we have a good idea what it most likely is."

"It doesn't explain what Jeremy and I saw in the woods last week though," Cheryl countered.

"You mean there's really something suspicious back there?" Emma asked.

"Oh yes, he thinks he has footage of a gray wolf which hasn't been seen in this area for a very long time. He also hasn't ruled out the possibility of a skin-walker."

"That's the second time this weekend I've heard reference to a skin-walker," Celeste said. "We definitely need to do more research on that. It's an Indian legend, isn't it?"

"That's what Jeremy said. He was very excited to get this evidence. He wants to show it at a convention. He's sure he has something out there in the woods beyond the house, but he's not sure if it's related to what's going on inside the house. In fact, it's highly unlikely they have anything to do with each other," Cheryl said.

"Why isn't he here today?" Robert asked. "His input could be helpful."

"He says he's not part of the team and since he believes the two things are not related, there's no reason for him to be part of the team," Cheryl said.

Robert shook his head. "I disagree. They still may prove to all be connected. We should at least be open to the possibility."

"I agree," Emma said. "There's nothing to prove they're not related, and they are on the same property. Anything is possible. Why not call him and ask him to come over now?"

"That's a bit last minute, but worth a shot," Robert said. "Cheryl? Will you call him?"

"You're preaching to the choir. I tried to get Jeremy to come with me, but I'll call and let him know that you all want him here."

"So," Robert said, "what have we learned about the spiders and spirits inside the house? Do I understand that we think they're hallucinations and nothing more?"

Emma took a sip of her drink. "Well, I've investigated a lot of legends from around the world. I found a few things that could cause hallucinations and even some things which could, according to legends, cause temporary mutations. Madam Celeste thinks we should be looking closer to home."

"We can look around the world for myths and legends, but it seems more likely to me that it would be something that comes from more local legends," Celeste said. "This is not the first time strange things have happened in the area . . . maybe not the same strange things, but strange, nonetheless."

"What did you have in mind, Madam Celeste?" Robert asked.

"The idea of a skin-walker can't be ruled out, but I—"

"What's a skin-walker?" Cheryl interrupted.

"In Navajo culture, a *skin-walker* or a yee naaldlooshii, is a type of harmful witch who can turn into, possess, or disguise themselves as an animal. The term is not used for healers. That's the definition from Wikipedia," Tony chimed in, never looking up from his phone.

"Does that mean they could disguise themselves as spiders?" Cheryl asked.

Robert shrugged. "I guess it could."

187

"As I started to say . . ." Celeste said, regaining the floor, "I don't think a skin-walker truly fits in this situation, though it may have something to do with what's going on outside the house in the woods. I think it's more likely that we're dealing with an agitated spirit, possibly a psychotic one at that."

"What if they're just a bunch of mutant spiders, after all?" Cheryl asked. "We know how huge they can get. Why does it have to be anything to do with spirits at all?"

"We've all seen those spiders on video compared to in person. They are or were huge, but not as large as they seemed in person. Something was manipulating what we were seeing," Celeste said. "We have not found a spider as large as what was seen with the naked eye. It was an illusion, probably meant to scare us away. So, the question should be, who would want to scare us away? And why?" Celeste looked around the room. "Is there any living person we know of who would want to keep everyone away from this house? Cheryl? Do you know of anyone?"

"No, ma'am, I don't. I could ask my mom, though. It could have to do with why she needed the paperwork in the first place."

"So, she could know something she's not sharing," Celeste murmured.

"She could," Cheryl said. "Do you want me to interview her a bit and see what I can find out?"

"I think that would be a good idea," Celeste said after thinking it over. "Is Jeremy on his way?"

"Oh, I almost forgot," Cheryl said. "He's on his way, should be here in a few minutes."

"Good, I'd like to hear his input on the creature he's found in the woods."

"Emma said you had some ideas, Madam Celeste," Robert said.

"As I said earlier, I think we are dealing with a spirit. A friend of Cheryl's mom suggested a skin-walker, which I find suspicious. What reason would this woman have for discussing it with me, and why would she want to send us on a wild goose chase looking for a skin-walker?"

"I have also been looking at the possibility of a skin-walker," Jeremy said as he entered the room. "It's a Native legend, and I don't like the idea of it. But there is a gray wolf out there, and that is equally impossible. I have gone over the evidence, and it is definitely a gray wolf, and there aren't supposed to be any of those in this part of the continent."

"But at least we know they exist on the planet," Celeste insisted. "Skin-walkers are strictly legend."

"There are a lot of Natives that would disagree," Jeremy said. "They count them as real as the wolf."

"But we don't," Emma countered. "There is no physical evidence that they exist. There are no photographs. You can't go see one in a zoo or stuffed in a museum. They only exist in the minds of believers. Did you get pictures of a skin-walker or wolf?"

"A wolf," Jeremy responded. "But it's a wolf that hasn't been seen in this part of the country for centuries."

"But it was here centuries ago?" Emma asked, her brows raised.

"Yes, but you don't understand . . .. Things don't just return once they have gone extinct," Jeremy said.

"So, you think it's more likely a mythical creature is wandering the local woods than that a past predator has returned," Celeste said.

"Well, when you put it like that . . . I don't know. I don't know what I believe anymore," Jeremy said softly. "I guess it's possible the gray wolves that were being held by the zoo settled in the forest and have managed to survive as a pack all these decades. And that does sound more plausible than a skin-walker." He seemed disappointed so Cheryl jumped in.

"If it is a pack of gray wolves, wouldn't that be an extraordinary find? Wouldn't that find go in some kind of college textbook or something?" she asked.

"Well, it would certainly deserve a paper, at least. And I have irrefutable proof of the gray wolf. I could probably get a grant to look for, document, and study them."

"That sounds like you've gotten far more than you came looking for," Celeste said. "Congratulations!"

"Here! Here!" Robert yelled as everyone joined in with congratulations for Jeremy's discovery.

"So, we are completely dismissing the possibility of a skin-walker on the property?" Emma asked as everyone settled down.

"I think so." Jeremy nodded. "I've reviewed my video, audio, and stills. The only real evidence is for a very large gray wolf. There was no evidence, except for a few tracks, of a man and those are obviously not related to the wolf. Though they may be related to whatever is going on in the house . . . .. I'll give you what I've got on those tracks. You may have a living, breathing human involved in your case."

"Well I'm glad you've made so much progress on your tracks. I think you may be right—we may have some paranormal activity, but it is probably being muddled by the human activity," Robert said. "It's good to know it doesn't bleed out to the woods and the lake. That means we can focus on the house."

"Celeste and I have been to the house a couple of times, and there are three spirits there for sure, possibly more. We haven't uncovered any clues that suggest which, if any, of these spirits may be causing the mass hallucinations we've been experiencing."

"Mass hallucinations?" Cheryl, Tony, and Brooke asked in unison.

"Yes, all the spiders in that house were either small common spiders or exotic spiders from your brother. None of them were actually the size we all thought we saw. It was a mass hallucination," Emma explained. "And after everyone left Robert's that night of the séance, we had a conversation with Pete and his dad. There is some hostility there from Pete to his dad, but after working with Celeste, that was reduced considerably. But we also found that Andrew is a stalker. He was when he was alive and apparently continues to be."

"So, is he the one causing all the problems?" Cheryl asked.

"We don't think so," Celeste said. "He doesn't seem strong enough to cause all the havoc we've seen, but we can't rule him out as a possibility either. Did anyone here know him when he was in school?"

"I did, obviously," Cheryl said. "He was, after all, stalking my brother and maybe my father."

"Is there anything you can tell us about him that would give us more insight into his motives or actions?" Emma asked.

"Just that my brother called him a dork and tried to get Andrew to leave him alone. Andrew told everyone they were friends. His mom and my mom have been friends since high school, so we had a lot of play dates with Andrew when we were little. He was an annoying little snitch. We couldn't get away with anything when he was around."

"I remember him from high school," Brooke offered. "It always seemed like he and Pete were friends. I would have never guessed him for a stalker. I thought they just enjoyed hanging out together. Andrew was very convincing."

"I never met him," Robert said. "But then again, I didn't go to school here."

"Same here," Mia and Tony both added.

"So, the only ones who remember Andrew at all were Pete's sister and someone who thought they were friends," Celeste said. "What are we missing? There's something to find out about the three of them. I can't put my finger on it, but there's something else there . . .. If either of you think of anything, please let me know, okay?

Cheryl nodded. "Will do."

"Me too," Brooke said.

"Was there anyone who knew them who seemed jealous of their friendship?" Emma asked.

"What about the tornado?" Celeste asked.

"Tornado?" everyone questioned together.

"Mr. Brently witnessed a tornado in downtown Oklahoma City. Andrew was there. It was where the picture with Andrew and Mr. Brently was taken," Celeste explained.

"Do you think the tornado is significant? I thought it was just the picture," Emma said, turning to Celeste.

"He was very proud of having seen that tornado," Celeste said. "It seems to be why the picture was so important to him. For Andrew, I think it was just the fact that he was in a picture with his hero's father."

"So, you think Pete was Andrew's hero?" Cheryl asked.

"Hero, idol, something like that," Celeste said. "I think Andrew is being held there in that room by that photograph. He may not know it, he may not even realize he is trapped there, but I think he is and it's all about that picture. The question is, is it on purpose. Does someone know they are keeping him there, and, if so, who?"

"Who is even aware of the picture?" Brooke asked. "Before you shared it with us, that is. Mr. Brently knew about it. Did Pete? What about Mrs. Brently? Whoever knows about it is a suspect."

"A suspect of what? What crime has been committed here? A bunch of big scary spiders? That's not exactly a crime," Robert said with an eyeroll.

"Actually, it is," Jeremy said. "Those particular spiders are illegal."

"But they were left to breed by a dead boy. It's not the same as a current crime. It's not like Pete did it intentionally," Robert countered.

"I'm pretty pleased with how it turned out, though," Pete whispered to Emma. Startled, Emma let out a quick gasp. She had not expected to see Pete here today. She looked around to see if anyone had noticed.

"What just happened?" Mia asked, picking up on Emma's frantic gaze.

"Pete is here and thinks the spiders are funny," Emma said.

"You tell him that we don't think they're funny at all!" Cheryl yelled.

"He can hear you," Emma said gently. "He's probably listening all the time."

"What does he think is going on?" Cheryl asked.

"I don't see a problem," Pete said while Emma relayed the messages. "It's not like anyone uses the house. The spiders are happy there. Andrew is as happy there as he would be anywhere. What's the problem?"

LINDA ANTHONY HILL

CHAPTER 29

"The problem is neither Mom nor I can use the house like it is," Cheryl said, her anger evident in her tone. "It's creepy and spooky and downright scary. There seems to be some sort of demon there, and even the psychics are afraid to go over there alone. In a few years, I'm going to want to live there. I won't be able to if it's going to be so active. Can't he get rid of Andrew and whatever else haunts the place?"

Emma had a brief discussion with Pete about this and then turned to Cheryl. "Pete says he doesn't care if you're afraid to live there. Pete doesn't haunt the place anyway. It's Andrew and another one that Pete doesn't know."

"Another one?" Celeste questioned. "Pete, what can you tell us about the other one? Is it someone you know?"

"I don't really see them. I just know others are there. Andrew talks about them a lot—he's afraid of them. He thinks I should be afraid, too, but I'm not. They don't bother me, and I don't bother them."

"Have you always known about them, or is it only recently?" Celeste asked.

"Now that you mention it, it's only been since I met you. I didn't know about a lot of things before I met you. I guess I was kinda blind to a lot of things before."

"What can you tell us about them now?"

"Not much. It hangs out at the house, but it's kinda in the shadows. I never really see it. I don't even know if it's a guy or a girl."

The rest of the group was sitting in awe. They understood Emma and Celeste were conversing with Pete.

"Is he here? In my apartment?" Robert asked excitedly.

"Yes," Emma whispered.

"This is awesome," Robert said as he sprang up from the couch. "I'm going to set up a recorder. Brooke, can you video it?"

Brooke nodded.

Mia was not comfortable. She didn't mind sifting through photographs and videos, but to be in a room with a spirit was more than she signed up for. She started to leave but Tony grabbed her arm and brought her back to a seated position.

"You can handle this," he whispered. "Nothing is here to hurt you or scare you. They're just talking."

"I don't trust ghosts," Mia whispered. "I just don't. We've already seen what they can do. How can you sit here knowing what they are capable of doing?" She blessed herself and made herself as small as possible.

Everyone else sat mesmerized. They hadn't even gotten together to ghost hunt, and they had one. How incredible was that?

"How often is it there?" Emma asked.

"I don't know. How often am I there?" Pete asked. "I don't know that either. Time is different where we are. It's there at least as often as I am, which isn't saying much. I try to stay away because of Andrew. Didn't like him when we were alive, and don't like him now."

"What about your father? Is he there very often?" Celeste asked.

"I get the feeling he hangs out at the lake a lot. He seems to still be upset about the accident. I don't see him at the house very much. But again, I'm not there very much, so I don't see anyone there a lot. But if I had to guess, I'd say Andrew is stuck there. I don't think he could leave if he wanted to and he doesn't seem to want to."

"Do you feel sorry for him, Pete?" Celeste asked, hoping she could get Pete to help with Andrew.

"Nah," Pete said quickly. "He's still a dork, and he's two-faced if you ask me. I don't trust him. He lies. Like that B.S. about him and my dad. He never did anything fun with my dad. Sure, we drove to Oklahoma City that one time and gave him a lift, but we ignored him. My dad would have never spent any time with Andrew if Mom hadn't set it up. Me either."

"Why do you think your mom set it up?" Celeste asked.

"She was friends with his mom. They talked on the phone a lot, and Mom would have them over for dinner sometimes. Andrew's dad was dead, and I think my mom felt sorry for him and his mom."

"Maybe they were just friends," Celeste offered.

"Maybe," Pete said before he disappeared as quickly as he had entered.

"He's gone," Emma said, looking at the others.

The room exploded in a flurry of questions, remarks, and sighs of relief.

"Did he just up and leave?" Mia asked, the only one who was really relieved that he was gone.

"Yes," Celeste said. "When they're finished, they're finished."

"Did we learn anything new?" Brooke asked.

Celeste nodded. "I think so."

"Yes, I think so, too," Emma repeated.

"Pete thinks Andrew is stuck there. Pete's father doesn't come around much and tends to hang out near the lake, presumably near the sight of the boating accident. I obviously need to spend some more time with him to get him past the shock of losing not only his life but that of his son," Celeste said.

"Not now, though, right?" Mia asked again.

"No, my dear, not now. This was a fluke. We didn't summon Pete. He just showed up," Celeste replied.

"He didn't say anything about the wolf, did he?" Jeremy asked.

Celeste shook her head. "No, not a word."

"So, I got from this end of the conversation that Pete thinks there is someone else there other than Andrew and him," Robert said. "Does he have any clues about who it is?"

"No, he's sure something is there, but he's not even sure if it's male or female," Celeste said.

"I wonder if that's what's causing all the trouble," Mia murmured.

"Next time we go over there, we'll have to look into that. We were looking for an evil entity at one point," Emma said.

Celeste put her hands out. "Let's not assume evil, please. Let's just assume trickster for now."

"Isn't that just kind of semantics?" Emma asked.

Celeste looked at her sternly. "I don't think so. But I think we must go back to the house."

CHAPTER 30

The house was less spooky with lights, even if they were dim lights at best. It was still Sunday afternoon, and everyone was there except for Mia, who had made it clear that she wanted nothing to do with the house. Even Rocky, the bug guy, made it. He was now ready for some more spiders to sell and hoping to get some of the oversized ones while there were people around to help. Even Jeremy was there, though he was now convinced there was nothing paranormal or supernatural going on outside. It was exciting to have found a gray wolf here, but not supernatural.

Cheryl was just as happy. There was no known method for getting rid of a skin-walker, and she wanted no part of anything so hateful. Jeremy was relieved on her behalf.

Whatever was on the inside, however, was being very elusive and she did not care for that, either. Cheryl didn't mind problems as long as they came with solutions. She liked her problems neatly tied up in a package with a bow on top.

"So, do we know what we're looking for?" Cheryl asked.

"Signs of Andrew, I guess," Emma said. "A picture of him would be very good. We know it's here. We just can't seem to hold onto it."

"We've used a very special sage solution and custom blessing to try to keep the trickster at bay long enough to search for Andrew, the picture, and anything else we can find that will help. I'm sorry we can't be more specific, but that's all we have to go on right now," Celeste said.

"That's okay," Robert said. "We'll just do what we would ordinarily do on an investigation—one where we didn't have two real psychics along. We will find something, I'm sure."

"Andrew must be hiding today. I don't see him anywhere. I don't even feel him," Emma said softly.

"That's strange. Neither do I," Celeste said. "If he's stuck here, he should be here. Where is he?"

"I smell smoke!" Brooke yelled from the living room.

"It's coming from there," Tony said, pointing to Mr. Brently's study.

Celeste and Emma were in the study and didn't see where Tony had pointed. They neither smelled nor saw any smoke. Emma went to the door and said, "Where is it?"

"What are you talking about? You're standing in it," Robert yelled. "Are you saying there is nothing on fire in that room?"

"This room?" Emma said, glancing around. "No, it's fine. Are you saying you see smoke?" She sprayed more sage around the group, the room. and the hall they were now gathered in. Everyone calmed down as she recited the spell she had written.

"I would have sworn there was smoke pouring out of that room," Brooke said, her cheeks turning pink.

"Me too," Tony, Robert, and Cheryl agreed. Cheryl had already dialed 9-1-1 and was now explaining that it had been a false alarm.

"So . . . Andrew could be here, and we're just not seeing him," Celeste said. "The trickster is at work today. Let's find that picture and get out of here, shall we?"

"I found it!" Brooke yelled, holding it in the air.

"Let me see." Emma moved toward Brooke and confirmed it was the picture they were looking for.

"I found one, too," Robert said excitedly.

"Well, there's something not right about this," Celeste murmured. "Let's gather the pictures and go outside."

They all headed outside, remembering to turn off lights this time. Robert had a picture, and so did Brooke and Tony.

Brooke's was the one they were looking for. Robert's was the one of Mr. Brently and Pete, and Tony held a picture of Pete and Andrew at the lake.

Emma inspected Tony's picture. "Cheryl, I thought you said Pete didn't like Andrew. What would they have been doing at the lake together?"

"I don't know," Cheryl said slowly. "I didn't take the picture, did I?"

"It does look like you may have been wrong about the two boys being friends," Celeste said, taking a closer look at the photo.

"I thought Pete told you they weren't friends," Cheryl barked. "Now you want to accuse me of making up stories?"

"Maybe they were friends, but Pete didn't want anyone to know it. Maybe he was embarrassed about it," Emma offered.

"I guess that's possible . . .. He kept those stupid spiders a secret, after all." Cheryl turned to Rocky. "Speaking of spiders . . .. Do you think you got them all this time?"

"I don't think so," Rocky said. "I found ten, and three of those are getting ready to hatch out. So, it's lucky for y'all that I found them. But I didn't find any of the super huge ones. They're hiding really well."

"Maybe they were never any bigger than the other ones, Rocky. We've imagined a lot of unusual things in this house," Celeste said.

"Shoot! I thought it was just me 'cause I got bit by one of 'em. At'll cause you to see and hear some pretty peculiar stuff, ya' know," Rocky said.

"Really? But the rest of us didn't get bit, and we saw things, too," Celeste said.

"I don't rightly know what to tell ya about that, Ms. Celeste. It's sure enough a mystery," Rocky said.

"That it is, Rocky. That it is," Celeste said. "And a mystery we intend to solve. It helps to know that a bite from one of these spiders could cause one to see things. Thank you."

"How does that help?" Cheryl asked. "They didn't bite any of us, and they sure didn't bite any ghosts!"

"Spirits!" everyone yelled. Madam Celeste and Emma were having an effect on them. They were pleased.

Cheryl raised her hand. "Hold on . . .. This picture isn't of Pete and Andrew, it's of Pete and Dad. I thought you said it was Pete and Andrew."

"It was," Robert said, moving closer.

"Let me see it." Cheryl handed the picture to Celeste. As she touched the photograph, Celeste began to see the scene play out like a video. "This was taken about a week before your father and brother died," she said. "They were getting things ready for the fishing expedition. Your father told Pete how much he was looking forward to spending some time with Pete. Pete seemed anxious about something else—something was going on at school that kept him from enjoying the day. There was some type of exam coming up that Pete was worried about. He was worried about how his father would feel if Pete didn't do well on the test. He was thinking of asking Andrew for help."

"So, he would have wanted to keep it a secret," Cheryl said slowly. "He wouldn't have wanted Dad to know he was getting help from Andrew. Dad didn't like Andrew any more than Pete did."

They heard a loud crash in the house. It sounded like furniture falling or being thrown. Leaving the pictures in Emma's car, they hurried back into the house. Emma went immediately to the study and the rest followed her. Andrew was there, and he was upset.

"Pete was my friend!" he yelled. "Why won't anyone believe me?"

"Because Pete told them something different, Andrew," said Celeste. "Where were you an hour ago when we were looking for you? You weren't anywhere around here."

"I was in New York," Andrew said, offering no explanation.

"I thought you were stuck here," Celeste said.

"I thought so, too," Andrew said.

Everyone waited for Andrew to explain.

Finally, Celeste said, "And . . .? How did you get to New York?"

"Someone thought me there," he said.

"Are you making this difficult on purpose?" Celeste asked.

"No," he said.

LINDA ANTHONY HILL

CHAPTER 31

Celeste was starting to lose her patience. "Then tell me how you got there, and why and by whom."

"It was all very strange. One second, I was here, and the next, I was there. It was near where the accident happened. There were a lot of people in a circle with candles and bells and stuff. They wanted to know why I hung out there, which I don't. So, I told them I don't, but they didn't like my answers to most of their questions. However, they couldn't see me or hear me the way you can. I would say no, and she would tell everyone I wasn't sure. I was sure. My answer was no. So, I don't know if she could really hear me or not."

"What kind of questions did they ask you?" Celeste asked.

"They wanted to know if I knew I was dead, which was rude. And wanted to know if my death had been painful and what year I thought it was . . . you know, things like that. They would ask the same questions over and over and over. They had some machines they said would help us talk to each other, but I didn't feel like they were helping much. They did have a really nice one that lit up with lots of pretty colors when I got close to it. I liked that."

"I know this is a stupid question but, do you know about how long you were there?" Emma asked.

"Nah," Andrew answered.

"How did you get back here?" Celeste asked.

"When they finished, everybody stood up, and I was just back here like I'd never left."

"So, someone in New York summoned you. They must have a haunting going on and thought it might be you because you died so close to where they were," Celeste said. "Did they call you by name?"

"Yes, they did. The one woman knew my whole name."

"Did you live in New York for a long time?" Celeste asked.

"Yes, but not that long. I was hit by a car after living there for a few months," Andrew said. "You know, you are much easier to talk to than those people in New York."

Celeste smiled. "Thank you, Andrew. I take that as a compliment."

"You're a nice lady," Andrew said softly. "I'll make sure you don't get hurt."

Celeste took a step back. "Why would I get hurt?"

"Oh, no reason . . . .. Forget I said it," Andrew said before he disappeared.

Celeste was quiet for a minute, staring where Andrew had vanished from. "That is a very strange young man."

"Which is what I've been trying to tell you," Cheryl said. "There's always been something not right about Andrew. He would be nice but creepy. It made you think he was up to no good most of the time."

"He seems to think I could get hurt by something and that he could protect me," Celeste said. "He's so fragile, I suspect I will have to keep him from being hurt."

"Maybe he's not as fragile as he seems," Robert offered. "He doesn't add up. We're looking for a trickster, but what if it's Andrew?"

Cheryl shook her head. "Nonsense. He may be sneaky, but I doubt he's powerful enough to pull off anything we've seen. He's just annoying."

"I can hear you," Andrew said, re-appearing. "I'm pretty much stuck here, so why do you hold it against me? It's not like I can magically transport to somewhere else."

"Let's look at that, Andrew. What do you think you're stuck to?" Celeste asked. "It would have to be something physical, and it would have to be in or around this house. Can you think of anything here you are especially fond of?"

"I always liked that picture of me and Mr. Brently. It made me feel like I belonged here," Andrew whispered. "It makes me feel good."

"It sounds like that's your anchor here," Emma said. "How do we test it, Celeste, and how do we fix it?"

"You make it sound so easy, dear. There is, no doubt, a problem with that in this instance because every time we get close, the circumstances seem to change. There is something else at work here. I haven't determined what it is, but I'm very sure there's more to it than say, the time Paul was stuck to his death certificate. That was easy to find and test. This presents something different."

"I don't understand," Emma said.

"Neither do I . . . yet."

"Shouldn't we try to take the picture away from the house and see if he comes with it? That worked with Paul," Emma said.

"We tried that the other night, and it didn't work at all, which makes me suspect there's more to this."

"True enough," Emma said. "So, what are we missing?"

"Assuming that Andrew is just a pawn in this little play, maybe we should look a little closer at Mr. Brently. He has every reason to want to keep people away from his house, especially his study," Celeste said. "Maybe he is manipulating both Andrew and the photo."

"How could he manipulate the photo?" Cheryl asked. "It's solid. He couldn't force it to stay in this house, could he? Can ghosts do that?"

"Spirits!" Celeste and Emma barked simultaneously.

"Okay. Spirits. Can spirits force physical objects to do things, even when the spirit is not around? Is that possible?"

"I don't know. Perhaps Mr. Brently is more than just a spirit?" Celeste offered.

"I heard that," Mr. Brently said. "What plot are you accusing me of in my own home?"

"We were trying to imagine what or who might be responsible for the goings on here in this house," Celeste said. "You are very protective of the house. Are you capable of manipulating physical objects to do your bidding?"

"I probably am, though I haven't tried it . . . there's really no need."

"We're just looking at all possible explanations, Mr. Brently," Celeste said. "Do you have any idea why Andrew is here?"

"My father is here?" Cheryl perked up. "Daddy, can you help us?"

"Tell her I will do what I can. I don't know why the boy is here, but it is certainly not because of me. I would have him out of here as much as you would. He is at the very least an annoyance," Mr. Brently said as he abruptly disappeared.

"This is getting us nowhere, and the sun is beginning to set. I think it's time to leave. My patience is running thin. I'm missing something important. Make sure we have the pictures." Celeste turned from the group.

"They're in the car," Emma called after her.

CHAPTER 32

Celeste didn't rest well that night. Her dreams made no sense, and she woke frequently. She knew, in her heart, that there was something she should be seeing, but she wasn't. It was like a spot in her line of vision was so illuminated that she couldn't see the area. What should have been obvious was being blocked. It was like being blinded, and the harder she looked, the less could be seen in the area.

Celeste met with a new client the next morning. She had been referred by an old friend, and Celeste could see her story just from shaking her hand. It would be an easy read, and Celeste felt she needed that right now—to not even bother with cards or props, simply telling Beth what she saw. Beth had cancer. She would be heavily involved with the medical community for a few months, but there was a light at the end of the tunnel. She would survive to live a healthy life again. It would be a bumpy road, and there would be setbacks. Celeste suggested they see each other once a week for a few months. Beth agreed, feeling an immediate bond with Celeste, which was mutual. The universe had delivered exactly what Celeste needed at exactly the right time.

Emma told Celeste about the new client so she could clear it with her. Celeste agreed this would be a good practice case for

Emma, who prepared her space with tarot cards and other paraphernalia that she hoped she wouldn't need, but better to be prepared, after all. Charlie Tanner arrived on time. Emma showed him to her desk noticing he was not alone. A tall, thin, elderly gentleman was with him, dressed in a suit, complete with vest and tie. Emma described the man to Charlie slowly, as not to frighten the man.

"That could be my grandfather," Charlie said. "Why would he be trying to scare me? Can you ask him why he's here?"

Emma asked, "Are you Charlie's grandfather?"

The spirit nodded.

She looked at Charlie. "Yes, it is your grandfather." She then turned to the spirit and asked, "Why are you here?"

The spirit shrugged his shoulders and wrinkled his face as if to say, I don't know.

"You can talk to me," Emma said gently. "I can hear you as well as see you."

The spirit shook his head.

"He either can't or won't talk to me," Emma said. "This is a new one on me. How long would you say he's been following you?"

"It's only been for a couple of weeks."

"How long has he been dead?" Emma asked.

"For as long as I can remember," Charlie said. "He died in Germany before I was born."

"Interesting," Emma said slowly. "You've never met him, and he shows up now. Has anything changed for you in the last few weeks?"

"Not really," Charlie shook his head. "Nothing I can think of. I've been toying with the idea of quitting my job and starting a business, but I haven't done anything yet."

The spirit held his arms in the air, crossing them aggressively.

"Bingo!" Emma said with a snap of her fingers. "We have found his button. Now, to find a way to communicate."

"Do you speak German?" Charlie asked.

"No, but he seems to understand English. He's responding to what we're talking about."

The spirit sat down on an object not even Emma could see. He put his hands together and brought them to his face, tapping them gently against his lips. Then he grabbed his head in frustration before he leaped to his feet and began to pace.

"Apparently, he's been trying to get your attention, and he's pretty frustrated. He seems to be able to understand us, but maybe he doesn't speak English."

The spirit pointed to Emma with his finger on his nose and smiled. It seemed this was about to turn into a macabre game of charades.

"Is this about Charlie quitting his job?" Emma asked.

The spirit held his hand flat and tilted it back and forth.

"So, it's about that, but it's also about starting a business?" she clarified.

The spirit pointed at her.

"Should he start a business?"

The spirit nodded.

"Should he quit his job first?" she asked.

The spirit shook his head.

"What kind of business are you thinking of starting?" Emma asked Charlie.

"It's an internet business. I'll have an internet store," he said.

"Couldn't you start that before you quit your job?" Emma asked, and the spirit became excited and pointed to her, nodding his whole body vigorously. "Uh, Grandpa seems to agree with me here. He's very excited."

"It would be harder to do it that way. It's going to take a few hours a day to set up, monitor, and promote the online store."

"But it could be done?" she asked.

"Yes."

"Grandpa likes the idea," Emma said. "But he's still here. Now that you know who it is, do you want him to leave?"

"I guess it won't be so scary now that I know it's my grandfather," Charlie said after a moment. "Maybe I could come to see you from time to time to help translate what he wants?"

"That would work for me," Emma said. "Let me ask you, was your grandfather a business owner?"

"I don't know a lot about him. I guess I need to start asking some questions and see what I can find out."

"He could be a big help," Emma said.

They set up an appointment for the following month, and Charlie agreed not to quit his job during that time. Emma had gained a regular client—two if you counted Grandpa. She smiled to herself and waited for Celeste to finish for the day so she could share the good news with her.

It had been a busy day, and neither Emma nor Celeste had had a chance to look at the photos taken from the Brently house. Emma was tempted to pick them up and get a "reading," but held off until Celeste could be there with her. This case had too many ins and outs to handle evidence without backup.

Celeste joined her within fifteen minutes and was as anxious as Emma was to see what the photos held for them. They huddled over them, each waiting for the other to touch one. Their eyes met, and Celeste realized she would be the first to read. She picked up the closest photo—the one with Mr. Brently and Pete. Mr. Brently had been scolding Pete before the picture was snapped.

Pete wanted to leave for a date, and his father wanted him to stay with Andrew until his mother arrived. He didn't want to have to stay with the boy nor did he want to leave him alone. Pete had made it clear he was leaving. No one was happy, and Andrew was hiding in the back seat. He really didn't want to be left alone to wait for his mother who was notorious for being late.

A stranger, seeing they had a camera, had snapped the picture for them. They had put aside their argument to pose and resumed it immediately after. Pete walked off, winning the argument by default. Mr. Brently followed him to the street where he saw the tornado.

Celeste handed the picture to Emma for confirmation, and Emma saw the same scene.

"This doesn't tell us much," Celeste murmured. "We already knew Pete and his father were not best buddies and that Andrew was an inconvenience on this trip. Let's try another. You go first this time."

Emma picked up the next picture, one she hadn't noticed before. It was one of Mr. Brently and Cheryl. As a young child, Cheryl was standing in front of her father with a smile on her face, and her father was smiling as well. The scene began in the garden with Cheryl chasing a butterfly.

Her mother was cutting roses, and her father was leaving for work. Cheryl was not paying attention and ran into Mr. Brently. He pretended to be hurt. Mrs. Brently grabbed her camera from her pocket and posed Cheryl and her father, taking the picture as the butterfly left the garden. Cheryl ran after it, and Mr. Brently left for work. Everyone seemed happy.

Emma handed the picture to Celeste and their visions matched.

Celeste looked for the picture of Andrew and Mr. Brently, but it wasn't there. It had, once again, disappeared.

"Curious," Celeste murmured. "The photograph itself seems to be attached to the house. I did not think that was possible. If we go back and find it there again, we'll know for sure. What manner of magic could attach a physical object to another physical object?"

Paul appeared. "Ladies, that's just not possible. Spirits get stuck to things, but things don't get stuck to things."

"Aha," Celeste snapped her fingers, "but could things get stuck to spirits? In other words, could the picture be somehow attached to Andrew, who is attached to the house or some other object within the house?"

"I think that's a stretch," Paul said. "But let me get this straight, you think Andrew is attached to the house?"

Celeste nodded. "Yes."

"And you think the picture is attached to Andrew, a spirit."

"Yes," Celeste said.

"Why? I mean, why would a picture be attached to a spirit?"

"Maybe the picture meant a lot to Andrew, and so it became attached to him," Celeste offered.

"That sounds more like him being attached to it," Paul said.

"What's the difference?" Emma asked.

"If the picture is attached to him, it can't be moved away from him," Celeste explained. "It would snap back to his location wherever he is."

"It sounds like what could be happening, but it doesn't seem right. That's just not possible, is it?" Paul asked.

"I'd love to hear a better explanation," Celeste said.

Emma glanced at Celeste. "Are we sure the picture is real? I mean can objects be spirits?"

"Don't be ridiculous!" Paul yelled. "Objects are physical."

Celeste rubbed her chin in thought. "I don't know . . . .. It's worth looking into. I've never encountered it, but this object keeps disappearing. Maybe it's not real."

CHAPTER 33

"It could be an illusion and nothing more," Emma chimed in excitedly. "It's *not here* more than it *is* here."

"True," Celeste said. "But who is creating the illusion? Andrew? Mr. Brently? Pete?"

Emma paused. "I don't think it would be Pete. He doesn't even like Andrew. It would make sense for it to be Andrew. He loves that picture . . . he acts like it proves that he and Pete were friends."

"And that does seem to be the most important thing to him," Celeste said slowly.

"Who died first, I wonder. Pete or Andrew?"

"I guess I just assumed Pete and his father had died first," Celeste said.

"Makes sense. Andrew seems older than Pete, so it would follow that Andrew was alive longer and grew up more before he died," Emma said and looked away thoughtfully. "I wonder how old he was. And why he was in New York. There's something we're missing . . . something that would solve the mystery of the spiders and the strange haunting of the house."

"I know. It could be any one of our spirit suspects or, it could be someone else manipulating them," Celeste said.

"Someone who was physically alive couldn't manipulate spirits, could they?"

"Seems pretty far-fetched," Celeste said.

The phone rang, interrupting their musings.

"Madam Celeste's. How can we help you fulfill your destiny today?" Emma asked.

"This is Darla, Teresa's neighbor. I met with Madam Celeste on Saturday. Is Madam Celeste available?"

"Let me check," Emma said before she put the phone on mute. She turned to Celeste and repeated the information.

"Interesting timing. I'll take the call. Darla may have some information that would be helpful," Celeste said as she released the mute button. "Hello?"

"Hi, remember me from Saturday?" Darla asked.

"I do indeed. Have you thought of something else that might be a clue as to who or what we're dealing with over there?"

"You know, I think I have." Darla paused for a minute. "There's a strange light that comes from that house sometimes at night. I don't think I mentioned that the other day. I was so busy worrying about the skin-walker. Have you found out anything about the skin-walker, by the way?" Darla said rapidly.

"What kind of light?" Celeste asked. She didn't allow time for Darla to answer before another question popped into her head. "Is it red or white or some other color? Is it bright? Is it large? Please tell me more about it."

Darla was quiet for a moment as if she was studying the questions. "It's not as bright as if say, the light was on, but it's not as soft as a flashlight. It seems to go from yellow to red, and I guess you would call it small, but larger than a flashlight. Do you think it's a ghost or a demon?"

"Well, let's hope it's not a demon. Demons are quite rare. It could be a spirit, though. We've found at least three spirits hanging out in the house occasionally. I'm surprised, that they can be seen from a distance though. Maybe it was on a night my helpers were over there, and you saw some things they accidentally stirred up."

"I can pretty much tell when people are in the house, especially now that the electricity is back on," Darla said.

"You realized that?"

"Oh yes, I try to keep an eye on the place for Teresa. She's such a good person. I want to help her in any way I can," Darla said.

"How well did you know Teresa's husband, Mr. Brently?" Celeste asked.

"Ray? He was a good guy. I didn't know him as well as I know Teresa. Is he over there haunting the place? That wouldn't surprise me. He didn't like people poking around in his things when he was alive, and I can't imagine he's changed his mind now that he's dead."

"Really?" Celeste asked. "What makes you say that?"

"I was over there one afternoon before he died, you know, and I walked into his study just to have a look-see. He came in and found me there, and I thought he was gonna' have a conniption. He got all flustered and told me it was his private study, and that I needed to leave immediately. He fussed at me like I was one of his kids. Imagine the nerve!"

"I can only imagine," Celeste murmured.

"Then one day after he died, I was over there helping Teresa box up a few of his things, and a saucer came flying across the room right at me. I told Teresa right then that her man was haunting the place and she needed to keep an eye out for what he might do next. She didn't seem too concerned, but we left the study and started in the living room instead." Darla paused to take a breath. "There's a very strange mirror in that living room . . .. I could swear that every once in a while, I see Ray's reflection in it. It fades almost as fast as I notice it, but I've seen it with my own eyes!"

"You make it sound like you've been in the house recently," Celeste said.

"Not really, but that's something you don't forget real easy," Darla said with a chuckle. "Deadman in a mirror will leave a mark on your brain, sure enough."

"Are you suggesting the light you have seen may be Mr. Brently?"

"Could be," Darla said. "Why not? You say there are ghosts over there. Wouldn't it make sense that it's him?"

"Actually, it would make more sense than you know," Celeste said, drifting off into thought about her most recent encounter with Ray Brently. He had more than one good reason to keep watch over the house. "Thank you, Darla, you've been most helpful today. Do feel free to call again if anything else occurs to you."

"I'll be happy to do just that. If it's Ray, can you get rid of him?"

"Maybe . . .. Thanks again," she said hanging up. Celeste turned to Emma. "Emma, what do we know about Ray and Teresa Brently?"

"Not that much, really," Emma said. "They were still married when he died in the boating accident. They lived in the house we're investigating. She doesn't like to go into the house but doesn't want to sell it, either."

"Would she benefit in any way from having rumors and legends spring up about the land of the house?" Celeste asked. "That could be a motive for her or for him to promote these occurrences."

"How would anyone benefit from people thinking their house was possessed by beasts or demons or skin-walkers?"

"That is a good question, Emma. Let's focus on that and see what we find."

"I'm not even sure where to start. What do you think about calling a real estate agent?"

"They could tell you what effect it would have on the value of the property. Are haunted locations worth more as tourist attractions?" Celeste asked.

"I'll make a few phone calls in the morning," Emma said, pulling out some paper to write down the note for herself.

"Very good," Celeste said with a nod. "I'm also curious about what Andrew was doing in New York. Do we know any of his people? Like his parents or siblings?"

"Who knew there was so much research involved for a psychic?"

Celeste gave her a look that said quite emphatically, "I did, and you should have, too."

Celeste's personal phone rang. Seeing Joe's name on the screen, Celeste excused herself and left Emma with the pictures and a lot of questions. Emma started to leave for the evening without reading any more pictures. She knew Celeste would be on the phone for more than a few minutes.

"Good Morning, Joe. Did you rest well?" Celeste asked.

CHAPTER 34

"This is my last week on the night shift," Joe said. "I'm looking forward to living like normal people, but I wonder how long it will take to get my sleep rhythm back."

"I imagine you'll live on caffeine at first," Celeste said with a chuckle. "Are you already at work?"

"No, I was thinking about stopping at a hamburger joint. Can I bring you something? We could at least share a meal."

"That would be lovely, Joe, but I have Emma here, and we're working on a case that's proving difficult. Maybe we could do it tomorrow night?" Celeste asked, motioning for Emma to stay.

"Tomorrow night it is. I'll talk to you then . . . .. You're not doing anything I should be worried or concerned about, are you?"

"Not yet," Celeste said. "But I'll keep you updated. There had been some talk of a skin-walker, but I'm not too concerned about it."

"A skin-walker? Those things are not to be taken lightly, Celeste. If there really is one, you could be in serious danger even being in the vicinity. Don't be too nonchalant about it, please."

"I won't," she said. "But it is hard to take the legend seriously when there's no empirical evidence of even one of them.

They've been reported many times, but none have ever been proven."

"That's because no one has ever survived getting too close to one. Skin-walkers are extremely dangerous, Celeste. Please, don't dismiss the legend. This one could kill you," Joe said.

"How does a legend persist if no one lives to talk about it, Joe? Have you thought of that? Who is telling the stories? They have to be coming from people who have confronted the legend and survived."

"Don't risk it. That's all I'm saying," Joe said with a sigh. "I have to leave now. You stay safe."

"I intend to. I'll see you tomorrow." Celeste ended the call and turned to Emma. "Let's try another picture, shall we?" she said with a smile.

"Sounds like Joe is pretty worried about the skin-walker. He actually believes in those things, doesn't he?"

"It seems so," Celeste said. "People hear stories from the time they're children, so they grow up believing without questioning. He will have a chance to examine those beliefs this time. Whose turn is it to read a photo?"

"I'm not sure," Emma said. "Why don't you go ahead and start?"

Celeste picked up the next picture in the small heap. It was a scene from the boat. A very young Pete and Cheryl were sitting together with life jackets on in the photo, but there had been a struggle to get them into those jackets moments before the picture was taken.

The children wouldn't stop playing long enough to get an arm through. Both parents were trying their best to get the job done, but both children were resisting with all they had. When they were finally suited up, Mrs. Brently snapped the picture. The children barely sat still long enough, and as soon as the picture was taken, they were immediately off and running again.

Emma picked up the image and confirmed the scene. So far, everything they were seeing was being confirmed. The spirits didn't seem interested in any of these pictures. The only one that caused problems was the one that wasn't here, and they were beginning to suspect it wasn't anywhere. Had there ever been a photo of Andrew and Mr. Brently? They had both seen it, but only in Ray Brently's study.

The rest of the pictures were of outings on the boat or picnics at a park or scenes from the garden. There were no apparent clues and no sign of Andrew. There were other children in some of the photos, friends of one or both of the kids, but no Andrew. He was either lying or delusional. Celeste and Emma believed it was the latter. The poor kid may have had friends, but not in this household.

"We need to go back over there," Celeste said, placing the photos back into a stack. "It's the only way we're going to get to the bottom of this. We know more now than we did. We can't be fooled by Andrew's story. We can put more pressure on him and get to the truth."

"It's not him I'm worried about," Emma said. "We're still not sure there's no demon there."

"I think a demon would have shown his hand by now. The only thing even close to demonic turned out to be an illusion."

"Yes, but what caused the illusion? Could it have been something demonic, in which case it has shown its hand?" Emma asked.

"Well, we're not going to find out from here. It's time to go back and confront Andrew and Ray Brently and find out who's responsible for that picture."

"Now?" Emma asked. "Let me call Robert and see if he can go with us."

Celeste nodded. "That may be a good idea. Tell him to bring a camera, too."

Emma contacted Robert, who agreed to come over immediately. He loved being there when the two psychics were working together.

LINDA ANTHONY HILL

CHAPTER 35

Robert tried to make small talk on the drive to Cheryl's house, but neither Emma nor Celeste were in the mood for it. Finally, he asked the right question. "What is your plan when you get there?"

Celeste answered, "We will begin in the study. We will first see if Andrew is ready to talk. I have far too many questions that could be easily answered if he just would. Then we will talk with Ray Brently, who is also hiding something."

"What about the spiders?" Robert asked.

Celeste cast a glance at Robert. "What about the spiders?"

"They were picking back up the last time we were there. It could be a problem," Robert said.

"We were just there yesterday. It didn't seem bad," Emma said.

"We'll see . . . .. Just keep in mind that we need to be on the lookout. Remember, one of them attacked Rocky."

"At least we have electricity now," Emma said cheerfully.

"How's that going to protect you from spiders?" Robert asked.

"It will make us feel better to have more light," Celeste said.

Robert dropped it, and there was no more conversation on the way to the house. They were surprised to find Jeremy sitting in his car near the street. Robert stopped to talk to him, so Celeste and Emma went on toward the house. Robert cut his conversation short and hurried to catch up.

"Jeremy said that he has footage of a gray wolf out back, and he thinks there may be more to find," Robert said when he walked up beside Emma.

"How nice for him," Celeste said. "Will you be joining us inside?"

"Yes, ma'am, if you don't mind."

"Stay out of the way and don't interrupt," Celeste said.

They walked in through the kitchen. The spider webs were a little heavier than they had been the day before. Turning on lights as they went, they moved toward the study. Robert led the way with a daylight-sized flashlight.

Emma had brought her cleansing kit and was chanting and sprinkling sage-plus as they walked. Robert started to question her, but Madam Celeste threw up her hand in a dramatic gesture that stopped even one syllable from leaving his lips.

As they entered the study, Celeste smelled smoke. Flames were licking the lamp in the corner where they had seen Andrew. "Emma, do you see the flames?" she asked.

"No, where are they?" Emma asked, her eyes quickly taking in the room.

"In the corner. You don't see it? You don't smell smoke?" Celeste asked.

Emma shook her head. "No, though there is a red glow coming from the corner. Which one of us is seeing things? How do we tell?"

"I think this is my vision. It's very real, though. We must find out if there was ever a fire in the study or . . . if Andrew was ever involved in a fire. I might be seeing a vision from Andrew. That would make sense. If he was traumatized as a child or even older, this could be a residual vision from him."

"Andrew? Andrew, are you here?" Celeste called out.

Andrew slowly appeared in the middle of the flames. "Why can't you just leave me alone? Everything gets worse when you come around. Go away!" he yelled.

"Emma, did you see or hear Andrew?" Celeste asked softly.

"Yes, I did. He doesn't sound too happy. Maybe we should leave?"

"I'm ready to get to the truth!" Celeste yelled. "We will stay."

"Are you still seeing a fire?" Emma asked.

"Yes. It is engulfing half the room and Andrew is in the middle of it. He doesn't seem to notice."

"Then what did he mean when he said things were getting worse? What is he seeing? Andrew? What do you see right now?" Emma asked.

"I see you and her and that guy over there, and you and Mr. Brently are all in my apartment in New York."

"New York!" Emma and Celeste said in unison. Though, Celeste was the one to question Andrew further. "Andrew, we're standing in Mr. Brently's house in Texas. Why would we be in New York?"

"You may be in Texas," Andrew said, pointing at Celeste, "but I'm in New York. I was getting ready for work when you showed up. Now I'm going to be late."

"Andrew, you're a spirit in Texas. You're dead," Celeste said softly.

Andrew gave Celeste a look of disbelief. "You're crazy. I have to get ready for work."

"Do you mind if I stay with you while you get ready?" Celeste asked.

"You need to get out of my apartment!" Andrew yelled.

"Andrew what are you doing right now?" Celeste asked, moving closer to him.

"I'm cooking bacon for my breakfast just like I do every morning," Andrew said.

"How big is your apartment, Andrew?"

"You're standing in the middle of it. You tell me," Andrew huffed. "Can't you see there's not enough room in here for the both of us?"

"I'll leave when you do," Celeste said. "Where do you work?"

"I deliver food for the Chinese restaurant downstairs," he replied.

Celeste's brows rose. "You have a car?"

"No, I use a bike. You can't make deliveries in a car. It would take so long with the traffic that the food would get cold, and there's no place to park anyway."

"Ah, that makes sense," Celeste said with a smile. "What time do you have to be at work?"

"What difference is it to you? I still don't know why you're here. You need to leave so I can get dressed for work."

Andrew's apartment was more of a one-room efficiency. There was a bed without a head or footboard. There was a small square table with one chair that doubled as a kitchen table and a desk. The bathroom had a curtain separating it from the rest of the room—but Celeste couldn't see that. Celeste could only see the flames leaping up the walls of the corner of the study in Texas, surrounding Andrew. He was obviously in trouble but apparently saw nothing at all from his vantage point.

He slipped into the bathroom to dress, leaving the bacon unattended. Celeste looked for him, but he had vanished from her sight.

"Do you still see him?" she asked Emma.

"No, he just vanished. But the room is still glowing. Andrew?" she called out. "Andrew, are you still here?"

"This apartment really isn't big enough for this many people," Andrew said. "You both need to leave. Besides, I said I'd like my privacy. Can you not even pretend I'm not here for long enough to put some clothes on?"

"Andrew, we're in Texas. So are you," Emma said more firmly.

"Then Texas sure looks a lot like New York City." He threw back the curtain to the bathroom and stepped into the kitchen/bedroom. He had put on a long-sleeved shirt and a pair of Hagar pants. Pulling on his boots, he looked out the window to the brick wall that was his only view. "Go away, ladies. You have no reason to be here," he said.

Then, as if someone had reset a television show, the flames disappeared and Andrew was back in Texas, and he knew exactly where he was. Had he been possessed?

"Andrew, what just happened?" Celeste asked.

"What are you talking about?"

"You were acting like you were in New York getting ready for work," Emma said.

"Why would I do that? I don't like to think about New York. It was not a very good time in my life, and it is, after all, where I died."

"Do you remember how you died, Andrew?" Celeste asked.

"Sure, I was hit by a car."

"You remember it?" Celeste asked.

"Well, it's kinda fuzzy . . .. I remember being in my apartment, then standing over myself on the street, then coming back here to the study."

"You don't remember getting from your apartment to the street?" Celeste asked.

Andrew shook his head. "No."

"We have some work to do here, Mr. Andrew. What is your last name by the way?"

"Bell," Andrew replied.

"Mr. Bell, we have some work to do. We have to free up those memories so you can move on. We have a place to start though. We will begin in your apartment that morning. Do you remember making breakfast and getting ready for work?"

"Yes, it was just like every other morning. I got dressed and . . .."

"And what, Andrew?" Celeste prompted.

"I don't remember . . .. I don't remember eating or going downstairs or unlocking my bike. I don't remember any of it. How could I forget that? I remember it from every other morning. How could I forget such an important morning? How could I forget the morning I died?" Andrew started to cry, and Celeste let him. He was holding in a lot emotionally, and it was bleeding out onto the living as well.

Emma and Celeste knew what was happening and were prepared for it. Robert had no clue what was happening to him as he began to weep. "I don't know what's wrong with me," he said, wiping the tears from his cheeks. "I never cry. What's going on?"

"You are empathizing with Andrew," Celeste said. "The tears are not yours."

That seemed to make Robert feel better, and much to his relief, he stopped crying. Andrew continued for ten or fifteen minutes before he was able to regain some composure.

"I can see it now. At least, I think I can. I stayed in the bathroom a little longer than usual. I couldn't get my hair right," Andrew said sheepishly.

"What happened next, Andrew? I want you to tell us everything," Celeste said.

"The bacon. It was black. It was starting to burn. I mean with actual flames. I grabbed the pan to get it off the fire. I burnt my hand, and I dropped the pan which sent grease and flames everywhere. My shirt sleeve was on fire. The walls seemed to be on fire. I grabbed a picture from the wall and ran down the stairs and out the front of the building. My shirt was going up in flames. I just kept running. Then I felt the car hit me. I must have run into the street without realizing it. It felt like a herd of cattle had run me down, it hurt that bad. Then, just as quickly, it didn't hurt at all. I was standing on the street with all the others looking down at myself. I looked at my hand and boom! I was here in Texas."

The flames Celeste had been seeing were dying down now. The study was no longer engulfed in flames. "Andrew, you say you grabbed a picture from the wall. What was it a picture of?"

"It was a picture of me and Mr. Brently in Oklahoma City," Andrew said.

"So, in many ways, you are attached to that picture, and it's attached to you," Emma said.

Andrew shrugged. "I guess so."

"So, Andrew has been projecting that picture all along," Celeste said. "It was never physically here."

"That explains a lot," Emma said. "We never actually confirmed anyone other than you and I could see it in the first place, did we?"

"No, I guess we didn't," Celeste said with a grimace. "I feel like an amateur. That should have been one of the first things we did. This house has such a confusing effect on me, and I don't think it's because of Andrew. There is still something else at work here. But at least we have cleared up the mystery surrounding the fire. Andrew was suppressing the memory of it, so it was popping out for me to see. I do love logical explanations."

"Wait a minute," Robert said. "You were the only ones who saw the flames, right?"

"That's correct. I was seeing flames and Emma was viewing a red glow and you, I believe, were looking at a fainter red glow."

"Oh, yeah, I almost forgot about that. So, is Andrew still here?"

"Yes, he is. We have a bit more work to do before Andrew is able to leave. But, now that we know what is holding him here, we can work through it with him," Celeste said. "It shouldn't take more than one or two more visits. He's played out for today, though."

"So, are you ladies ready to go?"

"Celeste?" Emma asked.

"Yes, yes. We may as well go. We've helped calm things a bit. I feel like we've accomplished something. Let's go then."

Robert turned on his flashlight and led them out, turning off lights as he went. He made a mental note that they had not seen one spider while inside. Approaching the car, they found Jeremy asleep in his. Robert didn't want to startle him with the sound of his car, so he went over and tapped on Jeremy's window. Jeremy was still startled, but at least Robert was standing there.

"Man, you trying to give me a heart attack?"

"We're headed out. Didn't want to startle you starting the car. Any luck tonight?" Robert asked.

Jeremy laughed. "Well, I guess I don't know since I fell asleep. I'll have to review the footage tomorrow."

"What are you hoping to see, bud?"

"I'm kinda hopin' for a wolfman, but I'll settle for a wolf." Jeremy laughed again.

Robert laughed with him and waved goodbye. What Robert didn't know, was that this would be the last time he would see Jeremy.

CHAPTER 36

"Emma?" Cheryl's question came over the phone. "Emma, were you at the house last night? Tell me you were at the house last night. Tell me Jeremy is with you."

"Calm down, Cheryl. I was at the house with Celeste and Robert last night, and Jeremy was there, too. But he was in his car. He's not with me. Why would you even think he might be?"

"One of the neighbors called the police and the police called Mom because his car was there all night and it's still there but . . . he's not in it. The neighbor said lights were coming from inside the house and another car had been there but left," said Cheryl, her voice shaky. "Emma, he's missing. They've searched the house and the woods. They can't find him."

"This doesn't sound good," Emma murmured. "Let me call Robert and see if he's heard from him. I'll call you right back."

Emma brought Robert up on her phone and hit the call button.

"Hello, gorgeous," he said.

"Is Jeremy with you?" Emma asked without acknowledging Robert's compliment.

"No," Robert said slowly. "Should he be?"

"His car is still at Cheryl's mom's house, but he's nowhere to be found. We were hoping maybe he was with you."

"Nope. Haven't heard from him. Maybe he ran his battery down watching those camera monitors and had to walk?"

"Why wouldn't he have called someone?" Emma asked. "Why would he leave in the night and not call someone?"

"Again, his battery could have died. He'd have been forced to either start walking or wait for someone to show up."

"That makes sense, and if his phone were dead, he wouldn't be able to answer, either. He could still be out there somewhere walking back home," Emma said, but the last few words faded off. "I need to call Cheryl! She's worried sick. We could go out and retrace his steps. You're right, he's probably out there walking. Talk to you later. Bye!"

Emma dialed Cheryl as quickly as she could. "Cheryl, I'm coming to get you. Robert thinks Jeremy could be walking home with a dead phone. We're going to go look for him."

"That would be a very long walk," Cheryl said. "Why would he do that?"

"Think about it . . .. He was running a computer and maybe more off the car battery. He could have drained it and his phone. I'm in my car. See you when I get there. Meet me out front?"

"Okay," Cheryl said, her mind already drifting to Jeremy on some country road trying to walk home. What if he got turned around? He could be anywhere.

Cheryl grabbed her bag and her phone, and she walked out to the sidewalk to wait for Emma. She felt better knowing there was a possibility Jeremy could be okay—maybe tired and hungry, but not really missing.

Emma pulled up, and Cheryl didn't notice her as she was that deep in thought.

"Get in," Emma yelled out the open car window.

Cheryl jumped at the sound, quickly getting in the car and fastening her seatbelt. "Stop at the Whataburger," she said.

"Really?" Emma cast her a sideways glance. "You want to stop for a burger now? I thought you'd be more anxious to find him. You sounded so worried over the phone."

"I am worried, but he's going to be hungry. We need to have a sandwich for him and some fries and a drink. Gawd! I don't even know what he likes to drink." Cheryl started to cry.

"It's alright, sweetie. We'll get him some food and a Dr. Pepper. This is Texas—everybody drinks Dr. Pepper. He'll be fine with that."

"Okay." Cheryl nodded and dried her tears. "I think you're right. I think I've seen him drink a Dr. Pepper. Yes, that'll work."

After getting the food, they headed to Jeremy's house. They would work their way back to his car. The police were in his driveway. Emma stopped and explained who they were.

"So, he had a reason to be there all night?" Detective Hillard asked.

"Well," Emma said, "I don't know about *all* night, but he would have been there pretty late. We're about to drive the route between here and there to see if maybe he's walking home."

"Why would he be doing that?" Detective Hillard asked.

"His car battery might have died and the same with his phone," Cheryl answered. "Can we go now?"

"You say you were there last night, Miss . . .?" Detective Hillard paused to let Emma fill in the blank.

"Emma," she said. "Emma Rivers. Yes, with my mentor and a friend of mine. We all spoke with Jeremy, who was sitting in his car when we left."

"What was he looking for with all the cameras?" he asked.

"He had found evidence there was a gray wolf in the area. They're not indigenous around here, so he was looking for irrefutable proof. He was excited about sharing his findings," Cheryl said. "We really need to go look for him. We've brought him lunch and everything. Can we go, please?"

"Let me get your contact information. I'm going to have more questions for Ms. Rivers," he said.

They exchanged numbers, then Emma and Cheryl were on their way. They weren't even out of town yet when they saw a man walking in their direction. Cheryl squealed, and Emma sped up. As they came closer, they realized it was not Jeremy. Cheryl quickly deflated, and Emma slowed down to a crawl. They were well out of town now, and there was little traffic. These were mini-ranches they were passing along the side of the road. Jeremy could have stopped at any one of them to rest or ask for help.

They had one more incident of thinking they saw him walking toward them, but it turned out to be someone else. Cheryl's spirits were wilting with each passing mile. Emma was running out of cheerful things to say.

"Who might he have called if he went up to a house for help?" Emma asked.

"Me. Jeremy would have called me," Cheryl cried.

"Maybe he doesn't have your number memorized. Maybe there is someone he's known a long time. Maybe there's a tracker buddy. Did you hear him talk about any other friends?"

"He's kind of a loner," Cheryl said after calming down again. "I've never met any of his friends. We didn't even hang out that much. He spends his free time watching those videos and watching the monitors in real time."

"Well, we're getting close to the house. We're going to need some other kind of clue because he doesn't seem to be on this road."

"He's a tracker. If he was walking, he might know of a shortcut that—" Cheryl was cut off by a short burst from a police siren. Detective Hillard was pulling them over.

"Do you have news of Jeremy?" Emma asked when he approached her car.

"I'm headed to the Brently estate now. A detective thinks he has found signs of a struggle in the woods beyond the house. I'll know more when I get there. I take it you two are working your way over there?" he asked.

"Yes, we've been going slow and visually searching the fields and side roads. He could be in any of the homes along this road," Emma answered.

Emma had a feeling Jeremy was in deep trouble. All her senses were telling her he was still alive but wouldn't be for long. But she dared not mention it in front of Cheryl.

"I hate to say it, but some of us are beginning to suspect foul play. I don't think you will find your friend along this road."

"You think he's dead?" Cheryl yelled.

"No, ma'am," Detective Hillard said. "We just think it's curious the way he disappeared. You said he had a laptop in the car. It's gone. But his other equipment is still in the car, and the car was not locked. In fact, the keys were in the ignition. Why would he leave all this equipment in an unlocked car unless he thought he was coming right back?"

"Maybe he was pulled away by a new track he hadn't seen before," Cheryl said, knowing how easily that could have happened.

"Maybe . . ." Detective Hillard said, "but what if he ran into something or someone in the woods that overpowered him and dragged him off to some location, we haven't found yet. You said he was tracking a gray wolf. There are wolf tracks all over the place out there. Maybe he tracked one a little too close."

"He wasn't trying to catch one. He was only trying to capture one on video. He wouldn't have gotten out of the car to track one at night," Cheryl said.

"So, you worked with him a lot when he was doing these stakeouts?" Detective Hillard asked.

"Well, no . . . not exactly," Cheryl said. "I just know from the things he told me. He was always going on about proper procedure and telling stories of some of the stupid things people did when they were on a stakeout. He talked about how fierce gray wolves could be, especially at night."

"Hmm," Detective Hillard murmured under his breath. "If he wasn't following a wolf, then what was he following?"

"Good question," Emma said as her phone rang; Madam Celeste's name flashed across the screen. Emma had lost track of time.

"Hello, Celeste. We have a situation. I'm with the police and Cheryl over at the Brently house. Jeremy has gone missing, but his car is still here," she said, trying to get in as much as possible before Celeste had a chance to get angry with her.

"I see," Celeste said with a clipped tone. "A phone call would have been nice, but I'm sure you've been occupied."

"Yes, you could say that. I've been driving Cheryl around looking for him. The police are beginning to suspect foul play. I'll tell you all about it when I get there, but it's going to be a while. I don't have any clients this morning. You can let the phone go to voicemail, and I'll deal with the messages when I get in if you don't mind."

"Of course, dear," Celeste said. "That will be fine. I need to take a walk to the creek so I may not be here when you arrive. I hear we're expecting rain for a few days and I don't want to lose any crystals to flooding now, do I?"

"Absolutely not, Madam Celeste. I'll see you later," Emma said before turning to the detective. "Madam Celeste said we're expecting rain for the next few days. Could that mess up the tracks and the scene?"

"We'll have pictures of the whole scene and video by the end of the day. Too bad we don't have Jeremy's footage," Detective Hillard said.

"You might," Cheryl said. "There are SD cards in some of the cameras."

"Really?" The detective grabbed his car radio and said, "Smiley, check the trail cameras for SD cards. We have a young lady here who worked with the subject. She's reporting that the cameras used SD cards, not a central hard drive."

"Roger that." Smiley's voice squawked over the walkie-talkie. A few moments passed before Smiley's voice came over again. "Hillard? There are no cameras mounted . . . at least none that we were able to find. Maybe he took them down, or was taking them down when the incident happened?"

"Then where are they?" Hillard asked.

"Another good question," Emma murmured. "Cheryl, I need to get to work. Do you want a lift?"

"Yes, I guess I'm not much use here."

They drove in silence for a few minutes before Cheryl turned to Emma. "What does your psychic intuition tell you, Emma? Is he okay?"

Emma hesitated, "I . . . uh . . . I'm not sure."

"What do you mean you're not sure? You're bound to be picking up something!"

"It feels like he's in trouble but . . . it feels like he's alive," Emma said softly. "When I try to see him or anything about him, it's like I'm blind. It's just dark. Maybe he's asleep."

"Asleep? Asleep? You've got to be kidding me. It's the middle of the day. Why would he be asleep? Why can't you get a fix on him? Why can't you find him? You're a psychic for crying out loud! You should be able to see what's going on," Cheryl cried.

"Psychics can't always see what they want to see, Cheryl. I know you're upset, but you can't blame me for not being able to find him. That's what makes me think he's alive. If he was dead, it would be much easier to find him, I think. I don't know because I've not dealt with anyone immediately after they died. I think it might take a few days. That's a question I'll be asking Celeste this afternoon. With that being said, my gut feeling is that you need to prepare for the worst."

"Then we need to go back and tell Detective Hillard, so he'll turn up the hunt. If Jeremy is still alive, they could find him before anything bad happens," Cheryl said.

"He knows," Emma said softly. "I could see it in his eyes. He knows he's racing a clock, and his best bet is to follow the evidence at the scene. We need to let the police do their job."

"I just feel so useless and helpless and frustrated," Cheryl said, looking out the window.

The rest of the ride home was quiet. Emma dropped Cheryl at her house and headed to work. She took the Whataburger in to nuke it and had it for lunch, but her thoughts kept drifting back to Jeremy. It was like she could see, but everything was just too dark.

CHAPTER 37

Jeremy came to slowly. It was dead of night dark. His shoulder was throbbing with pain and his left ear hurt and felt damp. As he regained more of his awareness, he realized he was bound to a chair. He could feel and smell duct tape across his face. But why was it so dark? A bag, there was a bag over his head. He squirmed to see if he could loosen the binding. The next thing he heard sent shivers down his spine—a low guttural growl. There was a wolf in the room—if it was indeed a room—and it was close.

He sat very still. *How did a wolf tie me up? Am I in a cave? How did I get here? What am I doing here?*

"What's the last thing you remember, Jeremy," he said to himself. "Think. Snap out of it! Where are you and how did you get here?"

Wait, he thought. *I saw something on the monitor. It looked human, but I wasn't sure. I went to collect the SDs so I could review them at home. I saw fresh tracks and started to follow them. Then what . . .? Think! What happened next?*

He shook his head as if to shake the cobwebs free. The wolf growled again—it sounded as if it had moved closer. Why had it not attacked him yet? He was a sitting duck. Was this the wolf he had captured on the trail cam? What kind of sick game was this?

Who would tie a man up, then leave him helpless in a room with a wolf?

Unless . . .. Maybe the wolf is also tied up? That would explain part of it—the fact that I'm still alive and in one piece. But what would anyone want with me?

He heard a sound, like a set of keys in the next room. The wolf growled, and Jeremy heard the door open. The wolf scratched its paws on the pavement as if trying to reach the newcomer to no avail. Jeremy was sure this was the wolf he had been tracking. It sounded huge. He heard a wet plop, and the sound of the wolf tearing at something. Assuming it was raw meat tossed to the animal, Jeremy wondered if the wolf had somehow been at least partially domesticated—maybe not a pet, but perhaps an asset.

Since the animal seemed to be placated for the moment, Jeremy asked why he was there. He was greeted with silence. His captor was smart. At this point, Jeremy didn't know whether he was being held by a male or a female. That meant there was hope since he could in no way identify them. As if on cue, Jeremy's hood was removed. His hopes were momentarily crushed until he realized that he had a blindfold on. His captor really didn't want to be identified. He felt better.

"What do you want with me?" Jeremy asked nervously.

No answer. Then he felt a fork at his lips. Was his captor attempting to feed him? They grabbed his jaw to force his mouth open, which brought him to cooperate. It was some sort of sandwich that had been cut into large, bite-sized bits. It tasted good after having had no breakfast. He wondered how long he had been here. Was anyone looking for him? Would they even notice he was gone?

His captor left the room, but not before replacing the hood. As he heard the door close behind them, Jeremy tried to reconstruct the night before. He had been tracking the wolf. It had come into view on the monitor, once again looking directly into the camera as if it knew it was being recorded. Then came a human with a hat covering their face. Jeremy couldn't tell if it was a man or a woman. He jumped out of the car to retrieve the SD cards from the cameras.

He wanted to examine what he had seen. Swapping out the cards on all the cameras took a few minutes since they all had to be labeled and replaced. He looked for tracks. The wolf tracks were everywhere, but the most recent ones stood out. There were no human tracks to be seen. Where had they disappeared to? They had to be there. He had seen someone. There had to be tracks.

Jeremy followed the fresh wolf tracks to the edge of the woods where the ground turned to rock, and the tracks were more difficult to see, but nowhere on the way did he pick up any human tracks.

"Very curious," he said out loud before everything went black. He assumed it was several hours before he regained consciousness to find himself in his current predicament.

"That explains my throbbing head," he said. "So, someone knocked me out and dragged me here, but why?"

The musky smell of the wolf was becoming more obvious as he regained full awareness. It permeated the room. He had smelled it before with part wolf dogs. There were people in the area that would breed wolves with dogs to the point of the resulting animal being far more wolf than dog. It was illegal to breed them more than a certain percentage wolf, but there was a market, so it was done. The smell was the same. It had an overpowering feeling of wild to it. Jeremy was glad it was chained up.

"Why are you here?" said Jeremy to himself and the wolf.

The wolf snarled and Jeremy felt the distinct slight breeze of the wolf lunging toward him. Another inch and he would probably be bleeding. He remained silent after that. No need to upset the big bad wolf creature.

Jeremy spent the rest of the day thinking about rescue scenarios. One involved the police being tipped off about the wolf breeding going on and finding him in the process. Another one had Cheryl and Robert finding him from following the clues from the scene. Another had the police doing the same. It lifted his spirits, but his hopes were dashed again when his captor came in to administer dinner.

"I haven't seen you, you know. Why not just take me back to the woods and release me? You can leave me blindfolded. I have no clue who you are or what you could possibly want with me."

Silence.

"Are you worried I'll keep investigating? Cause I won't. I know there's a gray wolf out here, but I don't need to prove it to anyone. Your secret is safe with me and even if I slipped up and shared it, it wouldn't hurt you . . .. I don't know who you are or where we are."

The wolf growled as if it knew Jeremy was lying. He assumed his captor was a woman from the way she fed him so gently with the utensil, coming from an angle low enough to indicate she was not more than five feet. This small woman may not have been the one who captured him, but she was the one keeping him.

She also had a fresh smell. Jeremy could smell it over the wolf whenever she came in. It was a blessing to get to smell something other than the animal. He had thought he would get used to it, but he hadn't yet. So, her entry was a gift. The food tasted like it was prepared by a woman, too. He couldn't explain it, but he could taste a woman's love in it. He understood he was giving her these attributes to make himself feel safer. After all, a kind and loving woman wouldn't hurt him, right? She would be more inclined to help him escape if the opportunity arose.

It was a little fantasy that helped the time pass easier, nothing more, but still . . .. It could be true. He tried to engage her in conversation, but she never slipped. He knew it was for his own good. If he could identify her, she would need to kill him. They had devised a system for bathroom breaks where he kept the blindfold on until inside the door and then replaced it before coming out.

She continued to keep him tied to the chair. His body ached from the lack of movement. He lost track of days.

"I know you're a woman," he said one day as she was feeding him. She immediately backhanded him, and then there was no food or contact for a time after that.

The next time she came in, Jeremy could hear someone shuffling around—the steps sounded heavier, more aggressive. The woman came closer to him to feed him. He was used to the routine. She removed the hood. But instead of offering a bite of food, she slit his tongue. She replaced the bag, acted like she was taking him on a bathroom break, but instead, led him up the stairs and out to the pasture.

He had been in the wrong place at the wrong time. His body would never be found. Did you know, hungry wolves will eat a carcass completely, not even leaving the bones?

CHAPTER 38

The investigation started the morning Jeremy came up missing. Detective Hillard had an All-Points-Bulletin with Jeremy's picture and last known location. The abandoned car suggested foul play. There was no physical indication he had left by foot in any direction other than the forest.

"These wolf tracks are significant. Arty, come with me and document them," the detective said to Arty, the videographer and media specialist.

The two men followed the tracks into the woods.

"Do you think the wolf got him," Arty asked.

"Makes sense," the detective said. "But there's no blood on the trail or any signs of a body being dragged. It's a mystery."

"Those girls were talking about a lot of eerie things going on at that house," Arty said. "Do you think the two things are related?"

"You mean, do I think we need to get involved in that mystery, too?"

"Kind of," Arty said. "If they're related."

"They probably are," Detective Hillard said. "They're too close to each other to be coincidental. We'll continue the search for another day, then switch to interviewing anyone involved in the incidents inside the house. For now, I want all efforts going into physically searching for this young man. Something tells me he's in serious trouble."

"Roger that."

They followed the trail deep into the woods where it cut back on them. Now they were headed back toward the house. There was a ranch house in the distance when they reached a spot where it looked like the wolf had curled up and laid down. The wolf then got up and trotted off in the direction of the ranch house. The two men followed the tracks quite a distance before they found footprints. They appeared to be small boots.

The person wearing them had walked around in the area then walked back to the house. There were several sets of wolf prints. They walked up to the ranch and were greeted, not too pleasantly, by three German shepherds. They weren't traditional German shepherds—they seemed to be mixed with something.

Detective Hillard and Arty stayed still and waited for the ranch owner. It only took a few minutes for a woman wielding a rifle to appear at the back door.

"What're you fellas doin' round here at my backyard?" Darla Weatheral yelled.

"We're with the police, ma'am," Detective Hillard said, flashing his badge at her. "We're looking for a missing person. We followed some tracks over here through the woods."

"I ain't seen anybody," Darla yelled. "Y'all need to get on outta' here. Nobody comes on this property the back way except for Teresa, me, and my dogs."

"Yes, ma'am," the detective said with a nod. "We'll head on back the way we came in. If someone had been through here, I imagine your dogs would have let you know, right?"

"They would for a fact."

"And you haven't seen anyone in the last twenty-four hours?"

"No, sir, I have not."

"Thank you for your help, Ms—?"

"Darla, Darla Weatheral."

"Is your husband around?" the detective asked.

"Not for years," Ms. Weatheral said. "Now git!"

The dogs began to growl, and the men turned to leave.

"Those were some mean looking dogs," Arty said once they were a safe distance from the ranch.

"Dogs, hell, those looked more like wolves," Detective Hillard said. "Are you thinking what I'm thinking?"

"That maybe one of those bad boys attacked Jeremy Maherg?"

"Or at least maybe one of them made an appearance on his tracker camera," Detective Hillard said.

"They do look like wolves. Seeing one in the woods . . . I'd sure think it was a wolf," Arty said.

"And we've just followed their tracks from the woods behind the Brently house," Hillard said slowly. "Doesn't explain what happened to him, but it might explain what he saw."

"I can't make sense out of why he took all the trail cams and the laptop with him, either. Maybe the girls are right. Maybe the car died, and he took off for home on foot."

"Makes as much sense as trailing a dog into the woods thinking it's a wolf, I guess," Hillard said. "Let's get a search warrant for his apartment and see what we can find there."

"You want me to document that, too?" Arty asked.

"Oh, yes! I don't want to lose any evidence to memory or hearsay. Why don't you go check for tracks around the Brently house while I get the warrant started."

Arty walked off to video anything out of the ordinary around the house and Hillard went to his car. As he was getting in, the phone rang.

"Officer Hillard?" came a familiar voice.

"Detective Hillard," he corrected.

"This is Emma. My friend Cheryl and I were out searching for Jeremy this morning?" she questioned whether or not he recognized her.

"Yes, I remember. I assume you didn't find Jeremy," Detective Hillard said.

"We didn't. I work for a psychic, and we're going to see what she can tell us."

"A psychic? You're bringing in a psychic. Wonderful. We have witnesses who've seen ghosts and phantom spiders and wolves, and now we're consulting a psychic. We don't need a detective . . . we need a circus director."

"Detective Hillard, I am a psychic, but I lack the experience of Madam Celeste. Please don't mock her."

"Madam Celeste," the detective scoffed. "Why does that name ring a bell?"

"Maybe because she's worked with the FBI on a case right here in Gloryville and was instrumental in solving it," Emma snipped, sounding rather miffed.

"Well, I guess if the FBI uses her, there must be something to it," Hillard said. "And what about you? You say you're a psychic, too?"

"That's right. I'm Madam Celeste's apprentice. I have abilities. What I'm working on is training and experience, which improves every day."

"I'll be interested in hearing what she has to say about this one. Your friend is definitely missing without a trace. Won't be surprised if someone brings up UFOs next." He laughed. "I have to get busy here, so if you'll excuse me."

"Certainly." Emma heard him close the police car door to what might as well be a mobile office. "I swear he's got a fax machine in there," she said to Cheryl chuckling.

"Really, Emma? Do you think this is a time for jokes?" Cheryl snapped.

"No, I was just saying, he has everything to run an office in that car," Emma clarified.

"Where do we look for Jeremy?" Cheryl asked.

"I'm going back to work and talk the whole thing through with Madam Celeste," Emma said. "I'll drop you off wherever you like."

"Will you take me to Jeremy's?"

"Sure. Detective Hillard will be over there soon. He's getting a warrant now."

"I know where he hides his spare key," Cheryl said. "I won't need to wait for the detective."

"Maybe you should, though. Maybe it would be best if the police had all the evidence in place as Jeremy left it. You could call him and tell him where the key is hidden and then wait on him. What do you say?"

"I'm tired of waiting and watching and not making any progress. I want to *do* something. I want to find him. I want to know he's safe," Cheryl said as the tears started to flow again.

"Sweetie, it's okay. Cry all you want. It's definitely a crying time. Let me drop you off at your mom's house. You can hang out there, and when I finish this afternoon, I'll come to pick you up."

"I guess that's as good a place as any," Cheryl mumbled.

CHAPTER 39

When Emma arrived at Celeste's, she was seeing a client out.

"What's the good news, dear?"

"Well, Jeremy hasn't popped up as a ghost yet," Emma said.

"I wouldn't expect him to right away," Celeste said. "Some show up immediately, but it's not that often. They'll show up for a few days and then disappear, or they won't show up at all for a few months or even years, if ever. No, I wouldn't count on any help from Jeremy right away. Are you certain he's dead?"

"No." Emma shook her head. "And I truly hope he isn't. But people don't disappear like this as a rule. He was actively investigating a sighting of something exciting to him. He couldn't wait to share it with his colleagues. That's not the kind of person who just up and leaves without packing a bag or leaving a note, is it?"

"When you put it like that, it is certainly suspicious. Still, we don't want to give up hope quite yet. He may turn up and be surprised at all the fuss."

"But we've looked everywhere!" Emma moaned.

"Obviously not everywhere," Celeste said. "No one has found him or any sign of him. So, it seems you have not looked everywhere."

"That's just semantics. You know what I meant. We've looked in every place we can think of to look," Emma said, clearly frustrated.

"Did you go into the house?"

"He doesn't have a key to the house and why would he go in there?" Emma asked, feeling like an idiot for not having thought to look. The police probably assumed they had looked in there, too.

"I wasn't suggesting he would be in the house. I was curious if the situation had changed since we had a breakthrough with Andrew. Are there fewer spider webs forming? Is the feeling less smothering? That sort of thing."

"Oh. No, we didn't go in . . .. We were distracted by Jeremy being missing," Emma said.

"There's nothing we can do that you haven't already done to help find Jeremy. So, let's focus on the job at hand, shall we?" Celeste asked.

"That's a good idea. Maybe the two are connected in some way we just haven't seen yet. Solving one may reveal a clue about the other. Would you like to go over there and see what the atmosphere is like now?"

"I think I have another appointment this afternoon, but as soon as I'm free, that would be excellent," Celeste said.

"What was I thinking? Of course, you have appointments. I guess I'm more flustered than I realized. I'll wait for you here and answer phones and catch up on some other work," Emma said.

"It's quite alright, dear. It can be quite upsetting, especially for someone who is gifted, to not be able to find someone. We're supposed to be able to just think of a particular person and know where they are, but most of the time that isn't the case, is it?" Celeste asked, trying to comfort her apprentice any way she could.

"No, no, it's not—" Emma was interrupted by the phone. She immediately picked it up. "Madam Celeste's. How can we help fulfill your destiny today?"

"I need to talk to the head witch," the caller said as though asking for the head nurse in a trauma ward.

"Witch?" Emma recoiled. "What are you talking about? Madam Celeste is a psychic."

"The two are not mutually exclusive," the caller snipped. "Is this Madam Celeste the person in charge?"

"Yes, ma'am, she is," Emma said.

"Then that's who I want to talk to."

"May I ask what this is about?" Emma asked, trying to remain as professional as possible.

"I need the help of a witch. I think my son is under the influence of a spell. I need it counteracted."

Celeste had waited in case she was needed. Emma muted the phone and told Celeste the situation. Celeste took the phone.

"This is Madam Celeste. Can you tell me why you think your son is under the influence of a spell?"

"He's not himself lately. He's spending more time on the phone than studying, and he's been talking about a girl at school he wants to see after school."

"That sounds like a typical teenage boy," Madam Celeste said. "This is a stage he could be in for a few years. I would be surprised if there was a witch involved. But even if there was, what do you think I would be able to do?"

"You could counter the spell. You could talk with the girl and get her to stop."

"I'm sorry. Do I know this girl?" Celeste asked slowly.

"Well, I think she's a witch," the caller said.

"You are making a lot of assumptions. First, I am not a card-carrying witch that belongs to a coven. Second, I don't know any witches. Third, this girl is probably just a girl who your son has become smitten with—which does give her a lot of power over him, but not because of witchcraft. Fourth, I cannot change that. If you'd like to make an appointment to come in and have your cards read, I'd be happy to give you back to my assistant who could set you up with an appointment." Celeste remained calm but firm.

"Um, well . . . yes, alright. Let me make an appointment."

Celeste handed the phone to Emma, who made quick work of creating an appointment for the new client.

"Celeste, you told that woman that you weren't a witch, but you told me you are a solitary," Emma said once she hung up.

"I don't like what the word "witch" means to people like that. They get their ideas from television and movies and the wrong books. They have no concept of what a witch is. They think I can snap my fingers and make things manifest out of nothing or make people do my bidding. And they think I serve a dark lord or Satan, or some other evil male being. They don't know how much they don't know. It's dangerous to tell someone like that, that you're a witch."

"But you do consider yourself a witch, right? I mean, you use spells and crystals and herbs."

"I do those things, yes. But I am a solitary soul. I am bound to no one for my beliefs or practices, and neither are you. I will teach you what works for me, but it's up to you to find what works for you. I will help you find your way. I will show you ways to expand your mind and soul. You will decide who and what you are."

"Was your mother a solitary or a witch?" Emma asked.

"Not to my knowledge, no," Celeste said as she shook her head. "She belonged to a Christian church and went faithfully every Sunday."

"My mother isn't anything. She doesn't go to church and doesn't seem to believe in God or souls or anything like that," Emma offered.

"Is she happy?"

Emma was quiet for a moment. "Most of the time, she seems to be."

"Then she has found what works for her this time around," Celeste said and patted Emma's hand gently. "Be happy for her."

"Do you think Jeremy is still alive?" Emma asked, changing the subject.

"There's always hope."

"Then I won't give up on trying to find him yet," Emma said.

"Good plan," Celeste said. "I need to freshen up before my next client, but we will be going to the spider house afterward, yes?"

"Yes . . . and Celeste?"

"Yes, dear?"

"Thank you for taking me on. I couldn't have found a better teacher," Emma said softly.

"You help me as much as I help you. Don't forget that. You are a wonderful student."

"Thanks," Emma said with a tear in her eye.

Emma's personal phone rang, and Cheryl's name flashed across the screen.

"When are you picking me up?" she asked before Emma could even greet her.

"It'll probably be around five or five-fifteen," Emma said. "Unless you need me to come later?"

"No, that will be fine. I'm just anxious to *do* something. I'm tired of sitting here waiting," Cheryl said, hoping that Emma would come earlier.

"That's as soon as I can make it. I'm bringing Madam Celeste to your mom's house to check on the situation with the spiders and the spirits."

"I still don't want to drive. I've been crying so much my vision is blurry," Cheryl said sadly.

Emma tried to think of something useful that Cheryl could do in the meantime. It wouldn't hurt for her to pump her mom for more information about the house and her neighbor Darla, or anything she might know about Andrew. Cheryl agreed to try. Her mom wasn't the talkative type, and she didn't hold much hope in learning anything new, but she would give it her best shot. Who knew? Maybe Mom would open up today.

CHAPTER 40

"Mom?"

"Yes, dear?"

"Did Andrew ever stay with us?"

"Andrew? Who is Andrew?" her mother asked distractedly.

"You knew his mom. He was that kid who desperately wanted to be friends with Pete. Maybe you had him over or something," Cheryl said.

"I don't really recall it," her mother said. "What was his mother's name?"

"Bell, I think," Cheryl said.

"I don't think I've ever known a woman named Belle, and if I did, I think I would remember it."

"No not Belle . . . Mrs. Bell. Bell was their last name. At least it was Andrew's last name."

"Mary Bell? That sounds familiar. We were friends when you kids were younger. We would have play dates at the park and sometimes at the ranch. Yes, if I recall correctly, that little boy was an odd one. Not what you'd call a happy-go-lucky child. As you kids grew older and started middle school, Mary and I drifted apart. I was more involved in your father's real estate business, and she was mostly involved with her child. I personally always thought she smothered the boy. But Pete is dead, so who's to say I did any better."

"He's not dead because of you, Mother," Cheryl said softly.

"He's not alive, either. And that is the primary job of a mother—keep them alive. I didn't do that, did I?"

"You can't blame yourself for a boating accident," Cheryl said.

"Let's agree to disagree. You are not the first person to have this conversation with me."

"Well, I'm more interested in Andrew today. You know he died, too."

"Did he really?" her mother asked. "How sad for Mary. I wonder what she's doing these days. He was her whole life. I hope she found another reason to live."

"You almost sound mean, Mother. You sound like she was beneath you."

"Not at all, dear. I just think Mary was too wrapped up in her child. It must have been devastating for her."

"Yes, I imagine it was," Cheryl murmured. She sat there watching her mother work. She was doing paperwork and Cheryl assumed it was some real estate deal. Teresa Brently enjoyed Real Estate the way most people enjoyed eating. She was a natural at it and had almost beaten Mr. Brently to getting a broker's license. And he had been in the field long enough to be successful when they met.

"Mother? Do you think I should learn real estate? I mean, I've learned a lot from you, but do you think I should get a license?"

"I just assumed you would do that, dear, but not until you're ready. There's enough time. Enjoy your youth. What's come over you today? You're so reflective. Is it only because that young man has been unavailable today?" her mother asked.

"He's not just unavailable, Mother. He's *missing*. He could be dead for all we know. The police are taking it very seriously."

"I'm sure he's fine," her mother said dismissively.

"I'm sure he's not," Cheryl snapped. "Mother, you don't know what's been going on over there. There are ghosts—Pete and

Daddy are there. So is Andrew, and we think there's one more. Jeremy was tracking something big, something potentially dangerous. What if he found it and it attacked him or worse? Do you care about all of these things happening on our property?"

"Well, I didn't think it was anything serious. There's no such thing as ghosts, and you determined that the spiders were left from Pete, and maybe there are wolves in the woods. He shouldn't have gone in those woods at night unarmed, and you don't know he did."

"They haven't found anything out there in the way of an injured animal," Cheryl said. "If he went into the woods, he didn't win a battle with a wolf or wolves. There would be evidence of that, and he wouldn't be missing. He'd probably be out there bragging."

"I'm sure he will be unless he found it was all a hoax and there was actually no wolf and nothing out of the ordinary happening. I remember someone talking about buying something to put on their shoes to leave animal prints. They would use them for Bigfoot hoaxes, but there are probably wolf paws, too," her mother said.

"You just don't get it, Mom," Cheryl said before storming out of the room in a huff.

Cheryl had learned nothing. She had forgotten her mission was to get more information on Andrew and also to find out more about Darla. Having accomplished neither, she collected herself and prepared to go back in. It was like walking into an arena with a far superior opponent. Cheryl had never gotten the best of her mother. But maybe there was something about Darla that her mother would be willing to share.

"Mother?"

"Oh, I'm glad you're back. I need you to run some errands for me."

"I'm not driving today, Mother. My eyes are too blurry. I'm waiting for Emma to give me a lift to look for Jeremy."

"I didn't realize you were that involved with the young man," her mother said. "Where do you plan to look?"

"We'll start at the house. Emma and Celeste want to see what the spider situation is now and to also see about the ghosts that have been there. They think that one of them should be gone by now. Then we may look around in the woods for clues the police may have missed. It's a long shot, but it's better than sitting here twiddling my thumbs."

"If it makes you feel better, then go for it."

"We may go over to Darla's place and look around, too. She tried to convince Madam Celeste there was a skin-walker on the loose."

"Don't pay that much attention to Darla, dear. She's not quite . . .. Well, her shotgun isn't fully loaded, if you know what I mean. Her picnic is a couple of sandwiches light." She chuckled to herself. "I mean, really? A skin-walker? I thought only the Indians believed in those. Oh, wait. Last time I saw her she was telling me about how she's part Chickasaw or Cherokee or something and is probably obsessing over it," Cheryl's mom said.

"So, is she dumb or crazy?"

"I'm not too sure, but don't underestimate her," Teresa said. "She seems dumber than she is, and she's only crazy some of the time. The trick is determining which time is which."

"That doesn't make a lot of sense, Mom," Cheryl said.

"Okay, but don't you think it's crazy to talk about skin-walkers like they're real?"

"Mom, I've been telling you about ghosts or spirits, as Emma likes to call them. Do you think I'm crazy?"

"No, dear, just suggestible. People you trust have mentioned them, and you've let yourself suspend reason where spirits are concerned. It's not crazy or stupid."

"But Darla is?" Cheryl asked.

"But you're not Darla. You can reason. Darla is subject to get wrapped up in things she shouldn't. Don't compare yourself to her."

"What kind of things, Mom? What has she gotten wrapped up in? You were neighbors for a long time. What kind of things did she do when we lived there?"

"Well, this whole nonsense about being an Indian," her mom started. "I remember her parents. They were not Indians. They would be livid to hear her talk about it."

"What else?" Cheryl prompted.

"She fell in love with a carnie once and suddenly was going to be a gypsy. Swore there was gypsy blood in her from the "old country." It was ridiculous," Teresa scoffed.

"Sounds like quite a character," Cheryl said. "And she seems to keep an eye out on our house and land, which is a plus."

"What do you mean?" her mom asked. "Keeps her eye on? She would love nothing better than to own it."

"Really?" Cheryl said in disbelief.

"She's been acquiring all the properties around that little pond for years. Ours is the last one on her list. And I'm not selling," her mom said firmly.

"That little pond will hold a john boat and has some good fish in it," Cheryl said. "It's really not that small."

"Thirty- or forty-acres tops," her mom said. "Nothing to get excited about. She approached me years ago wanting to buy the north side of my property so she would own the whole lake. But what good is my property without access to the lake? It's just another dry mini ranch. I said no, and she's not been civil with me since."

"But she called Madam Celeste and told her about seeing strange lights and told her about the skin-walker . . .. We thought she was being a helpful neighbor," Cheryl said slowly.

"She's probably up to something," her mother sneered. "If people are convinced my place is haunted, maybe she thinks I'll sell it. But she needs to think again. I don't care if it's haunted and has a skin-walker, I won't be selling."

"Why do you care, Mom? It's not like you ever go over there. In fact, you go to great lengths not to go over there. Why not just sell it and not have to mess with it anymore?"

"It has sentimental value, Cheryl. You understand that, don't you? That was your father's family homestead. He would have wanted it to stay in the family."

Cheryl's phone rang. "Cheryl, are you ready?" Emma asked.

"Yes. How far off are you?"

"Be there in five minutes. Meet me out front?"

"Okay," she said and ended the call. "Mom, I have to go now. My friend and I are going over to the 'homestead' to see what paranormal activity is like today. Do you need anything while I'm there?"

"No, dear," her mom said. "But be careful. If that young man really is missing, then you don't know what happened. It could be related to the property in some way that's not paranormal."

"Don't worry, Mom," Cheryl said, kissing her on the cheek as she left.

CHAPTER 41

As they drove to the house, Cheryl filled Emma and Celeste in on what her mother had said about Darla not being a good source of information.

"She actually said the woman's crazy," Cheryl said. "My mom doesn't say things like that. And, of course, if anyone were to ask, she didn't say it. But there definitely seems to be a grudge against Darla."

"All because Darla wants to buy your house?" Emma asked. "There has to be more to it than that."

"Darla does have some pretty strange ideas," Cheryl said. "That whole skin-walker thing was kind of bizarre, especially now that Jeremy's gone missing."

"About Jeremy . . ." Emma said. "Celeste thinks it's too early to try to contact him. There's no way to know for certain that he's okay, but there's also no way to know for certain that he isn't . . .. Unless, of course, he makes an appearance, which Celeste says is highly unlikely."

"I think he's still alive," Cheryl said. "I will believe it until we find concrete evidence otherwise."

"As you should," Celeste said. "As you certainly should. There is some piece of the puzzle we're not finding yet. Maybe today."

They arrived to find Detective Hillard poking around out by the woods. He had found the original path on the northeastern side of the yard—the same path Cheryl and Jeremy had followed toward the lake the first time Jeremy was there. Detective Hillard seemed to be retracing Cheryl's steps from that first day.

"Ladies," he called, "you should have called. We've wrapped it up for the day, but we'll be back tomorrow. Can I help you?"

"This is my house," Cheryl said. "We have some things to do inside."

"What kind of things?" Detective Hillard asked.

"What business is that of yours?" Cheryl snapped.

"Well, it's a potential crime scene, and you are the one who insisted a crime had been committed. We're just looking for evidence and don't need it disturbed by anyone, regardless of how good those people's intentions are," Detective Hillard said. "Now, I'll ask again, what are you here for?"

"We're here to check on the energy of the house and to see if any spirits that were here have left," Madam Celeste said in her most official voice.

"If you hadn't worked with the FBI, I would be laughing right now, but since you have, I have to admit I'm curious. You will vouch for there being spirits in this house?"

"Oh yes," Madam Celeste said, "I have spoken with them myself. It's all quite real, sir. You are welcome to join us if you'd like."

"I'll do that," the detective said. "I'm not busy at the moment. It won't hurt to see what you think you've found."

"I appreciate you humoring me, Detective," Madam Celeste said with a smile. "Shall we go in?"

Cheryl unlocked the kitchen door, and they went in. Celeste headed straight for the study, wanting to see if Andrew was still there and was reasonably sure she could contact Mr. Brently in that room as well.

"Andrew? Are you here today?" Celeste asked.

"Yes," Andrew whispered timidly.

"Why so shy today, Andrew?" Celeste asked.

"Too many people here lately. I don't like it."

"You mean all the police?" Celeste asked.

"Yes and no. The police don't come inside, so they're easy to hide from. There was a lady here, too. She was burning a stick."

"Who was it, dear?"

"I couldn't see her face. The smoke seemed to hide it. She kept saying all the spirits needed to leave and go to the light. I didn't see any light or any other spirits, so I guess she was talking to some other folks."

"What did she say exactly?" Celeste asked.

"I don't remember exactly, but it sounded familiar . . . maybe it was something from a movie or a book. I didn't know there'd be a test."

"You know you can go someplace else," Celeste asked. "You don't have to stay here."

"This is where I stay. I don't really know any place else except my old house, and I don't want to go there. I don't know where else to be," Andrew said sadly.

"I can help with that," Paul offered, popping in out of nowhere. "Buddy, didn't you live in New York? There are lots of great places to visit there."

"That's where I died. I didn't have any money or good times there."

"Well, you don't need money now," Paul said with a smile. "We can take in a show or a game or hang out in Central Park. It'd be fun."

"I don't know how to do it . . ." Andrew whined.

"No problem," Paul said with a shrug. "I'll teach ya' everything you need to know."

"Before you go," Celeste started, "were there any other people here besides the police and the woman?"

"There was another woman a couple of nights ago. She wasn't burning a stick. She was looking for something. Opening doors and looking at all the power outlets."

"Did she find what she was looking for?" Celeste asked.

"Not that I could tell," Andrew said. "She didn't seem very happy about it, either."

"And you're sure it was two different women?" Emma asked.

"Pretty sure. The last one was hard to see because of the smoke, but I think they were different people. Like I said, there's just too many coming and going. I liked it better when it was quiet."

"Can we go already?" Paul asked. "New York City awaits us!"

"Yes, yes, go have fun," Celeste said, knowing with Paul's sense of time, they could be gone for a few hours or a few days or even weeks. Andrew was in good hands.

Celeste filled Detective Hillard in on what they had just learned about the two women.

"I wonder if Cheryl's mother was here trying to smudge the place for ghosts," she said.

"Smudge?" Detective Hillard asked.

"Yes, some people believe burning sage by itself and telling the spirits to leave will cleanse a house of spirits. In their defense, it sometimes works when done correctly by the right person. But you can't simply copy something you've watched on TV and expect that to yield the intended results."

"So, you think Mrs. Brently would try that when no one was around?" the detective asked.

"My mom doesn't even believe in ghosts," Cheryl stated. "She said so to me just this morning."

"A lot of people claim they don't believe, but many do so secretly. Your mother is a businesswoman. She might not want word to get out she believes in anything paranormal or supernatural."

"She seemed pretty serious to me," Cheryl said to Celeste. "She made me feel superstitious for going along with you. She also said that the spiders were just pets that had taken over the house, like cats or anything else. The exterminator will handle it. She seemed very sure of herself."

"Again," Celeste said, "she's a powerful businesswoman. I would expect nothing less than complete self-assurance on her part."

"Didn't you claim to have contacted the late Mr. Brently here?" the detective asked, changing the subject.

"We did contact Mr. Brently and his son, Pete," Emma said. "We are going to see if they are still here tonight. Though, much of the original activity seems to have died down since dealing with Andrew's issues and, of course, Pete and his trouble."

"Mr. Brently?" Celeste called. "Can you hear me?"

There was a long silence as Celeste and Emma gave Mr. Brently a chance to respond. After several minutes, they tried again.

"Maybe he's gone for good," Emma said.

"Shhh," Celeste whispered. "I think he's here but doesn't want us to know."

"You mean he's hiding like Andrew was?" Emma asked.

"He could be afraid of being found out," Celeste offered.

"About what?" Emma and the detective asked together.

"That remains to be seen," Celeste said. "Why don't you want to show yourself, Mr. Brently? Does it have anything to do with either of the women Andrew mentioned? One of them was your wife, wasn't it?"

"Maybe," Ray Brently said. "One can't be sure."

"You don't think you'd recognize your wife?" Celeste scoffed. "Even if she were smudging, I would think you would sense it was her."

"Sometimes, maybe it's not always her. Maybe there is another woman that has been here."

"Recently?" Celeste asked.

"Maybe . . .."

"Is my father here?" Cheryl asked. "That's who you're talking to, isn't it? Daddy? Have you seen Jeremy? He was looking for wolves in the woods. Can you help us find him?"

"Who is Jeremy? Why does my daughter think I would know anything about him?"

"He's missing. The last place he was seen was outside this house. Your daughter thinks you might have seen him. She's worried he's dead," Emma explained.

"He was here last night but not inside the house. He was out in the driveway and in the woods with cameras set up to record a wolf. Would you have paid any attention to someone working on a project in the woods?" Celeste asked.

"I didn't notice anyone here except you," he said quickly. "And that was when you were in the house. I don't watch the outside much. I can see it. I just don't give it much attention."

"We think there has been another woman inside the house. Andrew said she was looking for something," Celeste said. "Was there a woman here who was definitely not your wife?"

"Maybe," Brently said. "You're all a little foggy to me. It's not like when I was alive."

"You seem most reluctant to give us any useful information today, Mr. Brently. Is it because your daughter is with us?" Celeste asked.

Mr. Brently remained silent.

"Your daughter can't hear you, Mr. Brently. Only Emma and I can hear or see you. Is there something you don't want to tell us because you don't want your daughter to know?"

"I love my daughter," Brently said sincerely.

"Your father says he loves you, Cheryl," Emma said.

"I love you, too, Daddy," Cheryl said. "Can you help us find Jeremy? Maybe he's in the woods? We need to find him."

"I thought you were looking for a woman," Brently barked as he barged into Celeste's space looking like evil incarnate.

"There may be a connection," Celeste said calmly. "The woman is part of this whole mystery. I'm not certain how yet, but she is involved."

"Tell my daughter I will go looking for her friend," Brently said before he vanished.

"I really had more questions for him," Celeste said, annoyance tinging her tone. "Cheryl, your father said he will look for Jeremy."

"Oh, thank goodness!"

"It doesn't sound like you know any more now than you did when we walked in," Detective Hillard observed.

"But I do," Celeste said matter-of-factly. "I have determined, whether he realized it or not, Andrew was the one projecting the hallucinations. We have had no problems since he left. And I would have sworn it was Mr. Brently protecting his castle, so to speak. I have learned Mr. Brently is still hiding something from us, but it may have nothing to do with Jeremy."

"Hallucinations?" the detective asked.

"Yes, when we started coming over here there were some pretty wild hallucinations shared with six people simultaneously. It made it impossible to investigate because none of us could trust what we saw or heard," Emma said.

"He's hiding another woman, isn't he?" Emma asked Celeste.

"My father would never have cheated on my mother," Cheryl said defensively. "We would have known or at least suspected."

"We still don't know what he's hiding, Cheryl," Emma said. "You might be right. But there is a woman, and she is involved somehow."

"I don't like to hear such talk about my father. There is no proof."

"Maybe it's not about him cheating," Celeste said. "Maybe it's only about him doing business with someone other than your mother. Maybe there was a deal she knew nothing about. That's a possibility, isn't it?"

"Well, yes, I guess so. They could have signed paperwork without my mother knowing, but why wait until now to try to bring it to light or keep it hidden or whatever he's trying to do. This is too confusing."

"It is," Celeste nodded, "and I think your father could clear things up a bit if he wanted to. For some reason, he doesn't want you to know about it. He doesn't seem ashamed, just secretive." Celeste turned to the detective. "Detective Hillard, do you think you could give Cheryl a ride home? I think we might make more progress here with a smaller group. I promise we will report our findings to you as soon as there is something to report."

"Funny, that's usually my line. Weird to have someone else say it to me, but I understand. Cheryl, may I offer you a lift?" the detective asked.

"I don't like it . . .. I could be helpful. What if my father comes back? I could talk to him. I might get him to do something he won't do for you."

"I'm sorry, I know you don't understand, but your presence is part of the problem. Your father doesn't want to say certain things with you here"

"What things?" Cheryl asked Celeste.

"We won't know until we get him to talk," she answered. "And that will be a lot easier when you leave."

"Come on," Detective Hillard said. "Let's clear out of their way. They need some room to work. Let's let them try this their way."

CHAPTER 42

"Mr. Brently? We'd like to speak with you again. Can you come back now that Cheryl is gone?" Celeste asked.

There was another long stretch of silence. Both Celeste and Emma tried calling out to Mr. Brently to no avail. It seemed they were finished for the day.

"My dad's not here," Pete said appearing behind them. Emma and Celeste both jumped at the sound of his voice.

"You startled me!" Emma yelled and clutched her chest.

"You're looking for a spirit, and you get startled when one shows up? That's rich," Pete said sarcastically. "I don't know what you want with Dad, but he's definitely not here. You're lucky I was passing through and heard you. Otherwise, you'd have been standing here talking to the air."

"Do you pass through often?" Celeste asked.

"Not really. I was curious about what was going on over here and the next thing I knew . . . I was here. It works that way sometimes. I think about a place, and I'm there. Pretty cool, huh? So, it looks like the spiders are under control, although I do see one in the living room."

"Thanks for letting us know. Does that seem to be the only one left?" Celeste asked.

"Only one I can see," Pete said. "Won't guarantee it, though, because there could still be some hiding."

"Is there anything else unusual you're picking up on?" Celeste asked.

"Like what? It seems pretty much abandoned at this point. What do you want with my dad?"

"We were hoping he could help us find out about a woman that may have been here in the last few days or even weeks."

Not wanting to be left out of the conversation, Emma added, "Your dad might have even known her or at least known who she is. He didn't seem to want to talk about it in front of Cheryl, even though she couldn't hear or see him."

"Dad doesn't always make sense," Pete said. "But we don't hang out together a lot, so I don't know. Maybe he thinks she could start seeing him and he doesn't want to risk it."

"So, you don't know anything about the activity around here over the last few days?" Emma asked.

"Sorry, I haven't been here for a while. It's pretty boring now that the spiders are gone, and I'm not mad at Dad anymore."

"Well, thank you for talking with us. Do you think you could find your father and convince him to come back and talk with us?" Celeste asked.

"I'll see what I can do, but don't count on it. My father can be hard-headed about some things."

"We'll stay around for half an hour just to give you time to try," Emma offered.

"This is really rather a pleasant house with all the craziness out of the way, isn't it?" Celeste asked as a way to pass the time. Emma just nodded. She wasn't interested in small talk with the living right now. She was anxious to find out what Mr. Brently was hiding.

After some time, he popped in. "Ladies, I don't think I can help you much. I don't know this Jeremy, and I definitely don't know where he is."

"But you do know who the woman is, don't you?" Madam Celeste said sternly.

"Okay, this is the part I never want Cheryl or Teresa to know about. Do you promise?"

"Yes, Mr. Brently, we are quite reliable at keeping secrets," Celeste said.

"The woman is a neighbor I got a little closer to than I should have shortly before I died. It was exciting, and I was enjoying myself. Teresa, Cheryl, and Pete never suspected anything. No one was hurt by it. We only saw each other when Teresa was busy with other things. I even started to think I might love this woman, but . . . I didn't."

"Was the woman's name Darla?" Celeste asked quietly.

"How did you know that?" he asked.

"Let's just call it a lucky guess. When did you decide you didn't love her?"

"It was after I died actually," Mr. Brently said. "I went to comfort her. I hadn't been to her place before. The things I saw made me realize she was crazy, and I didn't want anything to do with her."

"What kind of things, Mr. Brently?"

"It's all so easy to see when you're dead. When you're alive, you have to take people at their word. They can wear a mask, and you'd never know. They can tell you things they think you want to hear, and you don't question it. I was a fool to think that insane woman could ever replace my Teresa."

"What kind of things did she do? Or should I say, does she do?" Celeste asked.

"For one thing, she has a pet wolf over there. You can't domesticate a wolf—they're wild. If they get hungry enough, they will eat you. And what if it gets free? Do you know what kind of havoc he could set loose? And she's been breeding him with half wolves and more. Do not go over there!"

"She called me, you know," Celeste said. "Wanted me to know there might be a skin-walker around these parts. She claimed to be a friend of your wife."

"That's not true! They were never friends."

"What about the skin-walker? Do you think there is such a thing in the woods or anywhere hereabouts?"

"No. That's all Darla's wolf and her almost wolves. It's against the law, you know. It's against the law to own them or breed them."

"When was the last time you were over there, Mr. Brently?" Emma asked.

"It's been a long time. I was there for a few months after I died—that is, until I saw what she was doing. She's a prepper, too. There's at least a year's worth of dried food and emergency items in that basement. She's one of those people who believe in the apocalypse. Tell me, who would want to survive in such a world? Living off emergency rations and having to kill people to stay alive. She has all kinds of weapons. She could open a store. And ammunition? Buckets and buckets of it." Mr. Brently continued, "This is cattle country. What does she think she needs all that stuff for? Ranchers help each other out. Sure, they can fruit and vegetables and also dry beef for the hard times, but this goes way beyond that." He paused. "How does one get so afraid of the future? And how did I fall for her without realizing that she was nuts? It makes me look like an idiot, or worse."

"So, you haven't seen any sign of a skin-walker? And you're sure she's keeping full wolves," Celeste said.

"Oh, yes. I don't know why someone isn't dead already from the wolf I saw," Mr. Brently said. "Vicious and wild."

"Mr. Brently, could you go over there and take a look around? We hope it's not true, but it could be that Jeremy ended up at her house. She has an agenda, but we haven't discovered what it is. You could help us. We have no reason to tell the police anything yet because we have no idea where Jeremy is or why he would be over there."

"I could go check it out. You want me to go now? You want to wait for me?" he said.

"That would be ideal." Celeste nodded. "Very helpful, indeed."

"Wait here," he said.

Mr. Brently disappeared then appeared in the yard outside Darla's. The dogs started barking and howling as if they could sense him, which made him pause. He knew quite well they couldn't hurt him even if they could see him, but it was still unnerving.

"Who's out there?" Darla yelled. "You'd best get off my land. I'm prepared for the likes of you, sneaking up on a defenseless woman alone. Yeah, I know your type. Well, I'm not as helpless as you might think. I have a loaded shotgun here, and these dogs are part wolf. They'll tear you to shreds before you make it to the door. Come out where I can see you."

There was silence. Mr. Brently wasn't sure what to do. He could try to show himself, but he thought that might make matters much worse. She would remember him and know he was dead and after that? Who knew? The dogs were still barking and howling and she let them out.

"I gave you a chance. These wolves won't be so nice," she hollered.

The wolf-dogs ran toward him so fast it made him jump. They surrounded him, and for a second, he forgot he could easily escape. He decided to go stand next to Darla. That should confuse both the dogs and their owner.

It worked. The dogs came running to Darla. They were excited enough to make Darla even a little nervous.

"Settle down," she said. "What's gotten into you?"

They followed her back to the house, so she led them to the pen and gated them in. They were too wild to trust when they got overly excited. They were certainly excited now.

Brently stayed with her as she walked into the house. It was modest, and nothing seemed out of order. He wandered around until there was nothing left but the basement. That place gave him the creeps, and he was a ghost. He descended through the floor, not seeing any need to take the stairs. There was a wolf down there who immediately started growling, barking, and howling. Once again, Brently jumped back. This was not a wolf dog—this was a wolf.

LINDA ANTHONY HILL

Brently calmed down and looked around. There was a small room in the corner, and he peeked inside. There was someone tied to a chair with a hood over their head. Maybe this was the boy his daughter was looking for. He blinked back to his house.

"There's someone tied to a chair in the basement. Darla has a hood over the poor person's head. There's also a wolf in the basement and, I'm telling you, those wolves can see me or sense me or something. They started growling as soon as I got close. So, she's been alerted someone is interested in what's happening in her house and property."

"A hood? That's a good sign. That means she doesn't mean to kill him. She doesn't want him to recognize her face. That's very hopeful," Emma said.

"Maybe . . ." Celeste murmured. "Remember, Darla doesn't think like the rest of us. There's no way to know why he's there or what the plan is. We should call Detective Hillard and let him know we've found Jeremy or someone else who's in trouble.

"We have no proof," Emma countered.

"We have to try," Celeste urged.

She called the detective, and it went to voicemail. She left a message. "This is Madam Celeste. We have reason to believe Jeremy is being held in the basement of a neighboring house. We believe he is in imminent danger. Please call quickly." After she ended the call, she turned to Emma with a grimace. "There. Now, we wait."

"We can't just wait," Emma said. "We have to help him. We have to free him!"

"I'm not going willy-nilly into someone's fortress protected by wolves with nothing but a pistol," Celeste said.

"You have a pistol?" Emma's mouth dropped open.

"Of course, don't you?" Celeste asked.

"No, I'm a pacifist. I don't believe anyone should carry a gun."

"Well, we'll leave that for another time," Celeste said with a smile. "Everyone is entitled to their own opinion, and I wouldn't think of forcing you to carry. But we are definitely not armed enough to take on Darla in her own home."

"That's a fact," Brently said. "She's toting a shotgun, and it seems to be loaded."

"Can you go watch over Jeremy and let us know if the situation changes?" Emma asked.

"I won't be able to help him. I'll just be watching."

"That's better than nothing," Emma said with a frown. "We need to know if she starts to do anything to him."

"Then I guess I'll go watch him."

Celeste's phone rang.

"Celeste, this is Detective Hillard. How do you know Jeremy is in someone's basement?"

"The late Mr. Brently told me a few minutes ago. I had my suspicions, and we asked him to go take a look."

"That's it?" the detective asked. "A ghost told you? I can't do anything with that. I have to have something substantive to do a search. Do you have anything I can use that my supervisor wouldn't laugh at?"

"I'm afraid not," Celeste said slowly. "We know she has him in the basement. We don't know anything else."

"I guess I could pay her a visit in the morning. See what I can get out of her," the detective said.

"What if she does something to him before then? We need to help him now."

"There's nothing I can do to help him. I could go over and talk to her tonight if that would make you feel better."

"That would be better than nothing," Celeste said. "I would feel even better if we could gain access to her basement. What if Emma and I go over and visit with her and—"

"NO!" Detective Hillard yelled. "If she is dangerous, you don't want to go into the house. Let me go over and speak with her tonight, okay?

Celeste winked at Emma. "Oh . . .. If you insist."

"Ladies," Brently appeared while Celeste was still on the phone, "he's gone. She's moved him or worse. The wolf is gone, too."

"This is what I was afraid of," Celeste whispered.

"What?" the detective asked over the phone.

"He's not there anymore. Darla's moved him. She's also moved the wolf. This is not good. Jeremy is not safe."

"Your ghost told you this?" Detective Hillard asked.

"Yes, he's quite real, Detective, and I believe what he's saying. It's the only explanation that makes sense. You see, she's not entirely sane. Maybe she thought Jeremy was spying on her with all his equipment. If she felt threatened by him, she might do something like this, mightn't she?"

"It may make sense to you, but it makes none to me . . .. Since you think he's no longer there, do I still need to go talk to her?"

"More now than ever, we must find out what she's done with him. Did she let the wolf loose on him? Is he still alive? Is he hurt? There are so many questions," Celeste said.

"Wait a minute. If Jeremy's dead, wouldn't you be talking to his ghost?" the detective asked warily.

"It doesn't work like that, Detective. It can take time after death for the spirit to adjust to where it is and when it is. The afterlife is still a mystery in many ways."

"So, he could be dead, and you wouldn't know?"

"Unless Mr. Brently witnessed it and came back and told us about it, probably not."

"Alright, I'm on my way to Darla Weatheral's house to see what I can find out. Maybe I'll get lucky."

CHAPTER 43

"Are you telling me that she had him tied up in the basement and you knew it, and you didn't go over there to help him?" Cheryl screamed.

"There was nothing we could do," Emma stated calmly. "Barging in on her wouldn't have helped Jeremy. Besides, we don't even know for a fact it was Jeremy. He had a hood over his head. We're *assuming* it's Jeremy because he's the only person we know who's missing."

"You could have at least gone over," Cheryl said a bit more calmly.

"We sent the detective over," Emma said. "It seemed safer for Jeremy and for us."

"But Jeremy was already gone by then. You said so yourself."

"He's a detective, Cheryl. It's what he does. If there were any clues to be found, he would be the one to find them."

"I can't believe this is happening," Cheryl wailed. "I was really starting to like him, and I think the feeling was mutual."

"Don't talk about it like it's a done deal. Jeremy could be fine or, at least, still alive. We don't know yet. The detective may have found something last night, and he's going over today to look around in the daylight. He could find some tracks."

"I know. There's always hope until there isn't," Cheryl said, her voice shaking with tears. "There's no reason to believe he's dead. But, if he's alive, then where is he?"

"We're going to find out. Last time your dad saw him, he was alive. He's looking for him, so as soon as he finds him, we'll know, and we'll let you know," Emma said, not really knowing what else to say to the distraught girl.

"I'm going over there myself," Cheryl said firmly. "I'll make her tell me where he is. I have a pistol."

"That may sound like a good idea right now, Cheryl, but let me tell you, it's not. You wouldn't really use it, and she'd have to do something with you, and it just wouldn't play out the way you think it would. Trust me on this."

"You could go with me," Cheryl said hopefully. "You could read her mind and find out what she's done with Jeremy. You could find out where he is."

Emma sighed. "Again, it doesn't work like that. I can't just read people's minds like opening a book. I get flashes of things. Sometimes it's the future, but it can also be the past or even the present. I'm not sure it would do us any good to go over there."

"Yet that's exactly what we're going to do! I'm going, and you're going with. We'll get to the bottom of this. We'll find Jeremy. Your powers will work to help us because that's what we need."

"Fine," Emma huffed, realizing that Cheryl was desperate and would go alone if it came down to it. "I don't have any appointments until this afternoon. We can go now if you like. I can meet you there."

"Let's do it."

Emma pulled up to Darla's house and waited for Cheryl. Before Emma had a chance to text Cheryl to see where she was, she pulled up next to Emma.

They sat in their cars for a bit, each waiting for the other to actually get out and head for the door. Darla had been watching since Emma arrived. She had already moved Jeremy, so she wasn't too concerned about anyone finding him—but she didn't want all these people snooping about. She grabbed her shotgun and opened the front door.

"Y'all need to head on down the road," she yelled.

Emma rolled her window down and shouted, "We just want to ask a few questions about a friend of ours. We hope you might have seen him. He was tracking a gray wolf."

"There's no gray wolves here," Darla lied. "Y'all need to git. You're not welcome here."

"I work for Madam Celeste," Emma said. "She said you have been watching the old Brently place and had seen some suspicious happenings."

Darla lowered her shotgun a little. "I told Madam Celeste there might be a skin-walker out there. She said she'd check into it. Is that why you're here? Are you checking on the skin-walker?"

"Yes, she asked me to find out if you had any more information. Or maybe you might have seen it around here?"

"I never saw it around my house. It was over near Teresa's house. You need to be checking over there," she said raising her shotgun again.

"We were hoping we could look around your place and see if anything matches up with what we've found already. You know, like tracks or shoeprints or—"

"I already told you, you're not welcome here. You're trespassing, and I have every right to shoot you where you sit. I'm about to sic the dogs on you."

"Please, don't do that," Emma said quickly. "We just wanted to talk and look around a bit."

Darla turned and walked toward the dog gate. Three dogs were growling and barking fiercely on the other side of the fence. They were the biggest dogs Emma had ever seen, and they seemed pretty intent on getting out.

Cheryl started her car. Darla stopped and turned to see if the girls were actually leaving. Emma started her car as if to say, "We're going."

Darla wasn't convinced and turned back to the task at hand—letting those dogs loose. The dogs were in fact so much more wolf than dog, they were considered illegal. Darla reached the gate and turned to look one more time with her hand on the lock.

Emma and Cheryl backed down. Cheryl slowly backed out of the drive, and Emma followed suit. They both sped to Cheryl's house. On arriving, Cheryl jumped out of her car and into Emma's.

"I think we needed more of a plan," she said with a slight tremor to her voice.

"Were those wolves?" Emma asked, her eyes wide.

"Maybe not pure, but pretty close to it." Cheryl blew out a breath. "And I don't think that's legal. I'm calling the police."

CHAPTER 44

The girls told Detective Hillard their story once he arrived with backup.

"It's a technicality, but we'll use it," the detective said.

He sent two officers to Darla's house to investigate the claim of keeping—and possibly breeding—over 75% wolves on the property.

"That will keep her busy and possibly in jail for a few hours," the detective said. "It may also give us probable cause to search her property. With any luck, Jeremy is still there and alive."

"I found out she owns every property touching the lake, except ours. That's a lot of ground to cover," Cheryl said.

"I'll call Robert. Maybe he can get Tony and Rocky and the others to come help with the search," Emma offered.

"Tell them to meet here, not at the Weatheral place," Detective Hillard said. "We don't want to give her any cause to make any claims against us." He thought for a moment. "We have animal control on their way to remove the wolves. They, along with a vet, will help determine what percentage of wolf they are. We still won't be able to go inside the house, but you believe he's not there anymore, right?"

Emma nodded. "Exactly. We don't know where he is, but she couldn't have taken him far."

"Detective?" an officer called. "We're clear to search the next location."

The officer brought out a K9 to help with the search. There was also one with the officers at Darla's. The dogs had been given the scent from Jeremy's clothes, and they immediately picked up the scent. The one at Brently's was no surprise as Jeremy had been all over this property. But he had never had a reason to go to Darla's. Yet the dog was hot on a trail leading to the back fence. Had Jeremy gone there looking for the wolf and been caught by a crazy woman with a shotgun? Or had he been forced to go there against his will? Either way, he had been there.

The dog at Brently's was having a harder time. There were too many possibilities. He finally settled on one path that led in the direction of Darla's.

By now, Robert and friends had joined the search. They fanned out to look for hiding places, hoping that Jeremy had escaped and was hiding out away from the ranch house.

The detective came to a spot where there was a sign of a struggle. There was torn fabric and blood on the grass. It now seemed the wolf had dragged its victim as there were smooth tracks in the grass, along with darker smears of what they could only imagine was blood. But it also seemed the victim was putting up a fight. Farther along, they found a shoe. This was not a good sign, but at least it was a sign that Jeremy was still alive.

"How old are these tracks?" Detective Hillard asked the K9 officer.

"Hard to say. The tracks are relatively fresh. The blood hasn't turned black, but it's not bright red, either."

"Can you guestimate?"

"If I had to, I'd say five or six hours . . . maybe more." The officer stopped to take a break and a drink from his water bottle. "It doesn't look good for anyone . . .. Well, anyone but the wolf."

"Then why are we stopped?" Cheryl screamed. "We have to hurry. He needs our help. He could be anywhere around here by now. Let's go already."

Detective Hillard glanced at Emma and conveyed the hopelessness of the situation in that one exchange.

"Cheryl, honey, they are saying there's no way Jeremy could still be alive. He was already hurt and dragged hours ago," Emma said gently. "We're going to find him, but you probably don't want to be there when we do. It's going to be extremely ugly. You don't want to see him like that, do you?"

"I don't want to give up and leave," Cheryl sniffed. "I want to help find him. There's still a chance. I know there is."

Cheryl started to weep again. She had long since passed the raccoon look. She had now cried the makeup completely off her face.

In the distance, Robert and the others were jumping and shouting to get the attention of the K9 group. The excitement gave no hint of having found a body. There seemed to be a sense of hope. The K9 group ran to join Robert's group near an outcropping of boulders. The group had found a cave; however, the dog wanted to go west before reaching the outcropping.

"What did you find? The dog wants to go west," Detective Hillard said.

"There's a small cave here, and it looks like they might have stopped," Robert said quickly. "Jeremy left a credit card and a bag of trail cameras. I bet it was on purpose to help us track him, which means he could still be alive."

Detective Hillard looked at the K9 officer questioningly. The officer shook his head. The trail the dog wanted to follow—actually, both dogs as they had joined forces somewhere north of Darla's and northeast of the Brently ranch—indicated that the man was now being dragged. If he was alive, he wasn't conscious.

"Robert, you have been quite helpful, but it's time to round everyone up and take them home," the detective said firmly. "We'll contact you as soon as we find him. Emma that means you and

Cheryl, too. There is no need to stay any longer. These tracks show a wolf dragging a lifeless body."

"No!" Cheryl screamed. "I will stay. I'm not going anywhere except to find Jeremy, even if he's dead."

"I guess we all feel like that," Robert said as the rest of the team agreed.

The detective paced for a minute, heavily sighing when he faced the group. "Then from here on, you need to stay behind us. We seem to be pretty close now, and apparently, there's a dangerous wild wolf on the prowl. We don't want any more victims in this scenario."

"Agreed." Robert and the others nodded.

Emma tugged on Robert's arm. "Robert, will you stay here with me? I don't want to be alone, but I don't want to see what they're going to find. I've already seen it in a vision when I touched Jeremy's backpack. He's not okay, and it's going to be worse than any of you realize. Cheryl, I really wish you would stay here, too."

"When did you have this vision?" Cheryl asked, taking a step closer to Emma. "When were you going to tell me?"

"Just now when I touched his backpack," Emma said before she ran to some nearby bushes to throw-up.

"So, you believe he's dead?" Cheryl asked when Emma returned.

"Yes, and you, well, any of us really, don't need to see it."

"Then I'll wait here with you." Cheryl nodded sadly. "Robert, will you stay with us?"

"I think we all should. If what Emma is saying is true, it's no place for us."

They all sat down on any flat rock they could find to wait for what was only going to be bad news.

"Remember how funny he thought it was we had found chicken tracks?" Robert said, breaking the silence. "He had a good laugh on us that day." Everyone nodded, but no one laughed, not even a smile could be seen.

The time crept along like a snail. "What do you think is taking so long?" Cheryl whispered.

"Maybe they ran into the wolf," Emma said.

"Is that what you saw? The police fighting the wolf?" Cheryl asked.

Emma shook her head. "No. That's just a guess, a reasonable deduction." She pulled out her phone and called Celeste, who let it go to voicemail as she was with a client. Emma filled her in, and as she said it all out loud, her tears began to flow. She hung up before finishing.

CHAPTER 45

One of the police walked back to the Weatheral ranch house to meet the ambulance. They came back through a few minutes later with a stretcher. Cheryl expressed a measure of hope, but Emma assured her there was no hope to be had here.

"They have brought that for what is left of him. Nothing more," Emma said gently.

"You don't know that," Cheryl countered.

"Did you see them hurrying? No, you didn't. They have no reason to hurry. Our friend is dead, and I'm sure there is very little left of him to even need a stretcher."

"Emma is right," Detective Hillard said. "There was more than one wolf. It wasn't pretty. There were pieces of clothing left, but the rest had been torn apart and dragged off in opposite directions. We're searching for pieces now. You should go on home. We'll contact you when there's anything to share."

Cheryl burst into tears again. Robert and Emma tried to comfort her to no avail.

"I'll give you a ride home, Cheryl," Emma said.

"Why don't I give you both a ride home?" Robert offered. "You've been through enough today. You don't need to be driving. I'm parked at Cheryl's."

"This is so unfair," Cheryl cried. "He knew wolves. Why would he come out here unprepared? His whole point was to prove the wolf or wolves were here. He would have had a weapon. He wouldn't have followed a wolf into the woods without protection. It doesn't make any sense."

"We all know that's not what happened, Cheryl. Remember? He was tied to a chair in Darla's basement. She must have led him out to the trail, let him loose, and then released the wolves on him," Emma said.

"Are you saying that as a psychic or as an intelligent guess?" Tony mocked.

"The ghost who told me that Jeremy was tied up is completely reliable," Emma snapped. "There is no part of his story that I doubt. The rest is an informed guess. Maybe if I could touch something Jeremy touched while he was escaping, I might get some part of the facts. But know this . . . he was tied up in Darla's basement, and he was being guarded by a gray wolf. Did he escape or did Darla release him? That will make a big difference to me. I think she released him with some disadvantage and with a wolf right behind him."

"I don't want to hear any more about it right now," Cheryl whispered. "I don't want to think about it."

"Until we solve it, I doubt you'll think about much else," Emma said. "The sooner we know what really happened, the better for everyone."

"Except Jeremy, things will never be better for Jeremy, will they?" Cheryl cried.

"Emma, what kind of things do you need to touch to have a vision?" Robert asked.

"Anything Jeremy touched," Emma answered.

"Then lets you and I go back to the scene and find some things for you to touch. There's no reason to waste a good psychic while you're here and the trail is fresh. The police will find tracks, but you can find so much more. Tony can see Cheryl back to her apartment or maybe her mom's house would be better? You and I can go back and get some answers the police won't find."

"Is that really a good idea with a pack of wolves running loose?" Tony asked.

"There are police everywhere," Emma said. "We'll be fine."

"Be careful, at least," Tony said. "Be aware of your surroundings. Do you have a pistol?"

"No, I have been a pacifist. I'm beginning to change my mind, though, but we'll call you if we need you."

Emma and Robert walked back toward the cave. It was out of sight at this distance, but they would be able to follow the now trampled trail through the woods. Tony led Cheryl back to his car, though it took longer than he expected.

When Emma and Robert arrived at the cave, it seemed abandoned. Perhaps the officer who had been guarding it had been reassigned to join in the hunt for what was left of Jeremy.

Emma turned her phone into a flashlight and shone it into the cave. There was a piece of police tape pulled across the entrance. Emma ignored it and looked for the place Jeremy had sat, however briefly.

She touched a spot of blood on the wall of the cave. The vision was sharp and instantaneous. She saw Jeremy in the basement, but she was seeing through his eyes so it was dark. She could taste fresh blood as if he had been hit or cut and was bleeding from the mouth.

Someone untied him and herded him across the basement, up the stairs, and outside. The fresh air hit him and gave him hope. Then he heard the wolf. He was led to the gate to the pasture and the woods. He didn't know where he was. He looked back and saw someone standing behind the gate with the wolf. They had a mask on. Why?

The wolf was trying to get through the gate. The person was holding a rope. They yelled, "Run!"

In his disoriented state, Jeremy started to run north. He knew there was no way to outrun a gray wolf, but he had to try. It didn't take long for the wolf to overtake him. He was unconscious by the time the wolf had dragged him to the cave.

The vision ended. Emma knew there would be no more.

"Emma? Is that you?" a voice called from deeper in the cave. Jeremy drifted closer. "Why are you here? How did you find me? Where am I?"

"Jeremy, you're in a cave. The wolf caught you as you were running away from Darla's house."

"I thought that was Darla's house," Jeremy said. "So, it must have been Darla that had me tied up?"

"Seems like it."

"Seems like what?" Robert asked.

"Jeremy is here, but he's not sure where here is and I'm not sure what to tell him to do. I think I'd better try to get Celeste on the phone again."

"Should I just wait here?" Jeremy asked.

"You should do whatever you feel compelled to do. I'm going to find out what Celeste says that you should do if you don't feel drawn to do anything."

"So, you're talking to Jeremy right now?" Robert asked as Emma dialed Celeste.

"Yes," Emma and Celeste said simultaneously.

"Celeste, I'm in a cave on Darla's property. Robert is with me, and I'm having a conversation with Jeremy. He's very confused about what he should be doing or where he should be. I've gotten all the information he has for us, which is pretty sketchy. What should I tell him?"

"Are you talking to his spirit?" Celeste asked.

"Yes," Emma said softly.

"Does he know he's dead?"

"Should I ask that bluntly?" Emma asked.

"No, no, of course not. I meant, has he given any indication that he knows?"

"He's mostly confused. He remembers being at Darla's, but not that it was her place. He remembers running for his life, but after that . . . not much."

"Ask him how he feels," Celeste said.

Emma did.

"Now that you mention it, I don't feel much of anything," Jeremy said as he examined his hands and arms. The realization caught up to him slowly. "I should be dead . . . . That wolf went for my jugular, but now I don't feel it. I don't feel anything. There's no pain, but there's also no . . . I don't know how to describe it. Am I dead?"

"Yes, Jeremy, you are. It happened a few hours ago. I'm not really sure how it is you're here this quickly."

"Oh, dear," Celeste said. "Emma? You will want to help him see where he is and find his way home. It's too soon, and we don't want him to be stuck in a cave for eternity. Help him remember the details of what happened and then see if you can get him to go home. I'll see if I can get Paul to join you."

"Jeremy, we're going to help you. Remember Celeste's friend, Paul?"

"The ghost?"

"Exactly." Emma nodded. "Celeste is contacting him now to come and help you to where you should be, which is apparently not in this cave all alone. She said it might be helpful for you to remember the details leading up to your death. What can you remember?"

"I was running as fast as I could," Jeremy started. "I thought the trees in the woods would slow the wolf down, so I headed for the trees. It was harder to run, but I think it did slow him down. I saw a cave and made a dash for it, hoping to find a place to hide. I knew he could follow my scent, but you know what they say about hope . . . .." His brows furrowed as his voice trailed off.

He shook his head and continued, "Anyway, he overtook me in the open field between the woods and the cave. He found my jugular and ripped it out. Next thing I knew, I was here. Then you showed up. I saw you coming from a distance. There were lots of police, too. What do I do now?"

To Celeste, Emma said, "He's given me the details and wants to know what he should do now."

"Paul will be there in a second," Celeste said as Paul arrived.

"It's a shame about you dying and all," Paul said gently. "We'll get you fixed up in a better place than this while you settle into the whole situation." Paul then turned to Emma. "I'll take it from here. He'll be okay. Don't worry about a thing."

"Thank you, Paul. Where will you take him?" Emma asked. "That's not a question I can answer. It's not for you to know. Just take comfort knowing that he is in good hands and will be fine."

CHAPTER 46

As Emma and Robert made their way back to the Brently estate, Emma called Cheryl and filled her in on the details of what had just transpired. When Emma had finished, Cheryl was full of questions. What had Darla wanted with Jeremy in the first place? Was there any proof that she was behind the whole thing? Had she been involved in the spider situation? Did she really believe there was a skin-walker or is that made up to scare people away from the house?

"Those are all great questions. Let's go to Madam Celeste's and see what we can piece together with her help."

"I think I'd rather go to my mother's," Cheryl said. "Maybe Celeste could come over there. It doesn't look like we'll need her help anymore after tonight, does it?"

"Hard to say," Emma murmured. "There could still be a few things she could help with regarding Darla and her part in all of this. I suggest you not dismiss her yet. Play it by ear, but I'll call her to see if she can come to your Mom's with us."

"Robert, is your offer still open for giving us both a lift?" Emma asked.

"Absolutely! I'll need to free up some space if we're going to stop off and get Madam Celeste. Give me a few minutes."

When they made it to the Brently place, they were surprised to find Teresa Brently there waiting in her car.

"Mom, I'm so glad you're here. Jeremy is dead, and we think Darla had something to do with it," Cheryl rushed out. "It was awful."

"We were hoping to gather at your house to sift through the details we have and hopefully find some evidence for the police. All we have now are possibilities," Emma explained.

"Cheryl, is this what you want to do? Are you up for it?" her mom asked.

"Yes, Mom, I want to find out what happened to Jeremy, and if it's Darla's fault, I want her to pay."

"Please, do come to the house, then. We'll order in some food and go over your notes together. If Darla is involved, she will have made a mistake along the way. The woman is ten kinds of crazy. She's bound to have left a trail."

Mrs. Brently gave Cheryl a ride, while Emma rode with Robert. They would retrieve her car later and swing by to pick up Madam Celeste. The ride to Mrs. Brently's was somber until Robert arrived at Madam Celeste's. Emma took the back seat, giving Madam Celeste the front. She was full of questions that didn't need to be brought up in front of Cheryl.

"Did Jeremy see his kidnapper?"

"No, not even a glimpse. Not even after he was dead. Odd, it's like Darla knew he would be able to identify her after he died."

"Did the wolf involved act like an alpha?"

"I wouldn't know . . .. That would be a question for Jeremy, but Paul has taken him somewhere, and it didn't sound like he would be back anytime soon."

"I'm glad Paul is helping him. He might have spent ages in that cave not knowing what had happened," Celeste said. "It would have been nice to get some more details before he left, but we'll make do."

"What kind of details?" Emma asked.

"Things like, did he follow the wolf to Darla's or did Darla lure him there with a story or the promise of evidence? Was it a plan to capture him from the outset or did she just have a bit of luck when he happened upon her? Did he take those cameras down or did Darla? Those sorts of questions," Celeste clarified.

"I'm sorry, I didn't think of those things, Celeste. It was all a bit disconcerting at the moment."

"That's alright, dear. We will find our answers the old-fashioned way. And I'm sure the detective will have similar questions and may have already found some answers. I don't imagine we'll be able to talk to him before morning, though. By the way, dear, you stood up a client this afternoon. You'll need to call them later to apologize and see about rescheduling."

"Oh, no! I completely forgot. Did you explain to them a friend was missing and presumed dead?"

"I did. She was quite understanding and wants to reschedule for next week."

Emma nodded, relieved that she didn't lose the client. She made a mental note to call her in the morning. "Celeste? Even if Jeremy had seen Darla's face, would that really be any help? Would they let you testify to that in court?

"You mean, would they let *you*," Celeste said. "You are the one who spoke with him. The detective will want to hear what he had to say to you. But, to answer your question, no, it would not be admissible in court. However, the detective could use the information to let him know he's moving in the right direction. It could prove most useful to him."

They arrived at Mrs. Brently's just ahead of the Chinese delivery. Emma hadn't realized she was hungry until the scent of the egg rolls and fried rice and other delightful dishes tickled her nostrils. It had been ordered family style, and there was a wide variety to choose from—even Cheryl managed to eat a few bites. Mrs. Brently was amazing at entertaining a small crowd.

The mood was light as everyone ate and relaxed. Until Mrs. Brently mentioned Jeremy and the house grew quiet.

"Do we know about his family?" Mrs. Brently asked.

"He didn't like to talk about them. His parents were dead, and he had no siblings. Beyond that, I don't know," Cheryl said.

"Maybe the police will have that information," Celeste offered. "Do we know if they found his phone?"

"It was in the cave," Robert said. "I actually found it and gave it to Detective Hillard. He put it in a bag as evidence."

"What else do we know? Does anyone know what happened to the recordings from the woods? Are they on his computer or were they in the cameras or are they missing?" Celeste asked.

"They weren't in the cameras. It looked like Jeremy removed them as he took the cameras down. The SD cards haven't been found yet. It would make sense for them to have been around him somewhere, but," Robert hesitated, looking for words that wouldn't cause Cheryl any unnecessary pain, "they weren't."

"What makes you think Darla was involved?" Mrs. Brently asked.

The room exploded with people trying to answer. Celeste held up her hand to silence them.

"We know Darla lied when she first contacted me to discuss the skin-walker, claiming it was stalking the area. She has been raising and breeding wolves, yet didn't volunteer that information, and in fact, tried to hide it not only from me, but also from the police when they came asking questions about Jeremy.

"She was hostile when asked about Jeremy and claimed not to have seen him when his tracks lead directly to her house. We have it from a spirit we find reliable that Jeremy was tied to a chair in Darla's basement and guarded by a wolf." Celeste took a sip of her drink. "We believe she may have had something to do with some of the hallucinogens that were present when we first made contact with the house. It's not clear whether it was all coming from Andrew . . .."

"The spirit?" Mrs. Brently asked.

"Yes, exactly. We're pretty sure he was causing most of the hallucinations, but I have a feeling that Darla may have been contributing to some type of hallucinogens in the air."

"We believe she intended to get you to sell that portion of your estate to her just to be rid of it. She made it seem to be occupied by a demon and mutant spiders and possibly a skin-walker." Celeste took a quick break to answer any questions Mrs. Brently might have. "Need I go on?"

"It's all quite circumstantial, isn't it?" Mrs. Brently asked. "This all started out about my late husband and a house full of spiders. It's hard to believe it is now about the death and possible murder of my daughter's new friend. It's a lot to take in. Is there *any* evidence that would lead the police to believe Jeremy didn't just get tracked by the very wolf he was looking for?"

"That's what we're here to discuss," Robert said. "If we can come up with something tangible, then the police will pay attention. They already have Darla in custody. They know she was raising wolves. That's a start."

"We have to give them a solid reason to want to search her basement where there should be at least DNA evidence that Jeremy was down there. If we can show he was there, we can convince them it was not by choice," Emma said. "We know he was tied up against his will, but they're not going to listen to the testimony of a spirit they can't see or hear. We have to find something solid."

CHAPTER 47

"Do we really think she could have released something to cause hallucinations?" Tony asked.

"It's possible," Emma said.

"What were the spiders eating?" Brooke asked, who had joined them at Mrs. Brently's house to get the updates and help in any way that she could.

"Whatever spiders eat," Tony said sarcastically.

"No really." Brooke shot Tony a look. "Think about it. That was a lot of big spiders. They had to have a food source to keep them there. What was it? Is it possible someone was feeding them?"

Emma snapped her fingers. "Someone like Darla!"

Brooke nodded. "Could be. Robert, is it possible we could have caught her on video, at some point, entering to feed the spiders?"

"We can divvy up the SD cards, and everyone can inspect a share of what we have. The problem is that she could have been doing it for years before we showed up and stopped when we set up surveillance equipment," Robert said.

"True," Celeste said, "but it is worth looking."

"We need to let Detective Hillard know there are SDs out there somewhere with footage of the trails on the last night, in addition to the ones that may have already been transferred to his laptop or home computer," Brooke said. "There is definitely footage of the wolf, but there may even be footage of Darla."

"Yes, theoretically those would be out on the trail or near where Jeremy was found," Cheryl said as tears began to trail down her cheeks.

"They've been combing that area, but wouldn't know to look for those," Robert said.

"I'll call him now," Emma said as she pulled out her phone.

"So, everyone here is convinced that Darla directly or indirectly caused the death of Jeremy?" Teresa Brently asked.

They all agreed.

"There's really no other explanation," Tony said.

"Just to play devil's advocate . . .. He could have been tracking the wolf, and the wolf got the better of him during the hunt. So, the wolf was tracking him, caught him or came close. Jeremy took off running and didn't make it," Teresa Brently said.

"That wouldn't explain the three-day-old tracks of Jeremy leading to Darla's, and then the more recent tracks leading away from her house and toward the woods," Robert chimed in.

"Hmmm. Can there be no other explanation?" Mrs. Brently asked.

Brooke shook her head. "None that makes sense."

"Detective Hillard agrees," Emma said, still on the phone with the detective. "He's getting a warrant to search her entire property, including the house. Hopefully, they will finish searching before she's released on bond for the wolves she's been keeping."

"Has the game warden been called?" Mrs. Brently asked.

"I believe so," Emma said before posing the question to the detective. "Yes, yes, he's over there now finding all sorts of violations."

"It looks like our part in this is coming to an end," Robert said with a sigh. "We should probably leave Mrs. Brently and Cheryl alone now. They probably have a lot to talk about."

"You may be right. Though, I'd like to spend a few more minutes with Madam Celeste and Emma. We have some settling up to do," Mrs. Brently said.

"Tony, will you ride out with me to pick up Emma's car?" Robert asked. "That will give them time to talk."

"Sure. Let me get my car. I'll give you a ride and leave from there."

"Perfect!" Robert said and the group left.

"You have concerns, Teresa," Celeste said as the door closed. "You think we're all missing something."

"Most of your solutions are supernatural or paranormal or whatever the proper term is. You may be accustomed to that, but I am not. I'm more inclined to look for a mortal explanation. All these spirits and demons and Chickasaw legends leave me feeling like there is more human activity we may have missed. Was Darla acting alone or did she have help from a physical human being?"

"We know she had help from one or more wolves, and they are quite physical. No one is suggesting they were wolf-men. They are, indeed, capable of causing Jeremy's death and much of the business on the videos," Celeste said.

"Cheryl had fallen in love with him, hadn't she?" Mrs. Brently asked.

"I don't know about love, but they had certainly grown fond of each other."

Mrs. Brently looked away. "I don't know how to help her."

"You remember how you felt when you lost your husband. How did you want to be treated then? What made you feel better?"

"Time, empathy, a shoulder," Mrs. Brently said softly.

"Then give her that."

"Speaking of giving, I need to give you some money," Mrs. Brently said. "You and Emma. I want to thank you for all your time and effort on this. Finding out about my son and husband was a treasure I will never forget. And your help in determine what had happened to Jeremy? Priceless. Can you take a credit card?"

"Yes, I can, but I don't have an exact figure for you right now. Let me look over the numbers tomorrow, and I'll email you an invoice. There's no need to worry about it tonight."

"I would like to get it taken care of as soon as possible, though," Mrs. Brently said.

"Of course. Is that why you wanted to speak privately?"

"Yes, that and I want to say a word about Darla. It's been bothering me since you told me about the two of them being together. I don't think she had an affair with my husband. She just wishes she had. She's just hoping someone will believe her."

"It was your husband who told us about it and about how much he regretted it. He wanted to make it up to you."

"Celeste, would you tell her I'm here?" Mr. Brently asked.

"Of course. Teresa, your husband is sitting next to you. He wants you to know he's here."

"Here? In my house? He's not going to haunt this house, too, is he?"

"No, tell her no. I'm not going to haunt any house from now on."

"No, he won't be haunting this or any other house from now on," Celeste said.

"He told you? You believe him?"

"Yes, I believe him. He wants to be close to you, but not if it scares you," Celeste said.

Cheryl and Emma had started to listen to the conversation now.

"Are you talking to my dad?" Cheryl asked.

"Yes," Celeste answered.

"Will you ask him to look out for Jeremy when he comes back? If he comes back, ask my dad to help him."

"Of course, I will. Tell her not to worry about him. Or me, for that matter."

Celeste relayed the message.

"What do you plan to do with the old house, Mrs. Brently?" Celeste asked.

"I hadn't given it much thought. I knew I didn't want Darla to have it. But it always made me uncomfortable to be in the house. Cheryl, would you want to live there?"

"I'll have to think about that, Mom. It has some pretty spooky memories now. Jeremy and I spent a lot of time there. I can't decide yet . . .."

"No hurry," her mom said. "I may go ahead and open it up. Turn the den into a library. We can both use it for a weekender kind of place. We'll redecorate and do some updating. It could be a fun project."

Cheryl's mind had drifted off to Jeremy, and the smile had vanished again. "I'm not ready yet, Mom. I'm sorry."

"Never be sorry for feeling what you feel. I was just talking to pass the time. Don't give it another thought," Mrs. Brently said. "So, all the mysteries are solved then, Madam Celeste?"

"To my satisfaction, yes. The law will need to gather more evidence, but I . . . er, I mean *we* have given them everything we have. It is up to them to make a case from here. Detective Hillard believes he has enough to put Darla behind bars for a very long time."

"And the house is spirit free?" Mrs. Brently asked.

"I wouldn't say that," Madam Celeste said slowly. "There are still spirits that enjoy the house, but they should be leaving the living alone unless you decide to summon them. If you do, please call on me to do a proper séance for you."

"I will, Madam Celeste. You will be the first person I call."

THE END

EPILOGUE

In the following days and weeks, Darla was arrested for the murder of Jeremy, and the detective decided to investigate all the circumstances related to the sales of the surrounding estates. He found several instances of people selling off land at ridiculously low prices due to bizarre happenings, legends, and rumors.

Teresa decided to spend time at the old house and re-opened it to give Cheryl a better chance to decide if she wanted to live there. Cheryl embraced the project and helped bring the old place into the twenty-first-century by adding smart home features and plenty of surveillance equipment.

Celeste and Emma were well-compensated for their efforts in helping clear up the problems at the house and in solving the murder of Jeremy.

LINDA ANTHONY HILL

ABOUT THE AUTHOR

Linda Anthony Hill

was born in Sanford Florida. Growing up in Florida gave her a wonderful opportunity to meet people from around the world and from many different cultures. She now resides in North Texas with her husband, Del. Her first Cozy Mystery, The Anchor is the Key, has won the first-place award for literary excellence for paranormal fiction in the  PenCraft Awards, and was a finalist in the American Fiction Awards.

Linda also has a series of children's chapter books (ghost stories, of course.) The series is available on Amazon and B&N. *Amazon.com/author/hilllin*.

Linda and her husband own the infamous haunted house in Gainesville Texas known as Hill House Manor. You'll find more information at *HillHouseManor.com* Much of Linda's inspiration for ghost stories comes from the activity and her own experiences at Hill House Manor.

www.ingramcontent.com/pod-product-compliance
Lightning Source LLC
Chambersburg PA
CBHW021033030726
47496CB00006B/1519